Hot Pursuit

Dick Weller leaped sidewise like a frightened cat and fired at the flash of the steel in the sunlight. His own draw was so lightning fast that the advantage of the first move was quite stolen from the deputy sheriff. And the bullet, striking true by something far more than chance, knocked the heavy Colt out of the hand of Jacobs and flung it back against his body.

The deputy stared for an instant at his numbed, empty fingers, then snatched up the fallen weapon with his left hand. He should have been dead long before he leaned for the gun, and he knew it. He was expecting the shock of a .45-caliber slug through flesh and bones, tearing its way, every split second of this time of expectation. But the bullet did not come; the gun did not speak. Instead, a shadow flashed past him, skidding rapidly over the ground, and, as he half straightened, the gun in his hand, he saw tall Dick Weller, racing like a deer, dodging from sight among the great boulders down the gulley.

The whole of the posse was up now, and firing at the fugitive, shouting with excitement. But the deputy cried: "The hosses! He'll get to the hosses! Run, for God's sake! And shoot straight . . . straight . . . !"

Max Brand®

RIFLE PASS

LEISURE BOOKS NEW YORK CITY

A LEISURE BOOK®

November 2009

Published by special arrangement with Golden West Literary Agency.

Dorchester Publishing Co., Inc.
200 Madison Avenue
New York, NY 10016

ISBN 10: 0-8439-6079-5
ISBN 13: 978-0-8439-6079-2
E-ISBN: 978-1-4285-0763-0

Visit us online at www.dorchesterpub.com.

CONTENTS

The Nighthawk Trail

Frederick Faust's saga of the hero Speedy began with "Tramp Magic," a six-part serial in *Western Story Magazine*, which appeared in the issues dated November 21, 1931, through December 26, 1932. As most of Faust's continuing characters, Speedy is a loner, little more than a youngster, able to outwit and outmaneuver even the deadliest of men without the use of a gun. He appeared in a total of nine short stories in addition to the serial. The serial has been reprinted by Leisure Books under the title *Speedy*. The first short novel, "Speedy—Deputy," can be found in *Jokers Extra Wild*; "Seven-Day Lawman" can be found in *Flaming Fortune*; "Speedy's Mare" appears in *Peter Blue*; "The Game" is in *The Fugitive*; "Red Rock's Secret" in *Red Rock's Secret*; and "Speedy's Bargain" in *Treasure Well*. The Nighthawk Trail" originally appeared in the July 9, 1932, issue of Street & Smith's *Western Story Magazine*.

I

Al Dupray took the old river road with a feeling of shame and of guilt. He knew that many others in the town had visited the crystal-gazer in the Gypsy camp, but he was not the sort of man who the world would expect to give way to superstitions of this kind.

People had accepted him, ever since Tom Older's killing and the establishment of his own innocence, as an extraordinary fellow. After that he preferred to live on in the town of Clausen, because there, at least, they seemed to take it for granted that he was free from the stain of bad blood, and the town's newspaper was always singing his praises, both for his charities and public gifts to the place. For, from the beginning, he had donated to Clausen the whole of Tom Older's half in the mine. That made a tide of money that was more than enough to buy the favorable opinions of the people of Clausen.

But would it buy the favorable opinion of Sue Crane? Her opinion, just now, meant more to him than all the rest of the world.

At a turn of the road he looked back across the hills, and there he saw the trees divide and the front of the Crane house gleam out against the west, its windows turning to rose and golden fire in the light of a brilliant sunset.

Terrible old Joshua Crane was up there in front of the house at this time of the day, seated in his wheelchair, with a blanket wrapped around his

paralyzed legs and a rifle lying across his knees. He
never was without that rifle, day or night, and it was
said that he never knew when he would need it; he
had so many enemies from the old days when he
rode this range and started to win his fortune and
his way with an iron hand. He had never weakened
then. He did not weaken now that years and his
malady had made him a cripple. For five years he
had not been able to take a step, but in those five
years he had stretched forth the power of his mind
farther than ever across the range. Men knew him
and feared him more than ever.

This was the man whose daughter's hand Al
Dupray intended to ask—he, the nephew of
Charley Dupray, long-hunted bandit, robber, and
killer extraordinary.

Doubt in himself overwhelmed Dupray, and he
shook his head as he hurried his mustang down the
road. There was not far to go, and presently he came
to the camp. The Gypsies had put up their tents and
built their wretched lean-tos inside an elbow turn
of the river, where the ground was level. There was
a good growth of pines and brush, and in a number
of little clearings, where the grass grew thickly,
they had found pasture for their horses, mules,
and burros.

By this time, although the heads of the mountains
were still gleaming, the purple dusk of the evening was
sifting thickly through all the valleys and the ravines,
and under the dark pines it seemed as though night
had already come. The fires gleamed yellow; lanterns
hung from a number of the yellow boughs.

They were going about the ordinary camp work now.
Later on people would wander down from Clausen
to see the jugglers and the fire-eaters, the tumblers

and knife-throwers. Men would come to trade horses with these keen strangers, who knew horseflesh with a strange, intuitive knowledge. They would visit the tents of the fortune-tellers, also. Above all, they would consult the crystal-gazer, who was said to lay bare the past, present, and future at a glance.

One could test the truth of his predictions by his wonderful knowledge of the past, that strange old bearded man with the young and steady voice. Well, there was enough in Al Dupray's past that was hidden. If the old man could tell him about that, Al would willingly trust his predictions about the future.

He gave hardly a glance to the right or the left as he made for the tent of the crystal-gazer, which was distinguished by the flag above it with the yellow star and crescent on the crimson field. A mild breeze struck that pennon, and it streamed out in rapidly running folds. Al Dupray noticed that. He noticed many little things, as a man will do when his heart is ill at ease. It was altogether a bigger and more comfortable tent than the rest, and it was plain that the owner of the tent was the kingpin of the tribe.

When Dupray came to the entrance flap, he found it open, and a small fire burning on the ground with a pot steaming over it. Behind the fire, leaning against an Indian backrest, was the crystal-gazer. He sat with legs crossed upon the ground, smoking a long-stemmed pipe. A turban was wound about his head; a long white beard streamed down over his breast. It seemed to Al Dupray that under their dark and shaggy brows the eyes of the seer were keener and more glowing than the coals of the fire. There was no other light in the tent.

"Am I after hours?" asked Dupray.

"Enter, my son," said a soft voice.

He had heard that voice described before, but none of the descriptions had done it justice. There was a caress to it, and there was a menace, as well; furthermore, it was oddly, vaguely familiar, as though he might have heard it before, but never from one with such a face.

"Have you come in need or in folly?" said the crystal-gazer.

Al Dupray frowned. "I kind of thought that you'd be able to answer that question yourself, old-timer," he said.

"When I look in the crystal, yes," said the other. "Be seated. Cross my hand with silver. Tell me what you would know."

He spoke gravely. He had repose of manner. And Al Dupray sat down on the very low stool before the man of mystery.

"You can start back somewhere in the past with me," said Dupray. "Suppose that you lay in and tell me the worst minute that I ever had in my life?"

He crossed the extended, slender palm with a whole silver dollar, which the old rascal examined, turned this way and that, and then dropped into a capacious pocket, where it jingled against other coins.

The seer now produced a crystal ball, which he placed upon the raised point of the index finger of his left hand. With a twist of the fingers of his right hand, he started the ball rapidly whirling. It seemed to Al Dupray a miracle of cleverness that the man could support the ball in such perfect equilibrium, also that it would whirl so long. He saw the reflection from the fire in the crystal like a little, flickering sword blade of golden light.

The voice of the gazer murmured: "I see you manacled against a wall. The pale gleaming of steel bars is about you. On the floor lies a man, dead or senseless. Before you kneels a man who handles the locks of your chains."

Al Dupray almost rose from the stool on which he was seated. "By thunder," he muttered. He relaxed, and, as he blinked again, he saw that the crystal ball had disappeared. The old man had picked up his long-stemmed pipe once more.

"By the almighty tearing thunder, you've hit on it," said Al Dupray. "If you can see that, then see what's gonna happen to me tonight."

The other held forth a slender hand again.

"You get silver every shot out of the box?" asked Dupray.

"It is for the eye of the spirit," said the other.

"The eye of the . . . ," began Dupray, and stopped short. "It's worth it," he muttered, and handed over another dollar to the seer.

Once more the crystal ball appeared, was balanced with the same dexterity upon a fingertip, and once more the ball went spinning.

The soft, menacing voice began again: "This picture I see . . . a woman's face smiling on you."

"Smiling?" cried Al Dupray, starting joyously.

"Smiling sadly," said the old man, "as she bids you farewell."

Dupray groaned. "She says farewell," he repeated. "You mean for good and all?"

The crystal ball had disappeared again.

"As for the future," said the gazer, "that would need another crossing of silver. I have shown you the past and the present, one flash at each. For the spirit can see only one picture at a time."

Al Dupray gripped his hands hard. "I don't know but what I'm being a fool," he said. "And if that's what's gonna happen tonight, it'd be no good to me to know it, anyway." He added grimly: "Things that go wrong have gotta be made to go right."

The old man picked up his long pipe and puffed at it, the smallest white cloud of fragrant smoke issuing from his lips. His eyes looked steadily past the young fellow and toward the outer night.

Al Dupray stood up. "She gives me a smile and says good bye. Is that it?" he asked. "It's gotta be different." He pulled his hat lower down on his head and thrust out his jaw. People who found a great likeness to his terrible and celebrated uncle in his face would have had their opinion reinforced by a glance at the young fellow. He turned toward the door, with a wave of his hand to the crystal-gazer. As he reached the entrance flap of the tent, he heard quite a different voice speak behind him.

"Come back here, Al."

He spun about, bewildered. There he saw a man sitting in the robes of the crystal-gazer, with the turban still about his head, but the beard and the shaggy eyebrows were gone; the lines that had seamed and roughened the face had also disappeared, as if by magic. Now he was looking at a dark-eyed young fellow, not very much older than himself, a sensitive and handsome face that would have been too feminine except for the glint of wholly masculine humor about the eyes.

"Speedy!" cried Al Dupray.

II

In accordance with Speedy's request, Dupray closed the tent flap. Then he came striding hastily to grip the hand of his friend. "You rapscallion," said Dupray, "you're the crystal-gazer, are you? Gimme back that money!"

"Not a bean of it," answered Speedy. "I earned that coin, because you've broken every bone in my hand." With that he began to smooth and massage the right hand with the fingers of the left. Still he continued to smile at Al Dupray.

"I thought you were a thousand miles away from here. I thought that you . . . ," began Al Dupray. Then his voice stopped suddenly, as though he had bumped against an impassable obstacle.

Speedy continued for him: "You thought that I was on the trail of your uncle, Al. Was that it? Thought that I was drifting along behind Uncle Charley, looking for trouble?"

"Well"—the young man sighed—"that's what I imagined."

"Not I," said Speedy. "I'd leave him alone, but he can't forget me. Every now and then something happens that reminds him of the time that John Wilson and I snaked him out of his camp and landed him in jail, with a mighty good chance of having his neck stretched before he got out of it. Whenever he thinks of that . . . why, he's irritated, Al, and wants my scalp. I'm not trailing him just now, but he's trailing me so close that I thought I'd give him some elbow room in the hope that he'd settle down. That's why I slipped into this Gypsy tribe. Most of 'em, by the way, are no more Gypsy than I am. I've heard Mexican, Spanish, and Canadian French around here, but no lingo that sounds Romany to me. What's the trouble about the girl, Al?"

Dupray waved a hand that dismissed that subject.

"About Uncle Charley," he said. "I know he's a devil, Speedy. I know that as well as anybody. But he's been mighty kind to me."

"I know he has," said Speedy. "There's a good side to him about as big as the bad side, I suppose. I've seen something of it, too."

"You haven't seen all of it, Speedy," said the young fellow. "You haven't heard the way he talks about me leading a straight life, and what he'll do to keep me straight. Sometimes I think that he'd put up every penny he has in the world to keep me happy and contented and going right . . . and you know how he loves his money more than he loves his own blood."

"I know all of that," agreed Speedy, nodding.

"He has a lot of respect, and even liking, for you, Speedy," continued Al. "He knows that I'd have hanged for the killing of Tom Older if you hadn't showed that my hands were clean in that deal. He knows that, and he never forgets it. But there's the old grudge, Speedy. I think it comes over him with a sweep now and then. When he remembers how you mastered him in his own camp, it makes him feel foolish and helpless. Then, of course, the rest of his men never have forgotten, either. They all want to get back at you, and they keep your memory fresh in his mind. That's the reason he still takes to your trail now and then, and tries to run you down. I think he'd kill you in cold blood. Afterward he'd wish you back on earth."

"I think so, too," said Speedy. "Because it's been a long game between us. I'm just a trick ahead of him now, but half of the time he has me crowded against the wall, and, if he ever gets the upper hand, I'm a dead man."

"I know," said Al Dupray. "That's like you, Speedy. You'd keep at it for the sake of the risk."

"Al," said the other, changing the subject abruptly, "you're paying a lot more attention to your grammar than you used to, it seems to me."

"You mean I've fixed up the lingo I talk?" said Al Dupray. "I had to do that. Mostly I roll along just the same as ever, but I try to watch my step a little more. Well, Speedy, it's good to have you back."

Speedy smiled. "The same girl, eh?" he said. "You fixed up your lingo for her sake, Al. Is that it?"

The young fellow flushed. "Well, Speedy," he said, "I can't help wondering where you got the idea that I was to see a girl tonight."

"I suppose it seems queer to you that I should guess that," acknowledged Speedy. "But it's no more mysterious than most magic. You never were much for clothes, Al, and, when I saw you all dressed up tonight, I took it for granted that you were going to see a lady. Since you were so serious about it, I also took it for granted that you were even going so far as to ask her to marry you. Fellows who are simply vaguely interested in a girl don't waste their time going to see fortune-tellers. They don't do it even in the pinch, unless they're pretty uneasy."

"But what made you think that I would have had luck?" asked the young fellow.

"Oh, that's the crystal," Speedy said seriously, and yet with a faint smile of deprecation.

"You mean that you believe in that crystal?" asked the other quickly, and with a frown.

The smile of Speedy persisted. "What sort of a magician would I be, Al," he asked, "if I didn't believe in my own magic?"

Al Dupray stood back, frowning. "You get me sort of nervous, Speedy," he said.

"I'm sorry about that," answered the other. "Forget about me, and the fool crystal, too."

Dupray shook his head. "There's always something behind you," he mourned. "You never are shooting quite in the dark, like other fellows. Out with it, Speedy . . . tell me how you could guess that I'd hear the girl say good bye to me tonight?"

But Speedy resolutely shook his head. "I've talked a lot too much," he said.

"I don't say that," urged the young fellow.

"But I do," persisted Speedy.

"You know," said Al Dupray, "in spite of the fact that I know you don't even know her name, I feel like asking your advice about what to do."

"Don't," said Speedy quickly. "Ask my advice about everything else, if you want to, but not about that. Nobody ever follows advice about a woman, anyhow. It's no one's business. Don't ask me what to do."

"I'll ask you one thing," said Al Dupray. "D'you think that people around Clausen, here, have sort of forgotten and forgiven me for having Dupray blood in my body?"

"Are you ashamed of that blood?" snapped Speedy as he had snapped at Dupray once before in the past.

"No, not ashamed," said the young fellow slowly. "But you know the poem where they hang the dead albatross around the neck of the man who shot it. It seems to me, sometimes, that that name of Dupray is hung around my neck the same way."

"Well," said Speedy, "the Duprays have a pretty purple record. And some of the stain will rub off on you. Then, you were accused of murder."

"I was cleared of that, clean as a whistle," said the young man. "You cleared me yourself, Speedy."

"That isn't what matters. After a little while, all people will remember is that you were once accused of murder, not that you were cleared of it. Presently they begin to say . . . 'Where there's smoke, there's fire. There's bound to be.' "

"For every two dollars that I've made out of the mine," replied Dupray, "I've given one to charity, here in Clausen, in the name of Tom Older."

"People will say that you're trying to ease a bad conscience," said Speedy.

"Damn it, Speedy," Dupray cried, "you don't mean that!"

"I do," insisted Speedy. "For everything a man does, he's partly envied and partly hated, so long as the action has any strength in it. Not for things that are simply foolish and cowardly, but for everything that's outstanding. If you kill a man. . . well, half the people will envy your courage in doing it, the other half will want to help hang you. If you don't murder, but are a hero and save a life at the risk of your own, then envy is aroused again. Men shrug their shoulders and smile and sneer, as if to say that they know certain things about you, if they only chose to speak 'em out. We're made that way, all of us."

"Not you, Speedy!" cried the young fellow.

"Stuff," Speedy contradicted. "We're all cut out of the

same sort of flesh and blood. I have a good digestion, that's all."

Dupray considered uncertainly.

Speedy said: "Sooner or later you'll talk to her. Go tonight and have it over with, Al. Then come back here and tell me what's happened."

Dupray sighed. "I'll do it," he said. "She's expecting me after supper."

He held out his hand, and Speedy extended his left.

"I won't take your left hand, Speedy," said the young fellow.

"You've broken my right hand once already, Al," replied the other. "Get out and try your luck. When you come back, I'll be waiting for you here, with somebody probably crossing my hand with silver."

So Dupray went out, found his horse, and rode again up the river road, his head lifted at intervals to glance toward the hill where the lights of the Crane house were gleaming in the darkness.

III

Old man Crane sat on the verandah of his house. The night was chilly and the wind blew the cold straight to the bone now and then, but he hated to go inside the front door. Once within the house, it was a token that he had given up for the day. There followed the laborious undressing, the struggle of getting into bed, and then the long night, when 10,000 devils tormented his unhappy flesh.

As long as he remained on the verandah before his house, even through the darkness, his eyes envisaged the prospect of his fields and hills. The darker shadows of his woodlands were dear to his eye, also. At a time, thirty years before, when many improvident people were clearing their lands, taking down trees big and small with their reckless axes, he had worked with care, selecting only sufficient trees to clear the ground. Now his forests would go on and on under this sort of handling, growing bigger all the time. He had even extended them, planting new trees in districts that were likely to grow better timber than grass. It had needed foresight to accomplish these things. But now he had hundreds of acres of trees thirty years old, tall and straight, and growing more massive of trunk with the passage of every year. Perhaps they would not yield a penny to him, but they would be a sure source of revenue one day to his daughter. He never thought of her without a spasm of pain. She should have been a boy. An excellent boy she would have made.

He had reached this point in his reflections when a horseman came up the road, tethered his horse at the hitching rack in front of the house, and came up the steps almost to the top before he spotted the shrouded form of the old cattleman.

"Mister Crane?" said Al Dupray.

"Yeah, that's me," said Crane. "Come and set down. Here's a chair, if it ain't too cold for you out here."

Dupray sat down, and he and the old man had a few minutes' talk. At length Dupray said: "There's something I've been wanting to say to you, sir."

"Well, fire it into my face, then," said the rancher. "I ain't ever been one to waste time, at that."

"I want to marry Sue," replied the young fellow.

"You wanna marry Sue," said the harsh voice of Crane. "That ain't surprising. There's a lot of boys on the range that wanna marry Sue. What of it?"

"Well . . . ," began Dupray.

The old man broke in more savagely than ever: "You wanna marry Sue. Does she wanna marry you?"

"I haven't asked her."

"Then go and ask her now," replied the other. "There ain't any use of me having my say till she's had hers."

"I'll go, then," said the young fellow with a faint sigh of relief.

"Wait a minute," said Crane. "She might as well step out here. Hey, Sue!"

A voice came, far away, in answer. Footfalls hurried.

"Always running," the father said as harshly as ever. "Always runnin', when I pipe for her. She ain't no modern woman. Not one of these damn' new-fangled, high-headed, worthless mustangs. She's made proper, is what I mean to say."

The screen door opened; the girl came hurrying out. The light from the hall gleamed in her hair, then the darkness enveloped her.

"Yes, Father?" she asked.

"Here's Al Dupray wanting you," said the father.

"Hello, Al!" the girl called out.

He was only able to mutter words of no sense in reply.

"Here's Al," said Crane, raising his voice as though he were addressing an entire crowd. "He's come over here wanting to marry you."

"Ah?" said the girl.

It seemed to Al Dupray that all his heart's blood leaped, for when she cried out and moved it was a little toward him, not away. Only a trifle, a mere gesture, a mere leaning, but he had seen it, and he felt that he understood it.

"He's come here to marry you," said Crane. "Whatcha say about it, Sue?"

She went behind the wheelchair and laid her hands on his shoulders. "You're to say for me, Father."

"You like him all right?" asked Crane.

"Yes, I like Al," she said.

The music of the spheres hummed in the ears of Al Dupray.

"She likes you, Al Dupray," commenced the father. "Now, Sue, you say that I'm gonna have the disposing of you?"

"Yes," said the girl.

"Tell him why," went on Crane.

"Because," said the girl, "I'm all that Father has to leave the place to. I'm only a girl. He wanted a son. He prayed for a son. But he only had a daughter, so he wants to pick the right man for me. The sort who'll carry on with the place."

The heart of the young fellow sank.

"D'you understand that, Al Dupray?" asked the father.

"Yes, I hear what she says."

The old man swept an arm before him. "This here is my work. I made it," he said. "I growed most of them trees. I bred the cows that eat that grass. It's my place. It's all mine. It's gotta go down into the hands of a reliable fellow that'll handle it right."

"I understand," said Al Dupray. His strength and confidence were ebbing fast. He prayed inwardly that the girl might speak again, but she was silent.

"Whatcha know about cows, Al?" asked Crane.

"I can ride herd. I can handle a rope, cut, and brand . . . all that."

"I don't ask you if you can daub a rope. I don't ask you are you a cowhand," said the old rancher. "Any fool can throw a rope. But d'you know cows?"

"In what way?"

"Know how to foller the Eastern markets, so's to pick the right time for selling? Know how to keep your barns full of hay against a bad winter? Know when to keep your

whole herd over maybe three years, till bad times turn
into good times? Do you know any of those things, I'd
like to know?"

"I'm not much of a businessman, I suppose," Dupray
said faintly.

"Ain't you?"

"No, I'm not."

"Well, whatcha got to say for yourself? I'm listening
to whatcha got to say. I ain't gonna be in no rush about
making up my mind. Sue, she likes you all right."

"I don't know what to say," said the young fellow.
"I suppose you know that I'm pretty well fixed with
money. I've over a hundred thousand out of the mine
. . . and it's still producing."

"Damn money!" said Crane. "Damn your hundred
thousand and all mines, anyway. They never do
nothing but rot the hearts and the souls out of the folks
that dig the money out of the rock. Easy come and easy
go. Cows is the business for this country. Cows and
timber. That's what I got, ain't it?"

"Yes, it's what you have," Dupray said, turning to
ice.

"And it's the right thing to have," said the terrible
Crane. "Cows and timber is the thing to have. And
no fool is gonna marry my girl. Not if I'm living, and
she's true to her word to me. Listen to me, Sue. Am I
livin'?"

"Of course," she said.

"And are you true to your word?"

"Yes," the girl said faintly.

"Then, by thunder," said Joshua Crane, "I ain't
gonna throw you away on Dupray. Do you hear me,
Dupray?"

"I hear you," said the young fellow.

"You're a Dupray, ain't you?"

"Yes."

"And your own uncle is Charley Murderer Dupray, ain't he?"

"Charles Dupray is my uncle," groaned Al.

"Then," Joshua Crane cried, "I wouldn't have you married to Sue. By thunder, I'd rise right out of the grave and haunt you both."

"Father!" moaned the girl.

"Are you cryin' out for him?" asked Joshua Crane in a terrible voice.

"No, Father," she said.

"You cried out for him, but you didn't cry big," said Joshua Crane. "Al Dupray, you've heard most of what I've got to say."

"I've heard a good deal," the young fellow said bitterly.

"But mind you, it ain't nothing to what I could lay onto you if my girl wasn't here, and her liking you, all right. I'm holding off. I'm holding back, I can tell you."

Al Dupray said nothing. He turned his head and strained his eyes toward Sue Crane. It seemed impossible, if she "liked him all right," she would let him leave her as hopelessly and with such a cruel dismissal as this.

Joshua Crane broke in: "Sue!"

"Yes, Father."

"He don't seem to know that he ain't tied with a rope. You go and set him free and let him gallop. We don't want no more of him around here. We don't want no Duprays!"

She stepped across to Dupray, and, in so doing, a shaft of light fell on her face. It was sad, with a faint, wistful smile upon it. She held out her hand.

"Good bye, Al," she said.

He did not touch the hand, but another ghostly hand closed over his heart. He stepped suddenly back from her, gasping out: "Speedy! It's what Speedy said!"

That was his odd good bye to her.

Running down the steps, he mounted his horse and rode like mad down the steep pitch of the roadway and away into the darkness. The iron clanging of the hoofs against the stones came back to them in fainter and fainter rhythm.

"Look here, Sue," said Crane.

"Yes, Father," she said.

"Are you all right? You ain't grieving?"

"No, I'm not grieving."

"I thought I heard you sort of moan, like you'd stifled a sob or something."

"It's only the wind rising," said the girl. "It makes mournful sounds, you know."

"It does," he agreed. "And if the wind's rising, it's time for me to be getting back inside the house."

IV

Dupray's mustang sprinted all the way back to the Gypsy camp, while the stars flew above the trees as he stormed down the way.

He could not enter the tent, however. Young Ed Walker and Tommy Legrange were in there. He could hear their foolish, brawling voices that grated savagely on his ear. The long moments dragged on, while the voices of Legrange and Walker grew less and less boisterous; finally there was nothing but the pause and murmur of the crystal-gazer.

At last the pair came out. As they were passing close by the place where Dupray stood in the dark, he heard Walker muttering: "Dog-gone me, he seen right through us. D'you think that he really knows anything about it?"

Whatever that guilty secret might be, which Speedy had unraveled, or nearly so, Dupray cared nothing for it. The load on his own heart was too great for him to bear, and he hurried in at once before the seer.

Speedy raised a warning hand.

"It's all right," murmured Dupray. "I know it's business hours with you, Speedy." He sat down on the stool and said in a rapid whisper: "Speedy, tell me, did you know that Sue would refuse me?"

"I didn't know that her name was Sue," replied Speedy.

"You saw the whole picture just as it turned out, her hand out to me, and her face sad, saying good bye. How did you know that?" Al Dupray asked.

"I didn't know it, really," said Speedy. "Or, rather, the crystal knew, not I."

"That doesn't go with me," said Dupray. "I know that the crystal is only your own uncanny guessing, Speedy."

"D'you think so?" muttered Speedy. "I used to think that myself. Sometimes, now, I'm not so sure. I don't know where the guesses come from half the time."

"Tell me, if you can, where they came from this evening about what was going to happen to me," said the young fellow.

"I don't want to step on your toes, Al."

"Never mind my toes. I'm burning up, Speedy. She refused me. Not the girl, really, but that demon of a father. He forced her to." He added: "How did you know anything about her saying good bye to me?"

"It's like this," Speedy replied slowly. "You were worked up about a girl. That was easily guessed, as I told you before. And it was plain that you were about to bring the thing to a head. Well, then, from all of your excitement I gathered that the girl might be somebody important. And . . . well, partner, everybody in the West knows that you're the nephew of Charley Dupray, and Charley's record is a pretty long and black one. On the strength of that record I imagined that she would refuse you. If she was the right sort of a girl, though, she'd be sorry for the refusal in a way, and sorry for you, too."

Dupray closed his eyes and groaned. "Speedy," he said. "She likes me. She likes me a lot, and I'll swear it. It was only the old man who did me in, damn him. Old Joshua Crane, wrapped up in his blanket, grinning like an Indian, he did me in!" He dropped his face in his trembling hands.

"A girl that's worth her salt would never let her father give you the run, partner. Ever think of that?" Speedy asked.

"Yes, I've thought of that," said the young fellow. "But she's not like other girls. He's raised her in a special way. He's raised her to have a lot of respect for her parents, and all that. He's done the job brown, Speedy. Then, you see, she's the sole heir to his ranch, and he loves that ranch more than he loves life. He's worked all his days at it. The girl has known for years that her husband must be a fellow who can handle the ranch in the right way. Don't you see what that means?"

"I know. Businessman. Keen head, iron hand, and all that sort of thing," replied Speedy.

"That's it. Old Joshua wanted a son, but when his wife died a little after their marriage and left the girl, he wouldn't marry again."

"He's brought the girl up according to his own ideas, has he?" Speedy asked.

"She thinks that his word is a law from heaven," replied the young fellow.

Speedy nodded. "I've seen one woman in the world before this," he said, "that was the same way."

"So what she says when her father commands her doesn't mean much. You'll agree to that?"

Speedy nodded again.

"But the point is," said Al Dupray, "that I don't see how I can do anything about it. Nobody could think of what to do except you, partner." He made a brief gesture. There was a world of appeal in his face and his eyes.

"You're pretty fond of her?" asked Speedy.

"I can't live without her," answered the young fellow.

Speedy frowned. "That's caused more trouble than anything else in the world," he declared. "I mean that attitude that people our age get sometimes . . . that they can't live without a certain girl."

"It's true," Al Dupray said.

"It's not true," Speedy contradicted. "Suppose that Sue Crane didn't exist, d'you think that you'd never run into another girl that you'd want to marry?"

"Speedy, you might as well tell a tree after lightning has split it to pieces, that it's lucky . . . that there's stronger thunder than that in the sky," said Al.

Speedy smiled faintly. "If you take it that way, I guess I've got to help you, Al."

Dupray leaned back with a sigh, and then smiled. "I sort of knew that you'd come through for me in a pinch," he said.

"You act," Speedy said, "as though the thing were done this instant just because I take a hand."

"It is as good as done," said Al Dupray, his eyes shining with confidence. "You've never failed in anything you tackled before, and you won't fail at this job, either. It may take time, but you always win."

"You think so?" asked Speedy. He looked wistfully at the young fellow. Suddenly his expression was that of an old, old man who, down the great perspective of the years, peers at the face of modern youth and finds it very strange. "Well," he went on, "whether I can do anything about it or not, I don't know. Have you any ideas of your own?"

"Me?" Al said, as though greatly surprised. "Why, Speedy, when you step into the picture, I don't expect to use my own head. I'm just a hired man now. I do what you tell me to do, and jump when you tell me to jump."

"Even when there's a cliff ahead of you?"

"Yes, even when there's a cliff."

"All right," murmured Speedy almost wearily. "All right. I'll try it. But you ought to have some idea of how we can go about it."

"I could kidnap her," said Al. "Once I had her, I know that I could make her happy, some way or other." He sat up, hopeful with this suggestion.

Speedy lifted a hand. "That's no good," he declared. "It isn't the girl that we have to work on."

"You mean we have to tackle the father?"

"That's it."

"You can't manage that," said Al Dupray. "I don't pretend to do your thinking for you, Speedy, but I tell you that nothing will change the old man. He's as hard as rock."

"Are you sure?"

"Yes, I'm dead sure. I'm surer of that than I ever was of anything in my entire life."

"Just the same," said Speedy, "I've an idea that he may be changed. Anything that's human can be changed."

"He ain't human," broke out the young fellow. "He's an Egyptian mummy. The blood dried up in him five thousand years ago."

"He's pretty cold," agreed Speedy, "but I think that he can be handled one way or another." Then he shrugged his shoulders. "What will your uncle think about this?" he asked.

"What difference does that make?" asked the young man in his turn.

"He'll be on my shoulders all the faster, that's all," said Speedy.

"If he ever tries to harm you . . . ," began Dupray, his face contracting with a great passion at the very thought.

"Oh, that's all right," interrupted Speedy. "It would make the game all the better. But Charley Dupray on one side, and friend Joshua Crane on the other . . . well, we'll have to try juggling. That's all. Tomorrow I'll tell you what we're to do about it. Tomorrow, at noon, I'll meet you at your house. Is that all right?"

"Anything that you say is all right," said Al Dupray, rising to his feet. "Anything goes, as long as you're in the game on my side." He sighed contentedly and stretched himself. "I'm going to go and get something to eat, Speedy," he said. "The fact is, ten minutes ago I didn't care whether I lived or died. But now I know that I want to live, and that life is going to be a song."

V

Old Joshua Crane, once he was in his wheelchair, would propel himself considerable distances from the house. Although his legs were powerless, his strength seemed to have retreated entirely to his leathery arms, and their might was redoubled. Working the two-handed crank, he used to dash down slopes at a terrific speed in order to force his way up the next hill.

More than once he had upset himself in this manner. Also, as he went careening and dodging through the trees of his woodlands, he was likely to tip himself over. There was much danger of a serious or even of a fatal accident, considering his condition. For one thing, after falling, he could not manage to get himself back into the chair, and once he had lain in a heavy rain for five hours until the searching parties found him, in the dark of the evening.

On this mid-morning he sat two hills removed from his house, on a fine summit that commanded a wide view of the grazing lands that were his own. Now and then he shifted his look toward adjoining pieces of property. There had been times when he could not look on them without desire and envy, but that feeling had passed away from him by degrees, and he was coming to a pleasant, tranquil state of mind in which he regarded his estate as perfect. He would not have it smaller, certainly, but then he did not really wish it to be larger, either. Someday a younger man might run the place much further afield. But at present it was enough for him.

He closed his eyes presently to enjoy the heat of the sun and his own contented thoughts; when he opened them, he saw a strange figure coming up the slope not twenty steps from him, a form in a long red coat of silk, with red slippers on the feet and a black skullcap with a red tassel on the head. His step was light and long, but he wore a beard, and his face appeared to be seamed with age.

"Gypsy," said Joshua Crane to himself. And his face and his heart hardened.

The stranger paused before him, lifted a hand to his forehead, and bowed long.

"Don't begin your lingo. Get out!" said Joshua Crane. He handled the Winchester that lay across his knees.

"Brother . . . ," began the stranger.

"Brother to what? To you, you smoky-faced son of trouble?" broke in the rancher. "I told you to get out. Now budge, will you?"

The other stood up straight, and, folding his arms, his hands disappeared into the opposite sleeves. "Grief is come to you, Joshua Crane," he said, "and yet you give yourself up to vain passions."

"Grief?" said Crane. "I never felt better in my life. Whatcha mean by grief, you?"

The white beard wagged slowly from side to side. "Oh, brother," he said, "it is a vain thing to attempt to penetrate the future except with help."

"You get inside the future, do you?" said Crane.

"Brother, I do."

"I understand," said Crane, "you're the crystal-gazer that works down there by the river. Ain't that so?"

"I look in the crystal," said the Gypsy. "And I see in it a flood of light."

The ball of crystal appeared in his hand as he spoke, and the sun turned it into an intolerable blaze of white fire.

Joshua Crane blinked. "I've heard tell something about you," he said. "Somebody was telling my girl . . . some fool was telling her. But you ain't had your palm crossed with silver by me. There ain't nothing that you can tell about my future."

The Gypsy grinned as he received this retort, and thrust out his lean chin until, in fact, he looked very much like some Rameses in old age. "The silver is not needed," said the man of the red robe. "That is the wretched device to which I am driven by need. I am not rich. I am only the slave of the crystal, and it drives me. But by cheap and foolish tricks I try to earn my daily food." He sighed and shook his head.

At this the rancher thrust himself still farther forward in the chair, and stared earnestly into the eyes of the other. He could generally boast that, by such a glance, he was able to draw up something from the shadowy deeps of the soul. But now he was baffled. Eyes as keen and as steady as his own looked back at him. They seemed to be young eyes, in spite of the face, and they were dark and brilliant. Joshua Crane leaned back again in his chair with an ill-natured grunt.

"You say that you're half a fraud. I say that you're all a fraud," he said.

"Brother," said the stranger, "you say many things that are not the truth."

"Are you callin' me a liar?" demanded Crane fiercely.

"I am not a deceiver," said the man in the red robe. "And that you know, and that you fear."

"Hold on! I'm afraid of you, am I?"

"You are a little afraid," said the other. "Every moment your fear increases and your anger grows less."

"That's a lie as broad as it's long," said Crane, "and it's a mile long, the way that I see it."

The other waved his hand and shrugged his shoulders. He caused the blazing crystal to disappear.

"Well, I'll tell you what I'll do," said Joshua Crane. "I've heard that you can tell the future. Any fool can do that. I can do it. You bet I can. Put a white hoss and a black rider under a thin moon, with a wind blowing . . . pile up a lot of folderol like that, and folks are pretty sure to believe in you, eh?"

"Of course they are," said the Gypsy.

Joshua Crane blinked again. "You admit that you tell lies to folks that come to you?"

"If I did not tell lies," said the stranger, "they would soon stop coming. The pleasant lies are what most men wish to hear. I tell them so much that is pleasant that very soon they are crossing and recrossing my hand with silver. In that way I live, although I am only the slave of the crystal. But there is little that is pleasant in the truth as the crystal tells it."

"Dog-gone me," said Joshua Crane, "but you kind of interest me. I dunno that I ever heard nobody yarn like this before, and I'd like to know what you're drivin' at. You say that the crystal don't tell you much that's good about people?"

"How can it?" said the seer. "If I look through it into the mind of a young man, I see folly that shivers the glass, and if I look into the mind of an old man, I see death . . . at least, the darkness of a shadow that is soon coming. If I look into the mind of a bride, she is less happy than she is vain. If I examine the mind of a rich and great man, he sees in the whole world nothing but himself."

"Well," said Joshua Crane, "I'm old, and I'm gonna die soon, certain. But what's brought you up here to spin yarns with me?"

"I have not come for money," said the other.

"What has fetched you, then?"

"The crystal," said the other, "for I am its slave." He produced it again and raised it. Looking up at the crystal, its fiery point of light, gathered from the sun, seemed to glance into the eyes of the man in the red robe as if it were burning out the very nerves of vision, but he merely smiled as he looked up toward his treasure.

Old Joshua Crane exclaimed: "That's a lot of bunk! You can't talk to me like that, stranger. But, dog-gone me, you could fool a lot of people on the stage, you do it so good. You oughtn't to be wasting your time with a mangy lot of wandering Gypsies. You oughta be doing your turn on the stage with the lingo that you've got. I've heard lots that were worse." He nodded as he said this, and smiled upon the stranger with a good deal of self-satisfaction. "You ain't told me yet," he said, "why the crystal fetched you here to me. Lemme hear your lingo about that."

The Gypsy frowned, and then sighed again. "There is only one thing that I did not see clearly," said the man of the red robe, "and it makes me sorry that I have come. I saw that you were about to die, but I did not see. . . ."

"You seen that I was about to die, and any fool that knows what this here kind of paralysis is would know that," said the rancher, unmoved. "But what did the dog-gone crystal tell you that was worthwhile, I'd like to know?"

"It did not tell me, for one thing, or else I was unable to look clearly into it, that you were so old. I thought that I was coming to see a young man. Tell me, brother, if you have not a son, exactly like you in the face, but very young?"

"I've got a girl," said the rancher. "I ain't got a boy."

"Then," said the crystal-gazer, "it is true that I did not look closely enough. I saw the face clearly, so that I knew you at sight, but I did not see you closely enough to realize that you are not young."

"You mean that you looked into your crystal ball and all at once you seen me?"

"That is what I mean, and what I saw made me come in haste."

"Now looka here," warned the rancher, "I don't mind yarning with you for a minute, but you ain't gonna get a single penny out of me."

The man of the crystal ball drew himself up with a great deal of dignity. "Brother," he said, "do you think that all men who have dark skins are dogs, to be kicked from your path?"

Joshua Crane twisted his mouth and bit his lip. "Well," he said, "I dunno that I've been talking none too smooth to you, stranger, but I don't like cheats, and I don't like intruders. This here is my land, and all that I've knowed about Gypsies is that they're scoundrels and thieves, hoss thieves most of all. I've always thought that it might be one of your folks that stole the Nighthawk from me." His face darkened savagely as he mentioned the name. "One of your sneakin' gangs," he repeated. "Seven thousand dollars' worth of hossflesh, cheap at that price, too, and he was stole from me."

"To lose a horse," said the man of the crystal, "is a sorrow like the loss of a child."

"He was worth about ten ordinary kids," said the rancher. "Seven thousand dollars of him. He was

worth that in the stud, without never having raced.
Just his strain was worth that. And some one of you
damn' Gypsies or greaser hoss rustlers, you got that
stallion after I'd cured him up for running." He
flushed and sweated with his passion. Then he broke
out: "Stranger, I guess I don't wanna talk to you no
more. I'm tired of talk. At my age, lookin' is better than
talkin'. Just settin' and lookin' and thinkin'." He shook
his head and settled back in his chair, half closing his
eyes. When he looked up again, he found the stranger
still before him.

"Vamoose!" Crane shouted angrily. "Or," he went
on, letting his head fall back once more, "you don't
need to bother none about the future or the past. You
just tell me what I'm thinkin' about this very minute,
will you?"

He looked at the horizon as he spoke, and the man
of the red robe instantly produced the crystal, raised it,
and spun it so that it whirled rapidly on the top of one
finger. Yet so steadily was it balanced that the image of
the blazing sun in the ball trembled, but did not waver
from side to side.

Presently the voice of the gazer said: "I see the face
of a woman. She is young. Her eyes are like my eyes."

A great, stifled cry broke from the rancher; the gazer
caused the crystal to disappear once more.

VI

Old Joshua Crane had gripped his withered throat with both hands, but presently he drew them away and passed them across his staring eyes. Then, bracing himself forward in the chair, he demanded: "What devil told you that, stranger?"

"The crystal ball," said the man of the red robe.

Old Crane groaned aloud. "Can there be something in it?" he muttered. "Ain't it one more trick? Ain't it one more trick, I say?"

"How could it be a trick, brother?" replied the crystal-gazer.

"You've gone and pried into the story of my house!" cried Joshua Crane. "That's what you've done. You've gone spying on my past. You've got hold of a picture of my poor dead girl, and you dare, you sneakin', greasy-faced hound, to stand out here in the open day and speak about her." He paused, choking with emotion.

"Brother, no matter what I may have spied out about you, what am I to gain from it?" asked the Gypsy. "And what am I to do? And how could I spy on your own mind and see her face, except that the crystal showed it to me?"

The rancher, his eyes closed tightly, breathed hard and irregularly. "Look here," said Crane, "you came here for something. You came here to get something. What is it?"

"Brother," said the man of the crystal, "I came here to give you warning."

"You come up here to warn me that I was gonna die, eh? That's pretty smart, all right, seein' the age that I am."

"There was something else," said the stranger, "something worse than that . . . the image of a girl and a man, and you beside them, seated, and the girl holding out her hand with a sad face. She was saying farewell."

"To me?" snarled the rancher.

"No, to the young man."

"This is getting dog-gone strange," muttered Crane. "You seen sorrow in her face? How could you see that when there wasn't no light, hardly?"

"I did not see. The crystal saw. It can look, dimly, through the darkest night, brother."

"Is that all there was to it?" asked Crane, actual fear beginning to show in his eyes.

"That was not all," said the stranger slowly and impressively. "What else?" muttered Crane.

"The picture had come suddenly before my eyes," said the man of the crystal. "Therefore I looked very earnestly and long at it, and I prayed that the crystal might continue to spin for a long time. Then I was sorry that I had gazed so long, for the dark curtain fell." He was silent.

"What's the dark curtain?" asked Crane.

"Death!"

"Death?" said Crane. "I'm ready for that."

"You need have no fear. There are years before you . . . but not for the other. There are only weeks and months, perhaps. Over that face the dark curtain fell first with a sudden rush."

"Dupray's face?" said Crane. "I wouldn't be surprised none if he was bumped off almost any time. He's got bad blood in him, and bad blood is gonna lead to gun plays, and gun plays are sure death. I ain't surprised. It kind of shows me that you are able to see something."

"It was not the face of a man," said the seer.

"What?"

"It was not the face of a man."

"It wasn't?"

"No, it was not a man."

"D'you mean that it was my girl . . . Sue?" breathed Crane.

The man of the red robe bowed his head. "Ah, brother," he said, "is she your daughter?" He spoke gently.

Strange stories swarmed through the mind of Crane. Was there not the instance of the old woman who, seated at her door in mid-afternoon, saw the street darken and the image of a sinking ship, when, at that very moment, a thousand miles away, the ship that carried her son was going down in a storm? The strength went out of his iron heart as he said: "There wouldn't be nobody or nothing in the world that would touch Sue. She's plumb gentle."

"Ah, no, brother," said the stranger. "That which I saw in her face as the curtain fell was neither violence nor pain, but grief."

"What's that?" cried Crane.

The old man remained for a long time with his head bowed, considering. His hands were gripped into hard fists, and his body shuddered with the violence of the contest that was going on inside him. At last he said: "It might be. There's a romance, kind of, hangin' around the necks of scoundrels and scapegraces. Folks talked about him a lot. Folks have pitied him because of the name that weighs him down. Dupray! I'd rather that he was called the devil."

"Ah, brother," said the other, "I know nothing of names."

"Then get out with you," said the rancher.

"I go in sorrow," said the crystal-gazer.

"I'll make your sorrow a mite less, anyway. It's likely all a lie, but, by thunder, the like of it I never heard. Here's ten dollars in gold for you, you rascal."

The crystal-gazer made a sweeping gesture of refusal. "Do you think that I have come this long distance and endured many cruel words for the sake of winning a little gold? No, I came because grief makes us all brethren, and I, too, have known grief. Brother, farewell."

He turned as he said this, and hurried down the hill with the same strangely light, long stride that the rancher had noticed before. Crane watched him go. Evidently the refusal of the money had removed any final doubts. The old man was fearful of the future.

VII

The man of the red robe stepped over the hill and, passing through a small grove, came out on the farther side, minus white beard, manufactured wrinkles, shaggy eyebrows, and all; the robe, the red slippers, the skullcap were gone, as well. He called out softly as he approached a nest of rocks where Al Dupray was waiting.

"What's the luck, Speedy?" asked Dupray anxiously. "There has been luck . . . I can tell that, right enough." His eyes began to shine as he hurried toward the other, leading his horse.

"Jump into the saddle," said Speedy. "Ride like the devil for the Crane house, and get hold of Sue if you can. Old Crane will be back there before long, full of excitement and beginning to think that he's just seen an evil spirit or a prophet on earth. He won't be sure which." He smiled faintly as he said this.

Dupray was already in the saddle, but he lingered to ask: "What did you do, Speedy?"

Speedy gave a full account of the meeting. Then he added: "He has an idea that perhaps he's breaking Sue's heart by driving you away. Ten chances to one he'll go back to his house to make sure. When he gets there, he must find you already on the spot. He'll curse you, I suppose, and tell you to get out, but if you put a little pressure on him, then he's very apt to change his mind. Hurry up, partner. I'll be waiting here."

"Not at the camp?" said the other.

"No," replied Speedy. "I think that I'll leave them my empty tent . . . and they'll be glad to have that. The crystal tells me, Al, that there's likely to be a job for both of us before long."

Dupray did not wait to thank his friend, but drove his mustang with arrowy speed straight across the hills and toward the house of Joshua Crane.

The old man and the wheelchair he did not see as he approached, so he flung himself to the ground, threw the reins of his horse, and rapped at the door.

The old Negress who cooked for the house appeared at the door and wiped her hands on her apron, while she looked thoughtfully at the young man. She did not know whether she knew that Sue was at home or not, but she would go to see. So she went back, with a waddling step, through the dim hallway.

Presently Sue Crane came and stood before him on the verandah. It was plain that she was frightened, and that she was gathering courage to face him.

"Look here, Sue," he said. "I haven't any right to come back here, have I?"

"Not till Father permits you to come," answered the girl.

"Well, there's one thing that gives me a right," he went on. "I've never asked you yourself how you feel about me."

"I can't talk about that unless . . . ," she began.

He struck right in fiercely. He would not have dared to adopt such a tone, but he was fresh from Speedy, and he was inspired. "You're able to send me away spinning," he said. "You're able to say that your father doesn't want me around. Then why aren't you able to tell me whether you want me around yourself?"

"What I want doesn't count," she said, shaking her head. Her lip began to tremble.

"Don't cry, Sue," he entreated.

"I'm not going to," she answered. "But if you care about me, I must not give you any reason to hope. Father will never change his mind."

"What do I care about his mind?" demanded the young fellow. "There's only one important affair, and that's between you and me. Ever since I first knew you, you've known that I was crazy about you, haven't you?"

She was silent, and flushed.

"Look at me, Sue, and say yes or no," he commanded.

"I've thought you liked me pretty well," she said.

"Now," said Dupray, "I'm thrown off the place. Well, there are reasons. They're all summed up in my name. I'm a Dupray. That's poison. Your father can't stand that, and so he throws me off the place. But what I want to know now is was I making myself a fool from the very start?"

"No, no, Al," said the girl anxiously.

"You didn't think, then, that I was just a poison snake?"

"No, no!"

"You think it now, but you didn't think it then?"

"I don't think it now. I never thought it," she said, her voice growing uncertain.

"Then," he said, "you thought I was fair enough in the old days?"

She was silent, appealing to him with her eyes.

"I'm not asking what you think now," he pointed out. "I'm just asking about the beginning. I'm asking about the old days. You could have liked me then?"

"I did like you a lot, Al," said the girl.

"When I came to see you, you didn't mind that?"

"No, I didn't mind that," she admitted. "I liked it. I liked seeing you, Al. Only. . . ."

"Then I wasn't making a fool of myself?"

"No, you weren't."

"If your father had said to you one of these days . . . 'Sue, Dupray is the sort of man I want for your husband. I command you to marry him.' Suppose that he had said that. Would you have broken your heart about it, Sue?"

She half turned to escape, then she covered her face with her hands. At that moment a hard, high-pitched, nasal voice yelled out of the near distance: "Dupray!"

He turned and saw old Joshua Crane sweeping toward them, turning the double-handled crank of his wheelchair with all his strength.

The girl caught the arm of Dupray. "Al, nothing will happen?" she pleaded.

"Nothing'll happen," he assured her.

"Sue, get inside that house!" shouted the father.

She fled at once, while Dupray hurried down the steps and faced the tyrant.

"You damn' puppy!" cried out the old man.

Al Dupray stood silently. He was not very angry, for he felt that in some manner Speedy had turned this affair into a game in which he, through Speedy's clever machinations, was sure to win.

"You came back anyway, did you?" said Crane.

"I saw her once more," said the young fellow. "I wanted to say good bye to her."

"You did, did you?"

"Yes, I did."

"Are you through with it now?"

"No," said Al Dupray boldly. "You sent her back into the house before we'd finished talking."

"You . . . you . . . ," stammered old Joshua Crane. "You had her crying. Oh, I know the kind you are, Al Dupray." He brought out the name like an oath.

"Maybe I'm bad," said Dupray. "Maybe my blood's bad. But I never could be unkind to her."

"I'd oughta up with the rifle and shoot you through the head," declared Crane. "If I catch you around here again, I'm gonna do it. And I'll pass the word along to my cowpunchers, that, when they see you, they're to make you hop. Understand?"

Dupray said nothing.

"Get out!" yelled Crane.

"What a mean old hound you are," said the young fellow.

"I'm a what?"

"A mean old hound. You've got an idea that I want Sue because of this ranch you've got together. I don't give a damn about the ranch or about you. She's all I want. But you're never going to let go of her until you've passed her along to somebody that don't care a rap about anything but pasture land and cows. A sweet life she'll have of it."

"She'll have the sort of a life that I want for her!" shouted Crane.

"You look," said Al Dupray, "like the kind that could pick out the right sort of a life for a girl like Sue. You're a bully first. But second, you're a fool. And there's more fool than bully in you."

Crane grew suddenly cold sober. "If I was twenty years younger . . . ," he muttered, and then he was still, watching the young fellow with bright, hostile eyes.

"You'd get up and kick me off the place, eh?" said Al Dupray. "Maybe you'd try that trick. But I don't think that you've ever been a real man. You've talked your life away. You've never done anything real except to raise beef and sell it."

Joshua Crane drew in a great breath, as though he needed cooling. Then he made a sweeping gesture with his hand. "You're a man, are you?"

"You mean am I the right sort of foreman for your ranch? No, maybe I'm not," said the young man.

"What you ever done in your life, then?" demanded the rancher.

Al Dupray stiffened a little. "What ought a fellow do to prove that he's worthy of Sue?" he demanded.

"If you'd ever done one real, decent thing in your life, I might take another think about you and Sue," said Joshua Crane. "I might give you a chance at her, Dupray or no Dupray."

"Give me a job, then, and make it man-sized," said the young fellow. "As long as it doesn't turn into hay and beef, I could try my hand at it. Give me a chance to earn Sue, will you?"

"Earn Sue? Earn my girl. You?" said the other angrily. Then he changed suddenly, as though he felt a stroke of keenest physical pain. "Well," he said at last, "I dunno. Even supposing that I was wrong. . . ." His voice died out, then he began again: "Why, what do I care what you do, so long as it proves that you got the right stuff in you? Do something that takes brains and patience and courage. Well, do anything. Go and find the Nighthawk for me." He smote his hands together. "The Nighthawk," he repeated. "That's the trick. Go out and find him, and bring him back here safe and sound. When I see him out in front of the house, I'll know that a real man has rode up to our front door."

VIII

In the town of El Rey, far south of the Rio Grande, nested high among the mountains, there was an inn, and in the inn there was a large room overlooking the patio. In this room sat Al Dupray, giving orders to a slender, brown-skinned youth who stood on the threshold of the open door, bowing and cringing. His clothes were in tatters. His bare shanks showed from the knees to the sandals he wore. His coat was a mere rag; a rag of a torn red shirt showed beneath it.

"You have been gone three days," said Dupray, speaking a fair sample of Spanish. "The servants of this cursed *fonda* have had to look after my horses while you were away. How much moldy hay they've given 'em in the meantime, I can   only guess. I never had much use for you, and I've less than none now, you son of a rat. Close the door."

The door was closed. Young Al Dupray stood up and began to beat the floor with his quirt, while the brown-skinned youth skipped and wailed and bowed for mercy.

At length, panting, Dupray laid the quirt aside. Subdued laughter could be heard as Dupray said: "Well, sit down, Speedy. As a matter of fact, I thought you'd never get here. Two days is a devilish time to be sitting here waiting."

Speedy rolled a cigarette, lighted it, and threw himself flat on his back on the bed, his eyes closed with pleasure as he inhaled the smoke with great breaths.

"Anything turned up?" asked Dupray. There was no answer, and Dupray went on querulously: "We've followed a wrong trail for a long time, I think. The trouble is that it's not so easy to describe the Nighthawk. Plenty of horses are dark brown with black points. Plenty of horses are sixteen one. That's tall, but there are plenty more just as tall. He's no beauty, either, to fill your eye. It needs a horseman to read his points, as I understand it."

"It needs a horseman," said Speedy, yawning and puffing forth a great cloud of smoke.

Dupray glared at him. "Here I've been sitting like a fool these two days," he said, "telling lies to the greasers, Speedy, while you wander around and have the fun. What the devil have you been doing all this while?"

"Finding the Nighthawk," answered Speedy.

Dupray bounded to his feet. "Speedy," he said, "this isn't one of your infernal jokes, is it?"

Speedy yawned and puffed forth more smoke. "I'm tired," he said. "I haven't slept for a couple of days. Let me alone for an hour or so, Al."

Dupray, burning up with curiosity, nevertheless realized that he had better remain silent. If he importuned Speedy too much, the latter might defend himself with a still longer silence.

He occupied himself with walking up and down the floor of the room. He went to the window and listened to the monotonous sing-song chant of one of the house *mozos*, at work out of sight in the court beneath. Still the time wore on very slowly.

It might be a round of the clock before a man who had not reposed for forty-eight hours was able to lift his head again. But Speedy was a different problem, and Dupray knew it. What was hardly a pause in the course of exhaustion was to Speedy a complete repose. He could assemble a few catnaps and call them a night's sleep. He could sleep sitting. He could sleep standing, even—that is to say, he could profoundly doze.

Dupray waited two restless hours. Then that slight figure on the bed stirred and instantly sat up. There was one yawn. After that the magic fingers made a cigarette with what seemed no more than a gesture.

Still Al Dupray dared not ask a question, for he could guess that his headlong manner of questioning had offended the other.

Through a cloud of smoke, Speedy said: "It was a long trail, Al. I would have talked to you a lot more and argued out my plans with you, but most of the time I was going on instinct."

"What sort of an instinct, Speedy?"

"Well, that nobody but a Mexican could have done the job. Nobody but a Mexican would have picked out that one horse and gone off with it. There were twenty more in the field, and a good American rustler would have made a clean sweep of the lot. That is, that was my guess. But there was another chance." Dupray waited, and Speedy went on slowly: "It might have been some old jockey gone to the bad and on the road, someone who knew the breeding of the Nighthawk, and wanted to race the stallion. He's of a famous line, you know."

"I know," murmured Dupray. "Seven thousand dollars is a lot, but, even at that price, I understand old Crane couldn't have got him except that he'd broken down in training."

"He broke down, but two years on the range fixed him. He's hard as iron now, I believe, and, if he were taken to the big Eastern tracks, he'd make a lot of money."

Dupray nodded.

"It might have been that he was stolen like that," said Speedy. "There was a good chance of it. But there are more Mexicans than jockeys in that part of the range, so I put my bet on the Mexican idea. That's why we headed straight south. We were nearly to the Rio Grande before I hit another clue. That was only a hint . . . Vicente Bardillo, of the town of El Rey, who can't be caught in the open because he rides a brown stallion as fast as the wind."

"I do remember," said the young fellow. "That didn't mean much to me at the time, though. Vicente Bardillo would never leave his town long enough to ride as far north as the Crane place to steal a horse."

"That's true. On the other hand, any Mexican horse thief with half a brain would realize that no man south of the Rio Grande would pay as much for a perfect horse as Bardillo would. I worked on that chance. This morning I saw the horse."

Al Dupray turned white. "You saw the Nighthawk?"

"I saw him."

"There are lots of brown stallions in the world," said the young fellow doubtfully.

"Of course, there are," said Speedy. "I know that, but not so many just about sixteen hands high in this part of the world, with ugly heads, perfect legs, hip bones that stick out a good bit, and quarters that look too stringy and thin to be strong. At first glance this fellow seems all overbalanced, but when you look closer you can see that he's simply a running machine. He's an ugly devil, but he's hammered iron from head to foot. It's the Nighthawk, and no mistake about that."

Dupray said through clenched teeth: "If you've found him, then I'll get him, Speedy. You've done the miracle for me." He was walking up and down the floor in a tremor of exultation. He was not a handsome fellow, but in the fierceness of his determination he looked capable of great deeds.

Speedy regarded him with an approving eye. Presently he said: "You'd better find out where he is, Al."

"You'll tell me that," said the young fellow.

"Well, he's kept by the men of Bardillo, of course."

"Yes, I could guess that, naturally. Where do they pasture him?"

"They don't pasture him," said Speedy.

"What!" exclaimed Dupray.

"They take the Nighthawk out on a lead, and two men go out with him," said Speedy. "One is on a horse, holding the tether. The other is walking. And they're both armed to the teeth. They let the big fellow graze a while, and then they take him back into the barn. You can't very well call that pasturing him, can you? At least, he doesn't run loose."

Al Dupray groaned. "You mean that they guard him like a baby?"

"Like a king's baby . . . like the heir to the throne. He's always under guard," said Speedy.

"In the stable, too?" asked Dupray.

"You see how it is, Al," Speedy answered. "There isn't a chance in a thousand that any thief would dare to come up here to El Rey, right into Bardillo's home town, and then still try to get at the horse. But the Nighthawk means so much to Bardillo that he takes no chances. When he rides out, the Nighthawk goes on a lead. He's kept for the pinches. He's the horse that's to save the crook when his life's in danger. Looked at that way, the Nighthawk means more than twenty good men to Bardillo. Besides, I think it pleases Bardillo to treat the horse like some great thing. It flatters him. You see the idea? When such care is taken of the horse, imagine the greatness of the master."

"He's guarded day and night?"

"Day and night," said Speedy. "But we'll have to find the right key to the problem. I'm going up there this afternoon."

IX

It was not long after this that a clamor broke out in the upper hall of the inn, outside the room of the American guest, Al Dupray. Suddenly the door was thrown open, and that slender, brown-legged peon, Pedro, leaped out and dashed down the hallway, howling and yelling for help, while the blows of the whip cracked loudly about him.

Down the stairs he bounded, and leaped into the middle of the patio, where he stood dancing up and down, as though in pain, and rubbing his shoulders where the blows had evidently fallen.

Two *mozos* stood near, watching him and laughing at his plight.

"Now you see, Pedro," said one of them, "what it means to work for a *gringo*?"

And the second servant added: "It's a lucky thing for you that you're not in the *gringo* land north of the Rio

Grande. If you were, that master of yours would cut your heart out. Young fool!"

"The devil take him. And roast him ten thousand years," said Pedro, shaking his brown fist furiously toward the window of the room of Al Dupray. "I leave him now, and I am going to take service with another man and a greater man."

"What other and greater man?" asked one of the *mozos*. "With the great *Señor* Bardillo."

The two *mozos* broke out into hearty laughter.

"You are going to the *casa grande* to ask for work?" said one of them.

"Yes. Why not?" asked Speedy.

"Because," said one of the *mozos*, "you don't know what happens to people who ask for work at the gate of that house."

"What happens to them?" asked Speedy.

"Why . . . ," began the first one.

But the second snapped: "Let him go! He is one of those wise young ones that has to learn."

Speedy shrugged his shoulders. "Well," he said, "if you are friends, you'll tell me what they do to people who ask for work at the house of *Señor* Bardillo."

"A hundred men before you have tried," said one of the *mozos*. "And they've all. . . ." He broke off, laughing.

"You mean," said Speedy, "that nobody can get a place working in the *casa grande*, as you call it?"

"Go ahead and try it yourself," the *mozo* said after a while. "Then you'll know."

They both began to laugh again, and, although Speedy tried a few more questions, he got nothing out of them. At length he left them and stepped out into the street. Above and beyond its winding he saw the high wall of the big house that had once been the castle of a great man, and was still the open stronghold of a famous brigand. Law did not choose to ride so far as that nest of robbers in the mountains. Justice would cost too much bloodshed.

Bardillo, furthermore, knew certain palms that needed to be crossed with silver. When that was done, all was well, and he could be sure of another year of peace, at the least.

Speedy, looking up at that big, rough wall, shook his head and sighed a little. He was armed with a single slender-bladed knife with a weighted handle. Otherwise he had no weapon. He had only his bare hands, and yet he must open the door of that *casa grande*, enter it, and survive whatever grueling test was given to strangers. After that he would have to do the impossible—manage the liberation of the famous stallion.

He settled the ragged straw hat on his head, smiled, and started trudging up the street. Behind him, raucous laughter broke out, and, turning, he saw the faces of the two mozos of the inn. He waved a hand to them and continued on his way, wondering what the mystery might be.

He passed the last of the houses in this part of the little town and came into an irregularly shaped plaza before the walls of the great castle. Before him there was a single postern door with a strong arch above it, opening into the wall of the great house. Before the door sat a powerfully built fellow with wide mustachios, waxed, and turning up at the points like the horns of a steer. The sun shone on those mustachios. He was magnificently dressed for his type, with silver *conchas* down the side of his trousers, and a jacket covered with metal braid. It was plain that he was a grandee among his own particular order of men.

When he saw the young fellow coming toward him, he raised a hand. "What errand?" he asked.

"To ring the bell outside the door, *Señor*," Speedy said, bowing humbly.

The big man suddenly grinned and stood up. "You want to ring the bell?" he asked.

"Yes," said Speedy.

"You are a beggar, then? You want help?"

"I am not a beggar, *Señor*," said Speedy, bowing almost to the ground. "I look for honest work to do."

"You look for work?" said the other.

"Is that a fault?" Speedy asked humbly.

"Not a fault, but a folly," said the other. "Only men are wanted in this *casa grande*. Now then, go and ring the bell if you think that you are a man." He smirked as he said it.

But Speedy, making a wide, interrogatory gesture with both hands, stepped to the bell pull beside the postern door and gave it a tug. A deep-voiced bell answered, muffled by the thickness of the wall. Instantly the door opened.

Before Speedy stood a *caballero* even more gaudy than the man outside the postern. "What in the name of the devil is this?" he asked, looking once at Speedy, and then at the outer guard.

"Another fool," said the first man.

"Eh?" asked the second.

"Yes, another fool, who thinks that he's man enough to serve in the *casa grande*. He wants the test." He laughed suddenly on the last word.

"This young donkey," said the keeper of the door, "won't have the test. He'll only have the beating. Take him and tie his hands, Juan."

"Willingly," said Juan. "Come here, young rooster." He drew a cord from his pocket and came with a savage grin.

Speedy did not move. "What have I done, Señor, that I should be beaten?" he asked.

"You'll find that out later on," said Juan.

"Yes," said the second man. "You'll find out, all right."

"Hold out your hands," commanded Juan, taking hold of Speedy's shoulder.

"Ah, *Señor*," said Speedy, "I trust there will be no cruel injustice."

As he held out his hands, Juan shifted his grip from the shoulder to the wrist of the smaller man.

"No injustice," he said. "But we'll take all the skin off your back that a quirt can remove. That's all." He began to laugh.

With the first note of his laughter, one hand of Speedy rose and flicked down, striking with the hardened edge of the palm across the wrist of the other.

The Mexican leaped back with an exclamation of rage. "By the devil," he cried, "the little rat has broken my wrist! Oh, you'll pay for this!"

He rushed in with a poised fist to beat up Speedy. The latter made no apparent effort to avoid him. Only, at the very moment that the blow was shooting toward his face, he swerved suddenly, stooped, caught upward with one lightning hand, and Juan hurtled over his bowed back and landed half a dozen feet away.

He lay stunned upon the stones, merely gasping: "Clemente. Break the neck of the trickster. Clemente!"

But Clemente was already rushing to perform that task unbidden. He reached for Speedy's throat with one hand; in the other he held a clubbed Colt to rap his victim over the head. But the first hand closed on thin air, and on the wrist of the second came that same lightning stroke with the edge of the palm, as with a cleaver.

The gun fell from the numbed fingers; Speedy picked it up.

As Juan rose, staggering, and Clemente turned with a gasp of incredulous rage to find himself disarmed, the youthful stranger was gently saying: "You have rough games here in the *casa grande*, my friends. But I was raised where men are rough, also. You see that I am not very strong, but a game is a game, nevertheless. Now, will you let someone in authority know that a poor fellow is standing here at the door, asking for work?"

X

It would have been hard to say what answers might have been returned by Clemente and the other, but at this time a stern voice called down to them, bawling: "Juan! Clemente!"

"Mother of heaven," muttered Clemente, "it is that devil of a Diego Marañon. I might have known that he'd be near enough to see us. You've done this, Juan, you thick-witted blunderer, by allowing that fellow to ring the bell. You should have run him off the place." The voice of Diego Marañon now approached closer, and he appeared at a window just above the gate. He was a man of middle age, with a much wrinkled forehead, the face decorated with long seams that extended beside the corners of the mouth. He wore a very short mustache, and a pointed black beard that curled a little. In his youth he had undoubtedly been a handsome fellow; now he simply looked debauched and worn out.

There was a sardonic cast in his eye as he said to Clemente: "What's the matter, Clemente, with you and Juan? Two heroes, the pair of you, and both thrown about by a young fellow like that? Come along, Clemente! Come along, Juan! This will please Bardillo!" He paused.

They endured his sneer in gloomy silence.

Then Marañon changed his manner and commanded sharply: "He's won the right to have the test, has he not?"

The pair stared at one another and said nothing.

"Answer me!" shouted Marañon in a sudden fury. "Has he won the right or has he not?"

"He has won the right, Señor Marañon," Clemente said finally. But he looked down upon the ground as though he wished that it would open and receive him.

"Very well," said Diego Marañon. "Prepare the test for him. I'll have the bell rung so the people can come and look at the show. I'll fetch Vicente Bardillo, also, so that he can see the sort of people who are now admitted to the test by his guards. Prepare yourselves, my friends. Be ready for anything that may happen, for the temper of Don Vicente is a little on the short side these days."

He disappeared from the window, the glint of his evil smile being the last that was seen of him.

Clemente turned on Juan as he said: "Afterward I call you to an accounting. Now I go to prepare the test. Stay here and watch him. Shoot him if he tries to escape."

With that he strode on through the open postern as Juan, the sentinel, muttered to Speedy: "You see what you've done? You've raised hell. That's what you've done. You'll wish you hadn't, too, before Marañon gets through with you."

"He seemed to me like a great *Señor*," Speedy said innocently.

"He is a great *Señor*. He is a fiend, too," declared the other. "And you'll have time to find all of these things out about him. Dolt!"

Speedy merely shrugged his shoulders, as though bewildered. "What am I to do, *Don* Juan?" he said. "I do only what comes to my mind and to my hand. I'm sorry that I hurt you. But you seemed excited. You and *Don* Clemente, also. I was afraid. I only tried to protect myself."

The other grinned sourly. "You'll need to protect yourself a little later," he said. "Wait . . . there it begins."

A bell began to ring in the tower that stood up at the right of the *casa grande*. It had a broad, flat, unresonant stroke, as though the body of the bell were of a base metal. As it rang, voices answered from the town below the *casa grande*—children's voices, first of all, then the murmur of a crowd that began to pour from the end of the main street, thronging the plaza.

Presently there were others appearing on the wall of the *casa grande*, or thronging out through the postern. Everyone was grinning. All the people were laughing and shouting to one another, and it was plain to Speedy that their glances were upon him entirely. They expected from him some very dramatic conclusion of this incident, it was clear.

The bell of the great house still was beating, like a frantic, irregular heartbeat, when Clemente returned, carrying a fluttering bird upon his hand. Everyone shouted with redoubled violence at the sight of this. "The pigeon! The pigeon!" they yelled.

On the heels of their shouting, a great uproar of laughter began. Speedy saw women and children,

and even some old men, bent double, while they
wailed and yelled their delight.

His own blood grew a little cold, perhaps, for he
gaped about him in bewilderment. "*Don* Juan," he
said, "they are not laughing at me, are they?"

"Why not?" asked Juan, snarling.

"So many people have never noticed me before . .
. not even to laugh at me," said Speedy.

"Oh, they've only just begun to notice you, my
fine fellow," said Juan.

After this a *mozo*—he seemed no more—who
walked beside Clemente took the pigeon from him
and held it by the cord that allowed it to flutter
perhaps two or three feet just over his head.

There was a fresh yell of delight, and the general
cry: "The pigeon! The blood of the pigeon! Justice,
Bardillo!"

Here, into the opening of the postern, stepped
a man of magnificent presence, very tall, with
immensely broad shoulders that sloped away to
narrow hips, ideal for a horseman. He would have
made the perfect picture of a man at arms in the days
of armor. His broad-brimmed hat was of velvety
texture. He wore a cloak that flowed back from his
shoulders and gave to his gestures an imperial air
of command. His left hand was gloved, carrying
the glove of the right hand, and with this he made
his gestures.

That was Bardillo, as Speedy could have guessed.
He did not need the sudden silence of all the other
spectators to understand. As the man issued from
the postern, a stream of riders came out behind
him, eight of them, carrying long whips.

"Does this fellow understand the test?" asked
Bardillo of Juan.

"He wouldn't wait to find out what the test might be," declared Juan.

Bardillo smiled a little, and the people, who saw the smile of the master, gave one ringing whoop of cruel joy, and then were again silent.

"Well, Marañon," said the chief to his first lieutenant, "you may as well explain everything to the young beggar. Experience is apt to be a cruel teacher, and her lessons are not quickly forgotten, eh?"

"No, not quickly," said Marañon with a smile far more cruel than his master's. "They will be remembered, if I'm any judge of men and whips."

As he spoke, he looked toward the eight mounted men, then from Speedy to Juan and Clemente.

Speedy cleared his throat, although he was not preparing to speak. His heart and brain grew a little giddy.

"Tell him, Marañon," repeated the chief.

Diego Marañon stepped forward and gathered a solemn frown upon his forehead, although there was still a smile upon his lips. "Do you hear me?" he asked.

"Ah, yes, *Señor*, I do hear you," replied Speedy.

"You are about to learn the test that is to be given to you."

"I wait humbly . . . I wait with patience, as your servant, *Señor*," Speedy said, bowing again.

"The fellow has manners," interrupted the great Bardillo, looking calmly down at the scene, then surveying the townsfolk and his own armed followers critically.

"What is your name?" continued Marañon.

"My name is Pedro, if you are pleased with that name, *Señor*," said Speedy.

"And if it doesn't please me," said Marañon, "will I be able to change it?"

"Ah, *Señor*," said Speedy, "I would change my skin to win your favor, and what a simple thing it is to turn a skin inside out."

Brief laughter followed this, like a single shout with several echoes.

"Well," said Marañon, "perhaps you'll want to turn your skin inside out before long, unless there are too many holes worn through it."

"Alas, *Señor*, I tremble," said Speedy.

"Well," went on Marañon, "you are to understand, young fellow, in the old days, the first days of the greatness and the fame of *Señor* Bardillo, many men came to ask for service with him. Some were cowards, many were fools, a very few were traitors. Now everyone who wishes to join him must pass a test. You understand?"

"I understand," said Speedy. "I tremble, but I understand."

"Well, then," said Marañon, "the test is a very simple one." He pointed. "You see the pigeon?"

"I see the pigeon, Señor."

"Well, then, presently, at a word from *Don* Vicente, that pigeon will be set free with no more than the bit of string dangling down from its legs. All that you need to do, in order to pass the test, is to strike it with bullets from a revolver or a rifle as it rises through the air."

XI

Perfect laughter is never possible except to the hard-hearted. But at the sight of the dismay that opened the mouth and made the jaw of young Speedy droop down, every spectator broke out into noisy mirth, and the great *Don* Vicente as much as humbler people.

"And, *Señor* Marañon, if I fail?"

"If you fail," said Marañon, his cruel eye flashing fire, "then you will be very sorry for the failure later on, *amigo*. For you will have to run from this place and hurry down through the long, winding central street of the town. As you hurry along, these *caballeros* will follow with their horses, if they are able to keep up with you, and they will urge you to go faster. You see, Pedro, that they carry whips to spur you on and make your steps longer?"

Speedy looked at the long, sinister lashes of those whips, and he knew that the supple, long-seasoned rawhide thongs could be made to bite through the tough hide of a mule at every stroke. How much the more so would they slash his coat and shirt to pieces and cut his body to the bone? His eyes narrowed a little. They might curl a lash about his feet and trip him up as he fled. Once he had fallen, he would be beaten to death, like a dog.

There was no doubt that the riders would go as far as possible with him in order to avenge the insult to two of their men.

He looked back at the pigeon, which was fluttering eagerly at the end of the string, buoyant as a supercharged balloon, tugging to be off and into the heart of the sky.

"You have a gun already, Pedro," said Marañon. "*Señor* Bardillo, when you are ready, Pedro is ready to hear the word, I presume."

"I have a borrowed gun," said Speedy. "I don't want it. And here it is for the owner. *Don* Clemente, I thank you for the loan."

He offered the weapon, butt first, to Clemente, and the big guard snatched it with an oath, blood rushing up into his face at the suggestion of an insult.

"What sort of a gun do you wish, then?" asked the great Bardillo. "If you want a rifle, my son, you may have that, also. I warn you, however, you must exercise extreme care. Put him ten steps from the bird, Marañon."

"He is standing there now," said Marañon.

"Are you taking a rifle, Pedro?" Bardillo asked, not unkindly.

"No, *Señor*. I am prepared with a weapon of my own," said the young fellow.

"You are prepared? What sort of a weapon?"

"A weapon that fits my hand, *Señor*," said Speedy.

"He is a proud young fool," said Marañon in such a voice that Speedy heard him perfectly. "Let the whips give him advice, not your tongue, *Señor*!"

"You're right, Marañon," said Bardillo. "I am always too far from these people to understand them well. You are closer, Marañon. You understand them far better."

Marañon gave his chief one half-veiled but very sinister glance; the chief disregarded it, still maintaining a slight smile. Perhaps he failed to see it. Then, turning his long, aristocratic, ugly face toward the holder of the bird, he said: "Are you ready?"

"I am ready," said the *mozo*.

"Are you ready?" asked the chief, turning this time to Speedy.

"I am ready, *señor*."

"I raise my hand," said the robber. "When I let it fall, loose the bird . . . throw it into the air. Do you hear?"

"I hear," said the *mozo*. His chest was swelling a little, since he was, for a moment, the cynosure of all eyes.

So, for an instant, Bardillo stood, his gloved hand raised; suddenly it fell, and the *mozo* flung the pigeon high into the air.

There it hung for a moment, staggering, regaining its balance after being loosed so roughly. A second later it dipped away at full speed.

Now, as it rose into the air, flung up, it appeared, less by the hand of the *mozo* than by the shout of the mob, Speedy drew from his coat the knife that was his sole weapon, and slid it into the palm of his hand with a gesture so rapid that very few people were able to observe exactly what he was doing. As the pigeon fluttered in mid-air, he took a swift stride forward. As the bird darted to the side, he flung the glittering knife.

It dissolved in the air to a glint of light, while utter silence blanketed the amazed people on the plaza. The knife flew on in a broad, flat arc, and the bird shot away, apparently toward freedom.

A new yell of wonder and of savage triumph arose from the crowd, but Speedy sprang forward, and his fingers touched a broad-faced paving stone. He straightened again, and the tips of his fingers were red.

"He has missed! The whips! The whips!" shouted many voices.

Several of the riders spurred their horses and swung the lashes high, but Speedy had raised his hand. "*Señor* Bardillo," he said. "Look! It is the blood of the bird. It is on my hand . . . I have not missed. Look on the stones and you will find more blood. I have drawn it. The knife has found the body of the pigeon."

"Stop!" commanded the chief.

The riders reined back their horses, one of them so close that the beast reared.

"Fetch the knife," ordered Bardillo.

A panting *mozo* brought it in haste. Silence had descended on the plaza again.

The great man, taking the little weapon, stared at the point. "I think it is true," he said. "There is blood on the point of the weapon. Come to me, Pedro."

Speedy approached him. "There is the blood that I wiped from the stone where it fell, *señor*," he said.

"I see blood on your finger," said the other. "Wipe it away, now."

"It is done," Speedy said, obeying.

The chief looked closely at the two fingertips that had borne the stain.

"I thought that the clever rascal might have stained the knife with his own blood," he said, "but now I believe he has told the truth. By all the saints, that was either a very wonderful or a very lucky cast. Who are you, Pedro?"

"Ah, *señor*," said Speedy, bowing with his usual humility, "I am one to live as your gracious kindness permits me and teaches me."

Bardillo smiled faintly. "He is something above the ordinary peon, Marañon," he said. "Get him some clothes. After he has washed away the grime, send him to me. There is some little mystery about him."

XII

When Bardillo had passed through the postern and back into the house, the others swarmed after him, Speedy among them, and Marañon walking behind him.

In the inner patio they paused, and Marañon said: "Now, *hombres*, it seems that you are to have a new companion. You, Clemente and Juan, may think that you have reason to be angry with him. But there is no anger among the men of Bardillo. You know that of old. Don't venture to forget it now. Some of you have shed your blood already for *Señor* Bardillo, but his justice is, nevertheless, the same for every man among you. This new man is like the others. Do you understand?"

All answered in the affirmative, Juan cheerfully enough, and Clemente, last of all, remarked: "Pedro, here is my hand. We forget everything and commence again, do we not?"

"*Don* Clemente," Speedy said, "you are a brave man and a kind man. You forgive me my trick, and I shall try to make up for it another day with a good turn."

"Teach me the same trick to use in my time of need," said Clemente, "and I ask nothing better."

"I shall teach you every turn of my hand," Speedy said courteously.

"Good," said Marañon. Then, beckoning to Speedy, he said: "Pedro, come with me."

He led the young fellow into the house, up and down corridors and steps until he came to a door that he pushed open. Within, there was a small room with one narrow window, hardly a foot and a half square. For furniture there was a cot, a sheepskin rug on the floor and another on the bed, a stool, and a small table, on which stood a washbowl. There were some pegs along the wall. A battered hat hung from one of these. A pair of boots slumped in another corner.

"One of our men used to have this room," said Marañon cheerfully. "He was with us a long time, and was one of the best of the lot. No man ever rode better, I can tell you. His end was strange, for the bullet that killed him struck him in the middle of the back. We are sad still, but with you in this room, we'll be more cheerful about him before long. What is your last name, Pedro?"

"Garona, *señor*," said Speedy.

"Pedro Garona," Marañon went on, "you have begun very well. You have the eye of *Señor* Bardillo on you. You need only, for a few days, keep your eyes wide open, observe everything, speak little, and think much. Copy the actions of the men about you who are oldest and wisest. If you are in doubt, come to me to ask my advice. Live cheerfully, obey readily, keep faith, avoid brawling. Do these things and you are in the pleasantest company in Mexico. Break any of these laws and you will find yourself entangled in a jungle that is filled with tigers."

"*Señor*," said Speedy, "I learned when I was a boy to judge a wise man by his face and by his words. I follow you in everything."

"I'll send a *mozo* with clothes that ought to fit you," said Marañon. "And there'll be water to wash yourself. *Señor* Bardillo will send for you when he needs you."

So Speedy found himself alone in the room and looked curiously about him. He realized, as Marañon had pointed out, that he was in a veritable den of tigers, and there would be no way but death for him if the least hint of his true character should appear. He walked on a tightrope that might break under him at any moment.

However, he put such thoughts out of his mind as far as this was possible, and started to prepare for his change of clothes by stripping off those he wore. Then he fortified himself against the cold mountain wind that was blowing through the narrow casement into the room by performing some odd gymnastics.

He had barely finished this performance when there came a knock at his door, and a *mozo* walked in to find the newcomer to the *casa grande* panting in a cold room as though he had just run up several flights of stairs.

He put down the clothes and a bucket of tepid water, and then he hurried out to tell his fellow *mozos* that the stranger who looked so slender was, in fact, deep of chest, and that he was made of such rippling muscles as one sees in the panther as it crouches, ready to spring.

Speedy, in the meantime, had scrubbed himself thoroughly, glorying in the strength of the dye that clung to his skin so well in spite of soap and water. He was sure that not ten men in the world had the secret of its use, or the trick of the chemical that, when one chose, washed it away like so much surface dust upon the skin.

When he came to the scrubbing of his hands, he took particular care about cleansing beneath the nail of the forefinger on his right hand, for under the nail there was a deep but narrow prick, such as the keen point of a knife might make between nail and flesh. Such an incision was this beneath the fingernail of Speedy—such a one as could be used for the squeezing forth of a few drops of essential blood, after which the bleeding would be stopped at once by the pressure of the nail.

Speedy, as he regarded that spot beneath the nail, smiled a little. Yet, with all his forethought, his trick might have failed had it not been that he had thought of smearing some of that blood hastily over the point of the knife.

The wit of the great Bardillo had been quick enough to hit upon the proof at once. And there it had been, the precious, thin smear of blood in addition to what Speedy had squeezed out upon the surface of the stone, as though the drops had fallen from the wounded bird. The chief was convinced.

That Bardillo was a fellow to be watched. He would take some circumventing, unless his eyes were well closed in a false confidence.

There was something about this entire adventure that Speedy liked not at all. It was true that, as usual, he was preying upon thieves, but then, on the other hand, he had managed his entrance into the house by winning the respect and the admiration of the whole band of thieves. He might balance against this the fact that he had been in danger of being flogged to death. But for all that, his conscience was not entirely quiet.

He went on with his scrubbing, dried his body with a cotton towel, and then began to dress. Complicated clothes were these that he put on. A weight of metal ornament made them hateful to him, and the tightness of the jacket was disgusting to him, for he liked nothing that did not leave every muscle free to obey his will.

He was dressed, however, eventually, and now he made a few steps up and down, then went through a few movements to discover just how far and with what ease he could step or bend this way and that.

He had hardly finished fully this when there was another tap at the door. It was the *mozo* returning, with word that the great Bardillo wished to see his new recruit.

It was a great spread of rooms, halls and corridors through which that guide conducted him. Already he had mapped down in his mind the tortuous route by which he had entered the place, but he wanted to get hold of a good chart of the place. Let him be twenty-four hours in the house, however, and it would be strange if he did not know every corner of it down to the bottom of its cellar, no matter how deep.

The *mozo*, walking with him, was talking very respectfully about knife throwing. He admired, he said, men who were great with guns, but to his own particular heart nothing would be half so dear as mastery over the silent death. So talking, he brought Speedy to a farther corner of the big house and rapped at a door, whereupon a voice bade him enter. He pushed back the door.

"*Señor*, I bring you Pedro Garona," said the *mozo*.

Speedy stepped forward cheerfully enough, and saw that the robber chief stood beside a big window with a deep casement on the farther side of the room, a window through which so much light came that it blotted out with shadow everything else that was inside—at least, during the first moment. Then, as his eyes grew instantly more accustomed to the light, he saw in a corner the last object he wished to find there—the face of a man who knew him, who hated him, and who had reason for his hatred.

XIII

The great Bardillo, therefore, meant far less than that lean, pain-stricken countenance of the man in the shadow. As Speedy shut the door behind him, he expected the man to whip out a revolver and open fire, but the man with the one arm remained as expressionless as a mummy, while his hollow eyes followed the movements of Speedy across the floor.

Bardillo had turned from the window. His look was stern; for that matter, sternness was his habitual mask.

"Now, Pedro," he said, "I want to talk to you."

"Yes, *señor*," said Speedy.

"What's your last name again?"

"Garona, *señor*."

"Where have you lived?"

"North of the Rio Grande most of my life," answered Speedy.

"Oh, in the States, then?"

"Yes."

"Why did you go there?"

"My father took me there when I was a child."

"Why did he take you there?"

"He had killed a man, *señor*."

The chief nodded. "He had killed a man, so he ran across the Rio Grande."

"That is true, *señor*."

"And why did you come south, then?"

"Because, unfortunately, I killed a man, *señor*."

"Your father went north because he killed a man . . . you came south because you killed a man?" As he asked, the chief laughed. "There is killing in your blood, Pedro, is that it? How did you happen to kill this fellow?"

"It was because my knife's point happened to strike through his eye to the brain."

"That was the only reason, eh?"

"The only reason, *señor*."

"You're sorry for it, then?"

"Well," replied Speedy, "when I saw him drop dead, I knew instantly that now I must go to Mexico. That was something I had been wanting to do for a long time."

"What made you want to come here?"

"My country, my people, my blood," replied Speedy.

The chief stood a little straighter, and his eye flashed.

"There is something to you . . . there's a substance to you, Pedro," he declared. "What was your life in the States?"

"A wretched life, *señor*."

"You say that with a good deal of feeling."

"Because I suffered a great deal, *señor*."

"What made you suffer?"

"A wife, *señor*."

Bardillo laughed outright. "What was the matter with her?" he asked.

"*Señor*," said Speedy, "I endured what I could endure."

The bandit was apparently more and more pleased with his new man. "When you are working for me, Pedro, what do you expect?"

"Trouble," said Speedy. "Much trouble, *señor*. Long rides in the cold. Long rides in the heat. To starve often, lying among the hills. To endure gunfire. To be hunted and hated. I expect all of these things to happen to me."

The other, as he heard this catalogue of evils, could not help smiling a little. "Then what folly made you come to me?" he demanded. "What will you gain to make up for all that you lose?"

"Well," replied Speedy, "if I am treated like a wolf, I gain the right to be a wolf, also. If men snarl at me, I can use my teeth, too. I have a chief above me and another man or two, his lieutenants . . . outside of them I am free to do as I please. And what is it that I please to do? That which a hawk desires, *señor* . . . to sail through the sky with my eyes turned down, looking for smaller birds. If I find any very large ones, an eagle or two, I whistle and my companions join me. We drop down and make the feathers of the eagle fly. We eat eagle meat that day. That is the life for me, *señor*, and for the sake of it I have come to you."

The great Bardillo actually grew rosy with pleasure as he heard this speech. Finally he said: "Pedro, I have nothing to say to you for the present. Live in the house. Be happy. Get acquainted with the men. You will go far with me, Pedro."

"Ah, you are very kind to me," said Speedy.

"Tell me, furthermore," said the chief, "if you are treated well in this place or if you have complaints. The new are on a footing with the old in my band. We are a democracy, Pedro."

"Thank you," said Speedy.

"You are free to go now," said Bardillo. "There is only one thing remaining. I grant one gift to every man who comes to me after drawing the blood of the pigeon. What gift will you ask for, Pedro?"

Speedy appeared to hesitate. Then his eye lighted. "I can tell you that, *señor*. I came to the town in the service of a swine of a *gringo*. I was like a servant to him. The people of the *fonda* laughed at me. I ran away from his service. Now, *señor*, I am no longer in rags. Grant me one great wish."

"You want a brighter scarf, is that it?" asked Bardillo.

"No, no, *señor*. I am happy with these clothes. They are the finest that I have ever worn. But now let me ride out and strike the men of the town silent with awe. Let me ride down the main street of the town. And let me be upon the back of the great horse of the *señor* himself."

Bardillo started.

"You mean on the back of the Nighthawk?" he asked.

"Yes," Speedy said, bowing to the floor.

"That's a great deal to ask," answered the chief.

"Alas, *señor*, you send him out every day into the pasture with two men," said Speedy. "It is only to ride him through the main street of the town, that the people who laughed at me may now see that the great *señor* himself has placed his trust in me. How else can they learn that so well as when they see me sitting in the saddle of the great *señor* and upon the back of his horse, the great stallion. They will say to themselves . . . 'One minute ago we mocked him, but now see what a thing it is to have found the favor of *Señor* Bardillo.' "

Bardillo's frown, as he listened to this speech, relaxed, and at length he broke out into a roar of hearty laughter. "And why not?" he said half to himself. "You shall do as you please, then, Pedro. Go down and get the stallion when you please, and tell them that you come from me with that order."

"Suppose," said Speedy, "that they doubt you have given such an order, *señor*?"

An evil gleam shot from the eye of Bardillo. "In that case," he said, "I don't know what to say. Perhaps you will know how to convince them that you really come from me?"

Speedy bowed again. "You give me permission, in other words," he murmured, "to go and take the Nighthawk if I can?"

"Yes," replied Bardillo. "That's the permission I give to you."

"I will go," Speedy said. "And ten thousand thanks, *Señor* Bardillo. I am your servant. I am covered with a hundred thousand obligations, and I depart to find the great horse. Ah-ha, *señor*, you cannot tell how my heart laughs out in my body when I think of sitting on his back."

Bardillo, in fact, began to laugh a little as he heard this flowery farewell, and he was still laughing when Speedy reached the door, opened it, and backed out into the hall.

He had hardly turned down its shadowy length when the door opened again and the one-armed man stepped out behind him. He made a gesture, and Speedy paused for him to come up.

There was a casement at this point for the sole purpose of lighting the hallway, and Speedy stepped back in front of it. The one-armed man walked straight up to him.

"You remember me, Speedy?" he asked.

"I remember you dimly," replied Speedy.

"As a friend or an enemy?"

"That's hard to tell," answered Speedy. "You're simply back there somewhere in the shadows of my mind. I think I never saw you for a long time together."

"It was not a long time," said the other slowly. "It was a very short time indeed." His somber face seemed to shrivel with the great excess of his malice.

Speedy waited. All his nerves were tingling; his whole brain was thrillingly tuned for any eventuality.

"Do you not remember, *Señor* Speedy," went on the one-armed man, "the name of Benito Vizcaya?"

"That name I've forgotten," Speedy said, shaking his head.

At this the other grew livid, and, turning away from Speedy, he made two or three short turns up and down the hall as though gradually to master his emotion.

Then, coming back, he scrutinized the young fellow's face even more closely than before, saying: "*Señor* Devil, do you remember the pass of Las Hayas?"

Well did Speedy remember that pass, and from the very first he had recalled everything.

Benito Vizcaya went on: "I shall tell you a little to refresh your mind. The thieves had taken a good booty, and you had stolen it from them by your craft. You had taken it all and had ridden away. We followed. The others were weary. Their horses gave out. I, alone, I overtook you in the height of the Las Hayas pass. I saw you fleeing like a dog before me. Then you disappeared farther along the trail. I followed fast. Suddenly a tiger leaped on me from the brush at the side of the trail. Not a tiger, but you! I was dragged from my horse. I tried to fight, but the skill of a fiend, the fiend to whom you have sold your soul, was in your hands. My own strength you used against me. I felt a terrible pain, I heard a cracking sound as my arm was broken to slivers."

He groaned, half closed his eyes, and his head jerked back. "I rode back down the pass. The bone was thrusting out through the flesh and the skin, and the cold entered the wound. It was the next day before I could get to a doctor. The arm was infected. It had to be amputated." He paused, breathing hard: "Do you know what that means, Speedy?"

"A bad thing," Speedy replied calmly.

"Bad?" echoed the man. "To be pointed out by children, to be scorned by women, to be braved by men who would have run from me in the old days . . . that is what it has meant to me."

"I believe you, Benito," said Speedy. "I see that the pain has written its own account in your face. And I want you to believe me in my turn when I say that I am very sorry."

"You lie," said Vizcaya. "You rejoice in my agony."

Speedy raised a finger. "I don't lie, Vizcaya," he said. "Of course, I remember the whole thing perfectly. Tell me, then one thing, because I'm very curious."

"Why I did not denounce you to Bardillo in that room?"

"Yes."

"You forget," said Vizcaya.

"What, then?"

"You forget, as I lay in the roadway, in the broken trail of the pass, that you leaned over me and said . . . 'Perhaps I'm a fool to let you live. You'll certainly hate me, but murder is not the game I love. Therefore I'm going to let you climb back onto your horse and ride for it. Ride fast, because that wound is a bad one, even if there's not much blood from it.' That was what you said to me, and now I make an answer to you."

He paused at this point and drew himself up, with flashing eyes. "I saw you from a casement on that side of the house, *señor*. I saw you when you were making the trial of the pigeon, and I recognized the face that I have hated for so many years, and so heartily. I recognized you, *señor*, and knew at once that you were at your old game again . . . to plunder the thieves . . . to be the robber of the robbers . . . the bandit of the bandits. I saw at once that you had come here to prey on *Señor* Bardillo and the rest of us. For a moment I held my hand, because, to say the truth, I could not believe that any man would be so foolhardy as to adventure in such a place as this, surrounded by such men.

"So I waited, but presently I saw you enter the room of Bardillo. I saw that you not only had passed the ordeal and made yourself safe in the house, but that you were likely to win the complete favor of everyone at once. When I saw that, I was about to cry out your name. Then I remembered what you had said when you leaned above me in Las Hayas pass . . . 'Murder is not my game.' That is what I say to you now, Speedy. Murder is not my game. I shall give you a chance for your life, as you gave me a chance to save my arm. It will be not much of a chance, but it will be something."

He paused, and, compressing his lips, looked at Speedy with an odd mixture of hate and envy, admiration and rage.

XIV

"A small chance is a great deal better than no chance at all," Speedy said calmly. "And after the pain that you have had because of me, Vizcaya, I'm astonished to find so much generosity in you. Few men would do so much. Every day of your life you must have been saying to yourself, that to see me burned alive would be a proper pleasure."

"Perhaps," said the other, his smile growing ghastly, "I shall have that pleasure. In the meantime, I show you that murder is not the game I love." He drew in a quick breath, and then rattled out the following words: "I shall go back into that room. I'll tell Bardillo that I rushed out after you because it seemed to me that I had suddenly remembered your face. I'll tell him that now I feel almost sure that I can place you in my mind . . . but not quite, not quite. Maybe he will ask me if it is good or bad, and still I will say that I cannot quite tell. Only that you are blazed in my memory by some powerful recollection.

"I hold him in talk this way until he burns with curiosity, and then, at the end of five minutes . . . five minutes from this moment, *señor* . . . I bring out a single word that will shake the house of Bardillo to the foundations. Speedy! That is the word that I will speak. In ten seconds the alarm bell will be ringing, the horn will blow from the window, and the men of Bardillo will be after you, my friend. Twenty wild riders! And you can save yourself as well as you may.

Five minutes, *señor*, and then the game begins. It is not quite murder, however. There is not much difference, but a little. Perhaps you, too, will get through the trouble, and be able to face life after today with one hand, as I do."

With that he turned suddenly on his heel and walked back toward the door of the room.

Minutes, for Speedy, were instantly of such vast importance that even seconds counted heavily. He used some ten of them to speculate quietly on the strangeness of this speech, which matched the oddest he ever had heard. Then he turned and ran.

That finery that he had put on, he had cause to regret now. It was one thing to have bare legs and sandals as light as paper on the feet. It was another thing to be booted, spurred, and encased in heaviest cloth. Yet he made good speed down the corridor, down the stairs, and suddenly into the blazing light of the patio.

While he ran, he balanced his chances. They were small enough, if he strove at once to get away. They were infinitely smaller if he attempted to gain the stallion, but now the gambling instinct was aroused in him to such a point that he could not possibly keep from making the attempt.

As he hurried into the patio, the very *mozo* who had loosed the pigeon appeared, and stopped with a grin and a nod to see the new hero in his new uniform.

"*Amigo*, where is the great stallion of the *señor*?" asked Speedy.

"In the pasture," said the *mozo*. "Yonder in the pasture, *señor*." And he waved a hand toward the gate on the opposite side of the court.

"Good," said Speedy. "Now, then, do you wish to earn my friendship?"

"My father before me," said the *mozo*, "knew that friendship is worth more than gold." He smiled a little at the double meaning, which he conveyed with the word.

"It's a true saying," said Speedy. "Go to the inn. There find the young American. Say to him one word. Can you say one word of English?"

"It's an ugly language," said the *mozo*, "but I could try."

"It is an insult," Speedy said, "that is summed up in one word. The instant that you have said it, turn and run. Begin by explaining in Spanish that you have come from the house of Bardillo and from me. Tell him, further, that I have sent him a message, and that the message is . . . 'Ride!' "

"Ride?" asked the peon.

"Yes. That one word. You understand?"

"I understand." said the *mozo*. "When he hears this insult, will he be very angry?"

"He will be on fire," replied Speedy. "But what do you care for the anger of the *gringo* once you are back in the street?"

"I care less than the snap of my fingers," declared the peon. "I hurry to tell him, *señor*." And off he fled at full speed.

Even more rapidly, Speedy was through the opposite postern, and saw before him the rolling green hillsides beyond.

There strayed the cattle of Bardillo. There strayed the horses. And yonder was a tall brown stallion led by one man, while another sat the saddle of a second fine horse nearby.

How many minutes had passed up to this time?

Speedy went up to the men. One was that same Clemente who had quarreled with him at the first postern, and Speedy would gladly have had any other man of the lot to deal with. Forewarned is forearmed, and Clemente had had plenty of warning concerning the magic that the slender hands of Speedy were capable of working.

"Clemente," said Speedy, "I have just left *Señor* Bardillo and he gave me permission to take his own horse and ride it down the main street of the town in my new clothes. I'll lead him back to the stable for a saddle and bridle."

The stallion, as though he suddenly recognized the voice of the speaker, lifted his head with a jerk and turned toward Speedy. He was by no means a beautiful animal, but he was a running machine. Every bit of him was formed to drive him at sustained speed. Other animals had appealed to the eye of Speedy before this day, but never had one stirred him so completely.

Clemente, as he heard Speedy's remark, turned in the saddle, and looked down at the swarthy pirate who was holding the lead rope in one hand and a rifle in the other.

"Well, José?" said Clemente.

José shrugged his wide shoulders. "Are you a banker, Clemente?" he asked.

"A wise man asks wise questions," said Clemente.

"Well," said José, "if you had a bank and a stranger came in and asked you for half the money in your safe, do you think that you would give it to him at once?"

"I'd see him burn, first," said Clemente, eying Speedy.

The time was sliding past with dizzy speed. At any moment now he expected to hear the terrible clanging of the alarm bell and the great, braying voice of the horn.

He stepped forward and laid a hand on the rope. "*Amigos,*" he said, "I am sorry that you will not believe me. Tell me one thing."

"I could tell you ten," Clemente said grimly.

"Tell me this one thing," said Speedy. "Is it not true that this is the Nighthawk?"

"Perhaps," said the other two with one voice.

"If that is the Nighthawk," said Speedy, "do you think that I would be such a fool as to try to ride him without permission from the *señor?*"

José grunted. "That's true enough," he admitted. "That's true enough, I suppose. He would not throw away that uniform and be flogged till his bones were bare just for the sake of playing a prank."

"What do you know of Pedro?" said Clemente. "You don't know much about him, but you do know Bardillo. It's better to be too good a guard forever than a careless fool for half a minute."

"That's true, also," said José, in a quandary. "Take your hand from the rope, Pedro."

A great many things can be done with a rope, and Speedy did one of them. He pulled against the horse enough to give more slack to the loop. Then he snapped the rope back with a flashing movement of his hand. It flicked through the fingers of the surprised José, burning the skin.

He leaped back with an oath; Speedy leaped at the same moment and caught his knees on the round, firm barrel of the stallion.

"*Hai!*" shouted Clemente, and jerked out a revolver.

Speedy flattened himself along the side of the big horse, hooking one foot over the back bone and winding a hand into the mane of the great horse. The latter, obedient to the merest touch, instantly swerved away, presenting a sheltering side toward the gun of Clemente.

"He's tricked me, curse him!" shouted José. "*Hai, Clemente!*"

He got that far when the alarm bell began to beat with a rapidity that shocked the mind and the very nerves.

"Who is loose now?" said Clemente. "Pedro, off that horse or I'll shoot you, and the horse, too, if I have to."

"Something terrible has happened at the house," said José, seeming to forget all about the stallion. "Listen!"

The deep, braying voice of the horn was added to the bells, and all the air was filled by the clamorous vibration. José began to run at full speed straight for the house.

Clemente still handled his rifle as though he intended to use a bullet on the insolent Pedro, but the outcry from the house was too much for his nerves. At length he turned the head of his horse to follow José, shouting as he did so: "Keep the horse safe, Pedro, or Bardillo will have your head!"

Off he rode, while Speedy sat up straight, with a great sigh of relief, and turned the head of the brown stallion away from the house of Bardillo.

XV

If he had had one chance in a hundred before, he might be said to have one chance in twenty now that he was actually on the back of the horse and riding away from the house of Bardillo. An unsaddled and unbridled horse beneath him, and he himself was by no means an expert rider. However, he found to his great joy that the Nighthawk was as tractable to the touch of a hand on either side of his neck as though he were a circus pony.

In the meantime, Speedy had brought the stallion to a full-striding gallop. Looking back, he saw that the gate was open. Clemente and his horse had been turned back, and were now leading a charge of half a dozen riders, who must have been supplied from a store of ever-ready horses kept under saddle and bridle. At any rate, a fine and colorful procession it was that charged down the hill.

However, Speedy could at least be sure that his friend, Al Dupray, was enjoying freedom from interruption and suspicion. Dupray would have plenty of time to saddle his horse and ride hard, as he must be sure to do as soon as he received that message in one word.

Speedy himself must ride hard. He was followed by men as tireless as time and as savage; they could outride him, and they might be able to find horses for remounts here and there, but Speedy's only chance lay in the long, iron-hard legs of the Nighthawk, and soon the big fellow began to stretch himself. The grass flowed beneath them in a blur, like a stream of water.

He found a hill shoulder in the night, and there he dismounted at last and let the stallion graze. Twenty times he had been in easy rifle distance of death, and twenty times they had tried to close with him rather than risk a bullet that might strike the horse instead of the rider.

The green grass was no longer at hand. They had ridden into a lower and a far hotter belt of hills, where there was good, tough bunch grass, the best of grazing.

He tore up a quantity of this grass, and, twisting it into knots, he rubbed down the big horse, scrubbing him until his skin was dry—even taking particular care to go over his face, rimmed and water-marked by the salty evaporation of much sweat—and the great horse held out his head and pricked his ears for the grooming.

One good grooming is equal to one good feed in the twenty-four hours, Speedy had heard. He was no expert, but he was working according to the best authorities. And now his own weariness amounted to nothing. It was simply the horse that counted.

He sat down and watched the stars slowly climbing out of the east. The stallion he had hobbled with the end of the lead rope. The scattering trees, all stubbly second growth, stood up like an army of spears about him, black and thin. There seemed to be peace in the world.

After all, nothing was gained by keeping a needless watch. He lay flat on his back, and, in spite of the chill in the air and the ground, he was instantly asleep. An hour was all that he would ask from this resting spot.

But the full hour was not out when the horse sniffed at his face. Leaping to his feet, he saw a file of riders, a half dozen of them, coming across the brow of the hill, not a quarter of a mile away. One after another they came, with their long rifles balanced across their saddle bows.

They saw him at the very moment when he was loosing the hobble knots, and down they came with a charge that sent him flying onto the back of the stallion, and so scurrying off through the brush and trees, where the mustangs were hard to outdistance, for they ran like rabbits, dodging all obstacles, with their wild riders whooping and screaming like Indians.

For three days he wandered, resting the horse at every possible chance, working to find a safe way north out of the hills. The only food he had was on the third day, when he trapped a squirrel. He made a fire with dry wood that gave out little smoke, roasted the little morsel, and devoured it. It was tough meat, but delicious to the tooth of the hunted man. His only other provender was the bark that he chewed to keep away the sense of biting hunger.

Toward the close of the third day he ventured into a ravine running northward that sloped out toward the desert, and came almost to the mouth of it when a line of riders whirled out of nowhere and charged upon him.

He fled with the Nighthawk, the bullets nipping the air, and singing at his ear.

It was a very different game, this, because it showed him that the hunters had received desperate orders from Bardillo. They were to take no chances on losing this thief of thieves, this Speedy, this frigate bird who preyed on hawks of the air. They were to catch or kill him, even if in so doing they had to kill the stallion, too.

Other horses could be bought. But there was only one Speedy to be dreaded and destroyed. He accepted that compliment with a grim shake of the head as he sent the long-legged flyer back into the heart of the ravine, and steadily on, until he was again on high ground, from which he could watch the barren sunset sinking in the desert.

After that, for another day, he walked, never mounting the back of the horse, because even the iron strength of the Nighthawk was giving way in this life of constant alarms.

Speedy trapped a mountain grouse, and ate that, too, as if it were the food of the gods. The fifth day he was still walking. Yet every time, as he came to the edge of the hills, he saw the blurred forms of distant riders drifting here and there. Twice that day he had to mount in haste and flee from sudden attacks. One bullet clipped the shoulder of his gaudy jacket. That was all.

So, on the sixth day, in the gray of the morning, an emaciated form rode out from the hills. There was a thin mist rising, to make the hour yet more dim. Riders drifted here and there, eying him from a distance.

Aided by the mist all that day, he fled north through the line of guards. Sounds whimpered and mourned in the air about him, little deadly messengers of lead that searched for him with undying greed.

Those sounds also fell away, and still he thought, he heard the cry of—"Speedy!"—behind him, pronounced as the Mexicans always did that nickname, putting the accent on the last syllable.

He looked back. Only dimly and far away he saw the pursuers coming. He thought he heard them shouting, but no voice could reach him from them, and he knew that it was the fantasy of his own weary brain.

But he was through the line, and the horse ran strong and true, thin and weary as it was.

That northward march was a nightmare. They were in sight every day, those hovering riders, continually challenging, continually striving to close with him. Every night he shook them off and found rest and food for the horse, while he himself drowsed in catnaps. No other man in the world could have endured that terrible fatigue. Now the agony of starvation was upon him. No matter how tightly he drew his belt, there was no help for him.

Then something in the hot midday stung him under the left arm. Afterward he heard the report of the rifle, as the hot blood gushed down his side.

He turned and saw the rider, who had dismounted to take the long chance, now climbing back into the saddle and spurring on toward him to finish the kill.

What black madness and sleep had come upon his brain to allow an enemy to close in on him like this? He sent the stallion on, and the gallant horse responded to his voice and touch.

As he rode, he stripped away the gaudy jacket, tore out the lining, tore up shirt and undershirt, and, still without making a halt, he bandaged his wound.

It bled through the bandage. Nevertheless, he lived through that day, and dropped the hawk-like hovering line of riders far behind him. Suddenly they disappeared; yet he had not increased his pace.

At the very moment of their disappearance he saw before him a narrow strip of yellow, muddy water, twisting between low banks. Then he realized. It was not placed there by evil chance to block his way. It was the Rio Grande, and on the farther bank was safety for him.

The stallion swam across. On the farther bank Speedy fainted.

The damp cold of night air was in his face; voices were close to his ear when he came to himself again and heard a man saying: "A damn' greaser with a hoss that he's gone and stole. That's all he is. Leave the rat here to die, and we'll take the hoss."

But another voice answered: "Look there at his skin! Where the blood's washed it, and the bandage has rubbed. It's white. He's only stained his skin that color."

Speedy's dim eyes saw that a match had been lighted close to his wound. He sat up.

"Hello, and how's things?" asked the bearded ruffian who had spoken first.

"Things are looking up," said Speedy. "How's things with you, partner?"

"Well," said the other, "I ain't been clawed by any greasers lately, like it looks you've been."

"Who did this to you?" snapped the man in whose fingers the match had burned out.

"Why, there was quite a pack of them," said the young man.

"Greasers?"

"Yes."

"I'd like to get my hands on 'em! Know their names?"

"They're not hard to find," said Speedy. "Ever hear of Bardillo and his gang?"

He drew a gasp of astonished interest in reply.

"And who are you?" demanded the bearded man, lighting a match on his own behalf and letting it shine into the starved face of the young fellow.

"Why, people call me by any name that's handy," said the latter. "Speedy is a name that a lot of folks use."

The match dropped, a yellow streak of light that vanished as it touched the ground.

"Speedy," said two deep voices, hushed with awe.

XVI

It was a full two weeks after this, in the middle of the afternoon, that Al Dupray stood in front of the invalid, Joshua Crane, with Sue Crane at the back of the wheelchair, looking out of frightened eyes at her lover. For the words that Dupray uttered were enough to frighten older and braver souls than her own; enough, for one thing, to silence the terrible tongue of Crane.

Dupray was saying: "That was how I happened to take the trail at all. I never would have dared to go. I never would have known how to tackle the job, except that Speedy was along. He fought the whole thing out with me. He got south to the town of El Rey. Then, in his make-up as a Mexican, he got into the house, too. I know that much. The people in the town told me . . . he got in and joined the gang of Bardillo. Then the pinch came. I don't know exactly how. But the pinch came, and with those devils closing in on him, I suppose, he still thought about me before he thought about himself. He thought about me, I say, and sent me his last message, which was one word . . . 'Ride'! And I rode. I'm not Speedy. If I'd been in his boots and sent him such a message, he would have ridden, all right, but he would have ridden straight in to help me. He would have jumped the walls, tunneled underground, done something to come to my help. But I'm no Speedy. I rode to save my neck. And I barely got away with it, at that.

"I reached the river. I asked questions and sent messages, but no Speedy had crossed the river. No Speedy had come north toward this town. Then I got word that Speedy had been spotted. A rumor floated up from El Rey that he'd stolen the Nighthawk from Bardillo."

"He got the Nighthawk?" cried Joshua Crane.

The young man paused, and with scorn and rage he eyed Crane. "You see what it means?" he demanded hoarsely. "Even after he'd sent me word to run for my life, because he saw danger closing in, he must still have been working at his scheme to get the horse. Why? Because I'd asked him to. Why had I asked him to? Because you made that the price of Sue. Blood! That was what you wanted. And now one of the finest little fellows that ever walked the face of the earth . . . he's gone." He hung his head and groaned.

"How do you know that he's dead?" asked Joshua Crane. "The fellow that wore that disguise and made a fool of Joshua Crane . . . it'll take nigh onto all the greasers in Mexico to kill him, young man."

"The news came just a couple of days ago," said Dupray. "The rumor came up from El Rey that Speedy had been shot."

Joshua Crane put up a gnarled hand and pulled his hat from his head. He said, with bent head: "I kind of see that blame is comin' my way. I've been a hard man to you, Dupray, and a hard father to Sue." He had raised his head as he said this. Now, in the midst of the only contrite speech that human ears had ever heard him utter, he fell silent. With mouth agape, he stretched out a gaunt arm and pointed to a rider who was coming up the driveway, having just rounded the last turn.

He came on slowly, on a horse that wore neither saddle nor bridle, but only a lead rope, knotted about the neck. And he seemed painfully thin, that rider, for the slant afternoon light struck against his face and threw cadaverous shadows under the cheek bones.

"The Nighthawk, by the eternal!" cried Joshua Crane.

"Speedy!" cried Al Dupray, and ran wildly toward the horseman.

The Vamp's Bandit

"The Vamp's Bandit" was one of twelve short novels by Faust to appear in Street & Smith's *Western Story Magazine* in 1926. It was published in the March 20th issue under Faust's George Owen Baxter byline. It is a tale of redemption, told in the first person by the friend of the young outlaw, Bob Nelson. The fast-paced dialogue between the narrator, Bart Chambers, and the heroine, Mabel Crofter, lends a humorous tone to the story. This is the first time the story has appeared since its original publication.

I

I had my head in my hands. I was feeling so low that I could have stood up and walked under a snake without touching it. I was feeling so small that I could have used the shell of a hickory nut for a house and barn.

Tod Hunter came in, saying: "How's things, chief?"

"Curse your hide," I replied. "Don't talk to me. You're partly to blame for this as well as me."

He picked up the paper where it had fallen on the floor and he read the article out loud, spelling the words to himself before he pronounced them. Because Tod never had no educational advantages, like me. This was what he read out loud to me, and every word made me sicker and sicker:

FAMOUS OUTLAW HOLDS UP PORTER'S PASS STAGE—OUTFACES THREE GUARDS AND ESCAPES WITH LOOT

Last night, under a full moon, the celebrated bandit, Bob Nelson, waited in a gap of the Porter Mountains until the Porter's Pass coach came through and then stepped out with a rifle to. . . .

"Shut up!" I yelled.

He went on running his eye through the column as fast as he could, bringing out important words, here and there.

"'Three guards . . . a sawed-off shotgun . . . lady fainted . . . when last seen riding west. . . .' Dog-gone me, Bart, it looks like he might be heading for us. Might be coming back to pay us a visit. That would be pretty good, eh?"

"Shut up!" I repeated. "I've been thinking too much for my peace of mind."

Just then Lee, the cook, came in.

"Hey, Lee," said Tod, "Bob is drifting back this way. You savvy? The kid . . . maybe he's coming back to pay us a visit."

"Kid come? By golly!" said Lee, and he looked at us with eyes as big as saucers and a grin that tickled both ears.

The kid had always been the favorite with Lee. He always had managed to shy the best chuck onto the kid's plate when Bob was working with us on the ranch.

It didn't cheer me up much, to see that Chinaman's face. I could only groan and say to Hunter: "Maybe Bob is coming, and, if he does, I want you to tell me how we're going to be able to do something for him . . . how're we gonna be able to stop him, Tod, before he goes on with this bandit stuff of his, long enough to jam his head right into a hangman's noose?"

"He's killed nobody yet," Tod said very cheerfully.

I told Tod what I thought of him in language that can't be repeated here, incidentally pointing out that Bob was smart enough to be able to shoot for a leg or a shoulder, instead of for a head or a heart, but someday he would get cornered and have to fight for his life. Then the killings would come in flocks and bunches. Of course, Tod had to admit that it was sense, and he went outside right away, which was his way of showing that the puzzle was a bit too hard for him.

It was all left to me, and that was right and proper, in a way, because, of course, I was the man who had hired the kid and gave him his first job.

When I went outside and looked the landscape over, it was a blue day—oh, what a blue day it was. Nothing but high, gray clouds across the face of the sky. The cows had their backs to the wind that was blowing their tails between their legs, and the yearlings was roaching up their backs and dropping their heads, real miserable, as though winter had come already. Somehow, the sight of those miserable cows was too much for me. I had to get away from the ranch, and it was easy for me to remember a lot of things that ought to be done in town.

With a tough pair of buckskins hitched to the buckboard, I started out on the long trail. I tell you how mean I was feeling. All of the errands that I had to do would be better done in Bar Valley, of course. But Porter's Pass had the call over the good town this morning. I think that the lowness and the orneriness and the meanness of Porter's Pass just fitted into my own mind like clockwork, that day. I busted off down the trail, popping the buckskins with the whip one minute and sawing on their mouths with the reins the next, the way that a man will do when he's too down to be decent.

I got into Porter's Pass at dark, with two horses pretty near too tired to step. I shoved them into the livery stable and got me a room at the hotel.

Of course, I had what you'd half expect in Porter's Pass—a room right over another where some gents was playing poker and arguing a lot over their cards and their liquor. I listened to them yapping for a long time, and then I went stamping down the stairs and I kicked open the door of their room. I leaned in the doorway and used up a few minutes passing bad language, while they sat pretty dumb and scared, thinking that I must be nothing less than a deputy sheriff or a celebrated gunfighter, by the proud talk that I was using.

"Now, you sons of goats, you tinhorn cheapskates, you corn-fed flatheads, you loud-mouthed loafers, if I hear another peep out of you during the night, I'll come down here and chaw you up so dog-gone' small and fine that you'll blow away in the first night wind. You hear me yap and remember."

I gave the door another kick and went back to my own room. You would think, maybe, that I was a pretty hard fellow by the line of talk that I used, but I wasn't. I'm harmless, most generally, but when I get depressed, it acts bad on me—like low-grade whiskey, coming out in wrong language and such things. You understand how it is. Those fellows thought that I was some terrible fighter, and they didn't let out a peep.

Just the same, I couldn't sleep any. I lay in bed a while glorying in how I had bluffed out those pikers. Then I began to remember about the kid, and that took the joy out quick. All these weeks since he had cut loose and started burning up atmosphere and crowding the headlines of the newspapers, I had figured that someday, somehow I would have to work things so that this here Bob Nelson would be tamed down and made safe for democracy. But I never could figure it out no way at all. Planning on how to handle Bob was like planning on how to handle the next comet that heaves into sight. You may do a lot of looking and you may do a lot of thinking, but by the time you get turned around, the comet has gone kiting through another dozen light years, and you got to think all over again.

Just before dawn, I did fall asleep, and it was well after sunup when I wakened; that gave me a guilty feeling to start the day. I had breakfast, feeling grouchier than ever. Then I started out to get my errands done, and, when I was coming out of a harness shop, after having a fight about the price of some saddlebags, I heard a girl cry: "Hello, Bartie! What's the good news?"

There ain't much that makes me any madder than to be called Bartie. I don't know why. It's all right for a nickname. Only it don't fit in with my idea of myself. I always imagine that name going with blue eyes and pink cheeks. Besides, when a man is running a big ranch and gets to be forty years old, he's got a right to be a little particular about his moniker.

I turned around with a growl and there was Maybelle Crofter, sashaying across the street and waving her hand at me. She looked prettier than ever, which might have come of her wearing a blue jacket and a blue skirt, with a big twist of her hair coming over her shoulder and hanging down in a pigtail. It was like the outfit of a sixteen-year-old girl. Well, Maybelle—or Mabel, to spell it the right way and the easier way—could look sixteen when she chose to. She was every inch of twenty-five, but that didn't bother her. When she felt extra young, she could dress extra young. And when she felt old, she could dress herself up and look like the mother of a family, on her way to church. And I suppose that Mabel never seen the inside of a church in her whole life.

As I was saying, this girl came sashaying across the street, waving her hand at me. Then she come up, saying: "The finest sight I've seen since I had measles. But what makes you go down the street singing right out loud?"

Some of my grouch melted out of me. She had a sunny pair of eyes, that kid did. I knew that there was tons of bad in her. Everybody else knew that, too. But I knew that there was some good, too. Anyway, she was company above the average of what you get in Porter's Pass.

I said: "What dropped you in this dive, Mabel? Have you gone and got yourself another husband?"

"That's what I ain't done nothing but," replied Mabel. "I got me a fine six foot two or three inches of husband."

"He may be big," I said, "but if he lives in Porter's Pass, he ain't so fine. You take it from me, will you?"

"I know," said Mabel, "this town is full of pikers and strong-arm blackjacks, all right."

"What might be the moniker of the guy that you caught, Mabel?"

"Arthur Rand is his name," she said.

"Hey! Arthur Rand? The rancher? How did you ever pick up anything as good as that, kid?"

"Don't be nasty, Bartie," said Mabel, getting a little cold. "I don't mind an old friend speaking his mind, but I'm not such a poor looker, when you come to sling your eye over me." She picked up her head and dropped a hand on one hip and done a pirouette very slowly. "How am I?"

No, I had to admit that she was pretty, although she wasn't half so pretty as she looked. It's not just a beautiful face than can poison men and make them mad for a woman. It's something inside the soul of a girl.

"How do you do it, Mabel?" I asked. "You've traveled some, but you don't look as though you'd as much as gone across the street."

"I don't take things to heart," said Mabel. "When some folks make a slip, they write it down in red and study that passage a lot. But I . . . well, I just tear out the page."

She laughed and shook her head. She had a fine laugh—hearty as a man's, but musical, you know.

"Which husband is this?" I asked her.

"Second," said Mabel. "Third, I mean to say."

"You sort of lose the count?" I said.

"I never had much education," said Mabel, grinning.

"Well, how comes it that Arthur Rand is letting you drift around by yourself like this? Is he in town buying cattle, or something?"

"Oh, no," she answered, "he's back in Nevada getting a fresh start."

I asked her what she meant.

"Oh, I got tired of him," said Mabel, "and he suspected it. He made a scene, and I had to tell him where to get off. So he grabbed the Overland and . . . hello, Missus Potter."

A lady come down the street past us, and, as she come by, she slowed up enough to look the pair of us over. Then she stuck her head in the air and went sailing on. It was easy to see that Mabel's reputation had come to town with her, at last, but it didn't bother Mabel none.

"Missus Potter is hard of hearing," Mabel said loud enough for Mrs. Potter to hear. "The years will tell, won't they?"

You could see a shiver run through Mrs. Potter's back as she went sashaying down the sidewalk.

II

"Well," I said, when I got through laughing, "you're after alimony now, I suppose?"

"Sure," said Mabel. "By reason of not causing hubby any bother about leaving me, I get a pretty good slice off the estate. When the dough arrives, I get myself a vacation."

"Vacation!" I exclaimed. "Why, honey, you've had nothing but vacations since they tried to keep you in school back in our home town and couldn't."

"Don't make me think back that far," said Mabel. "It gives me a headache. I never remember anything before the time when I crowded a few extra letters into my name. But it hasn't been all a vacation. When I get my money, I'm going to get me a shack in the mountains where there's nothing nearer to men than grizzly bears and mountain lions. That's the way that I feel."

"You've got enough scalps to retire on," I admitted. "So long, Mabel."

"Wait a minute," she said. "Take off your pack and rest a while. What's gone wrong on the ranch?"

"Curse the cows and the ranch," I said. "This is about a man, old-timer, and you can't help."

"Can't I?" she asked. "Why, young fellow, I'm a professor in just that line of work. Tell Aunt Mabel."

I gave her another look. It wasn't that I really expected any solution from her, but I needed help so bad that I was willing to tell everybody how low I felt. We sat down on the front steps of a vacant house.

"You haven't been here long," I said, "but you've heard about Bob Nelson?"

She showed life right away. "The bandit. I know about him, of course."

"But you don't know much, and nobody does except me and a few of the boys out at my ranch. If that bandit showed out there, do you know what way we'd act?"

"Like the rest of the poor fish around here every time they hear his name mentioned," said Mabel, "you'd dive through the window or any way to get clear of him."

"You're wrong, kid," I said. "We'd shake hands all around and pull up an easy chair in front of the fire."

She blinked at me. "Since when have they had easy chairs on a ranch?" she asked.

"Don't get too literal," I said. "I say that Bob Nelson is the best-liked kid that was ever on that ranch."

"Did you say kid?"

"He's about twenty."

She put up her head and whistled.

"Let me tell you the story all in a nutshell," I went on. "I was drumming up a crew last fall for riding range on that ranch . . . which it's the meanest bit of range in the world . . . and I picked up this Bob Nelson. He was going around looking for a hero and he elected me to be the goat, you understand? I took this kid out on the ranch, and he went around worshiping me, wearing his clothes like me, and practicing with his Colt day and night to make himself half as good a shot as he thought I must be."

Mabel yawned. "I know," she said. "Men are a silly lot of fools . . . thank heavens! Go on."

"No," I said, pretty serious. "That's where you're wrong . . . he ain't a fool. And if you want proof, I'll point you out my gang on the ranch . . . all hard-boiled

. . . and every one of them would die for the sake of that same kid. The most cheerful, best-natured, happy, smiling, willing kid that ever chopped wood for the fire on a snowy morning. Never seen anybody so willing to do a double share of work if he thought that it would help out a pal. A clean sport . . . white all the way through. But the result was that he got tired of just posing and started out to be real hard-boiled. Then he goes cavorting around the mountains, holding folks up. Of course, he's not with us any more, but I feel sort of responsible for the kid. You understand?"

Mabel sat there with her eyes closed, and her face wrinkled up with pain. "Oh, don't I understand," she said in a sort of a whisper.

"Don't cry about it, Mabel," I said.

"I'm not crying," she said. "It just hurts too much for tears, and that's all. Why, Bart, there's only one thing in the world for you to do."

"Go on, Solomon," I said. "If you can show me how to get Bob out of this mess, I'll be your slave for life. Because I feel I want to look out for him."

"Shut up," said Mabel. "I thought I had the right idea, but it slipped away from me. Lemme think." She sat there with her face in a knot. Pretty soon she said: "This here is gonna give me wrinkles bad. Bart, what you got to do is to give this young fool something to be a hero about that is harmless to the rest of the world. Y'understand?"

"No," I said, "I don't."

"Why, what does a hero do?" asked Mabel. "He goes around and fights bad men."

It began to dawn on me. But still it wasn't clear.

"Has he raised so much trouble that the law won't let him alone?" she asked. "Has he killed men?"

"Only one," I said, "and that was a low-down head-hunter that needed killing. No, I think that the kid has a lot more friends than he has enemies. But he couldn't show his face in public, you know."

She nodded, still biting her lip and thinking. "How old did you say he was?" she asked.

"About twenty."

"A baby!"

"Not a baby, either," I began, "but a hundred percent. . . ."

"Shut up," said Mabel. "All men are babies . . . and spoiled ones, too!" Then she said: "I'll tell you what, Bart . . . that boy needs a woman, and he needs her quick. No mere man could handle him. If he's the sort of fire that you describe, the thing for you to do is to get hold of a mighty safe, mighty sweet girl with a level head on her shoulders, and let him start guarding her if he can. I gather it won't make much difference even if there's nothing to guard her from. You can just tell him that there is."

It sounded like sense. It hit me where I lived. I had to get up and walk around, exclaiming: "Mabel, I think that you've hit the nail on the head, maybe! I feel that you've come close to it. But still, there's something wrong. He's got to have something to worship as well as something to guard. He's got to think that he's taking care of something that is really taking care of him."

She nodded. "You get me perfect," said Mabel.

"But," I said, "how are you going to make him think that there's any danger at all in the way of one of these Western girls? A girl in this country never has anything to fear from men. Besides, no girl young enough and decent enough to make a wife for him would have the brains to handle him. If there was any mistake made in the handling of that bunch of lightning, believe me, it would make an explosion that would just blast a few lives, and you make no mistake about that. This kid is the concentrated essence of dynamite."

"D'you want him to fall in love with his grandmother?" asked Mabel, very peevish because her idea wasn't panning out so very well.

Then a light ripped across my mind. I thought it was an inspiration. "Mabel," I cried, "you're the girl! You're the girl for Bob Nelson!"

III

I had to have a girl with looks, brains, and a sense of humor—if I wanted one to handle the kid. Where could I find a better layout in all of those respects than in Maybelle Crofter-Rand, or whatever she happened to be calling herself at that time?

Mabel looked me up and down, and then she shrugged her shoulders like a man. "What a guy," said Mabel.

"What's wrong?" I asked. "Are you too proud for the job?"

"I've done a lot of stupid things and a lot of crazy things," said Mabel, "but I've never used my face and my chatter to rob the cradle. Not yet, I haven't, and I'm not going to start on this baby to please you."

The idea that Mabel herself would put any obstacles in my path made me mad. I couldn't answer for a minute.

She went on: "The boobs that I've picked out and made simps of have always been old enough to know better. Something over thirty and something under fifty. That's my motto."

She was funny that way. You never knew how she was coming at you, always something unexpected.

You might talk to her a hundred years, but on the last day she would flabbergast you with something that you'd never guessed about her before.

I said: "Now look here, you can save that talk for Sunday, but every day of the week is Monday so far as I'm concerned. Don't try any of the bunk on me. I want you to start in and plan out a campaign for taming down this here young outlaw."

She shook her head.

"Listen, Maybelle," I said.

"Even when you put the 'y' in my name," said Mabel, "you can't persuade me on this. I'm adamant, y'understand?"

"All right," I said, pretty disgusted, "you lean back in your chair and give yourself time, will you?"

I put a match to a cigarette and began blowing rings very deliberate.

"Now you try it in words of one syllable," I said.

"Try what?" she asked.

"Try to explain why you won't tackle this job for me?"

"Old son," said Mabel, "you hear me talk. When I get in my work on a man like that, it isn't any joke. I don't just pop into his head and out again. I stay there for a long while. The pikers and the tinhorn sports may forget me quick enough, but the hundred-percent men are different. This kid is a ham, of course. But he's a man. And suppose that he should really tumble head over heels in love with me?"

"Don't be such a fathead," I said. "You're not such a bright light as that, Mabel."

She just grinned at me. Then she turned the grin into a smile—which is a lot different thing, if you know what I mean. She reached out and dropped a hand on my arm and looked straight into my eyes.

"Dear old silly Bart," she said, "don't you think that even you could love me if you tried a little?"

I could only blink a little. Then I shook off her hand and took a deep breath. "Leave me be, Mabel," I said. "I never done you no harm."

"All right," said Mabel, "I never hit a man that's down."

I explained: "I understand what you mean. To get a hold on the kid, you've got to pretend that he's knocked your eye right out. You've got to pretend to be pretty woozy about him, and that may make him fall into something a couple of pegs deeper than calf love. But we've got to risk that. You understand what I mean. It's this or a hangman to make his finish."

"Why," said Mabel, "he seems to have been doing pretty well for himself, thank you very much. I don't notice that he's crowding the jails very much."

"You don't follow my drift," I explained to her. "Sooner or later, he'll have his back against the wall, and then, when he fights, he'll have to shoot to kill. And when that happens, there'll be a slaughter. Y'understand, Mabel? We got to plan on saving him from his future."

She saw that point, at last. "All right," she said, "but what am I to do first? Ride out on the mountains and lasso this young rip?"

"Leave me to corral him," I said. "He's too much of a friend of mine not to try to drop in on me at the ranch, now that he's working this section of the country again. When I lay hands on him, I'll try to get him interested in you."

"That's easy," said Mabel, opening her purse and taking out her photograph. "I pack some of these around with me all the time. You never can tell when they'll come in handy, you see? Hand the kid one of these. Wait a minute. Here's one that looks younger. That was last year."

You would say that she had a lot of brass, that girl. Well, she did have brass—but part of it was just frankness. She knew what her bad spots were and she was willing to confess to them. She knew what her good points were and she was just as ready to talk about them. She was just different from other people, if you know what I mean.

I looked this photograph over. She was dressed up in a girlishlooking thing with a sailor collar on it, y'understand, and a broad hat with the brim furled up a mite, like her nose.

"What deviltry were you up to when this here picture was taken last year?" I asked.

"That was when Sammy Marvin . . . no, I mean that that was when Jack Roxburgh was paying attention to me. Anyway, it's a good picture, isn't it? My mouth doesn't look so big in it."

"No," I agreed, "it doesn't. You looked kind of sad and sweet."

"That's the devil of a big mouth," said Mabel. "You got to smile sad and sweet, or else not smile at all. However, maybe the kid won't mind sadness?"

I said: "Now, you get this wrote down in red and don't you never forget it while you're on this case."

"After all, Bart Chambers," she said, "I'm a woman and not a doctor."

"You are a devil," I said, "but let's get down to business. While you're working on this kid. . . ."

"Remember," said Mabel, "I haven't got my alimony . . . not yet."

It took me up sort of short, but I set my teeth and decided to weather it.

"I'll mail you fifty dollars to start with," I said.

"All right," said Mabel. "It sounds like chicken feed, but beggars can't be choosers."

She didn't even blush, although she certainly knew that I was no millionaire, with no big pay to fall back on and not very many savings. She was a hard one, in her own way, was Mabel.

"You mail me fifty," she said, "and then what? I start dressing like that picture . . . real girlish? Matter of fact, I'm togged out sort of young today."

"How does it happen?" I said.

"One of my neighbors came in the other day. A sour-faced old dame. She happened to see a pretty young-looking hat lying around and she says . . . 'I really don't see, Missus Rand, how a person of your age can wear a hat like that.' Real catty, you see? So I says . . . 'Keep your eyes open tomorrow, and you'll see for yourself.' So here I am. And not so bad at that, Bartie. Not so bad at that."

Dog-gone me if she didn't have a little mirror out, studying herself and nodding and smiling, agreeing with herself every minute. You couldn't beat Mabel.

"Very well," I said. "I suppose that you might dress young for this part you're going to play . . . if I can ever get him to you. But look here, Mabel, I want you to understand that the face won't make much difference to the kid. You got to work by hypnosis on him. That's what you got to do. Rock him into a sweet dream, and then everything will be easy. He'll never see the solid earth again. He'll be miles above the clouds."

"Well," said Mabel, "I'll think it over. But right offhand, it seems to me that the best thing that I can do will be to be a wronged woman. That sort of stuff usually goes over pretty big with the youngsters."

She let her head fall back and laughed just as free

and hearty as any man. My, but she was a rascal, and a pretty one, too.

IV

On the whole, I felt a good deal better after talking with Mabel that way. It gave me more heart, and I went around town and did my chores. I decided that I had ought to have one more chat with Mabel before I left Porter's Pass. But when I went to see her, she was out. When I got to the hotel again, I intended to start right back for the ranch, but I didn't.

A man blew in from Montana that said he owned most of the silver mines in that part of the world, and besides that he said that he had corralled about all the luck that there was. He added that in his spare time he had invented a little game with cards, by the name of poker.

I allowed that I had heard of that game and would like to learn a little about it. Three more of the boys of Porter's Pass said that they were always willing to learn, and so we all sat in. Dog-gone me if he wasn't a good teacher, too! There was a time that night when my watch and my hunting knife and my Colt was all lying on top of that table. After a while I got them back into my pockets, and then luck turned my way a little—particularly when I suggested that we hire a gent for a dealer. After that the gent from Montana wasn't so dog-goned sure about his invention, and his silver mines didn't seem to be worth half so much.

Anyway, about two o'clock we got him parted from the last of his wad, and, although only about thirty dollars come to my share, it looked pretty fair to me for one day's work.

I went up to my room, singing, with the gents that I waked up on the way cussing me hearty on either side of the hall. When I opened the door and stepped into my room, the first thing that I seen was a shadow against the stars beyond my window. That was nothing much to make a fuss over, I agree, but this shadow happened to wear the shape of a man.

"Who is it?" I asked, but I was so scared that my voice wasn't any louder than a whisper. I looked closer and I could see that his head was lying on his arms where he sat at my table, then I could hear the breathing of the sleeper. Of course, I just thought that it was some drunk who had got into the wrong room and had fallen asleep before he could get into bed. I lighted a match, but the minute that the flame flared, I dropped that match and stepped on it, for fear somebody else might see what I was looking at.

The face that was turned sideways toward me on those folded arms was the face of the bandit, the outlaw, the stick-up artist that the whole range was howling to get at—Porter's Pass howling loudest of all. It was Bob Nelson.

"Bob!" I gasped out at his ear.

He woke up and stretched and yawned. Then he jumped up and shook hands with me and started saying how glad he was to see me again. "Except that I'm not seeing you," Bob said, scratching a match and lighting a lamp.

It drove me wild. "Suppose that someone looks in?" I said.

"Not much chance of that," he said. "It's a pretty far climb to get up to this window. I know, because I tried it myself this evening."

"But if they catch you here, they've got you trapped and helpless, sure."

"Maybe not," said Bob.

"What could you do if they got under that window and watched you there?"

"I might try to force the back door, or rush right out the front way. Or I might go up to the top of the house and jump for the next roof . . . that's not more than fifteen feet away, you know."

It was—fifteen feet across a regular ravine, with hard rocks underneath if you missed your foothold on the far side.

"Do you even know how to get onto the roof?" I asked.

"Oh, yes," said the kid. "When I found that you weren't in your room here, I looked the hotel over to get acquainted with it."

"How did you know that I was here?"

"I stuck up a farmer driving a buckboard out of town and I was asking him about what had been happening in town. He told me pretty freely. The idiot seemed to have an idea that I'd murder him at the first slip he made."

"But you held up a fighting man for the sake of getting news out of him?" I asked the kid, sort of sick and weak.

"He wasn't a fighting man," he said.

"They all pack guns . . . they all can use them . . . these gents in Porter's Pass," I said. "And it's time for you to know that . . . if you haven't gathered it already."

He only shook his head. "There's a difference between a dangerous man and a weak one," said Bob Nelson. "You can tell them by something in their eyes . . . the way that they look at you and the way that they carry their heads." He went on: "I heard about the poker game you were sitting in at. And then that you were staying at the hotel. So I came in after dark and drifted through the rooms, until I found the one that had your things in them. It was like seeing a friend's face when I laid eyes on them, Bart."

He laid a hand on my shoulder and smiled at me. But all I could think of was the incredible daring of this young fool, wandering from room to room in a hotel where he might run into danger at any time, and where every exit could be barred against him in no time.

"Then you sat down and went to sleep," I said.

"Well," said Bob, "you see there was only about one chance in five that anybody would come into the room before you did . . . I needed sleep . . . haven't had any in two days." He added with a crooked smile: "Four chances out of five is as good as a sure thing . . . to a man who's living in danger of the law. So I had to take it. And I've won out, you see. I've had . . . let me see . . . why, four whole hours of sleep. It bucks me up no end." He straightened himself a little and shook back his shoulders. You would never say that young dandy had gone forty-eight hours without sleep. He said: "You look downhearted, Bart. What's wrong?"

"Well, old-timer," I said, "I'll tell you what's making me blue. And it's a thing where I need help."

"Ah, Bart," he said, "if I could do a good turn for you, it would be the happiest day of my life."

V

He meant it, too. He was as deceiving and mysterious as a good pane of polished plate glass. He was as subtle as a bull buffalo and as hard to outguess as a hen in a chicken yard. He stood up there with his face shining at me and his eyes snapping. He wanted me to go tell him to fight ten men or find a gold mine or hold up an express train, single-handed, or do something else man-size like that. It would have made you laugh to see his face fail when I said to him that my trouble had to do with the affairs of a woman.

He lost interest right away and began to smile down at me in a very superior sort of way, as though I was to be pitied and wondered at, for wasting my time on anything as low-down and useless as a woman.

He said in an easy way: "You've fallen in love with some girl, I suppose, Bart."

"Yes," I said, "I have."

"Just lately, then?" asked the kid.

I thought back. "No," I said, "it's been about four years since I first fell in love with her."

That was not a complete lie—only partial. In a way, I had been half in love with pretty Mabel Crofter from the time that she got out of childhood. She had such looks and such ways about her. Anyway, this speech made a terrible hit with the kid.

He stepped back and took a long breath. "Bart," he said under his breath, "you don't mean that you have loved a woman for four years . . . and not said a word about it, ever? Bart, you're a wonderful man!"

Yes, sir, the raving young idiot was going to start in worshipping me again. I never saw a boy like that. He was positively miserable unless he found somebody to make a hero out of.

"You see, old-timer," I had to put in, "it's this way . . . she was only a kid four years ago."

"Don't explain to me," said the kid. "It's like something out of an old romance . . . like the way the knights used to love their ladies in the old times. Here you are, and me knowing you so long and so well, but I never guessed it. Never dreamed that you ever so much as thought of a woman."

There he was at it. He was always reading some sort of rot in books that he picked up, and then trying to apply what he read about knights in armor to real cowpunchers in chaps and bandannas. I only shook my head. I didn't know exactly what to say next.

"But tell me," said the kid, very excited, "why you're so sad, Bart? Won't she have you?"

"She won't," I said, "and she can't. She's married."

"Heavens!" cried the kid. "Heavens, old man!" He went over and leaned out the window with tears in his eyes.

Yes, I mean what I say. There was tears in his eyes. He was actually standing there and suffering for me. There was a frown on his face, he was working so hard to keep from showing his emotion.

He said, deep and quiet: "I always knew that there was a secret sorrow in your life, chief. I always guessed it when I sat and watched you when you were silent."

That was typical. Seeing me when I was too tired to talk, he turned my ache in the shoulders into an ache of the heart.

"Never mind that," I said, "what matters now is. . . ."

"I've got to mind that," sang out the kid, so excited that I was afraid that somebody close by my room might hear him through the tissue-paper walls of that crazy old shack of a hotel. "I've got to mind," he said, "how you've swallowed your troubles, and never winced. Why, chief, when I look at you and think what kind of a man you are, it makes me feel like . . . like a fool and a baby."

He got rid of the tears that were in his eyes—tears of sympathy for my grief. He got a new set—tears of joy because I was so wonderful and so great and so grand, because he could have the pleasure of looking at me with his own eyes. And he could stand there in the same room with me and breathe the same air. Oh, curse such a boy as he was.

"Bob," I said, "is this a time to think about me? No, it's a time to talk about that poor girl."

"Ah," said the kid, "I thought that your trouble was just because you never could marry her, chief. But I see, now. You wouldn't trouble yourself about such things. You wouldn't ask help for yourself. It's because you want to help her out of some sort of trouble."

He was busy putting some more gilt on my wings.

"Son," I said, "I can't tell you what it would mean to me if I could help this poor girl."

"Bart, Bart," he said. "Could you use me? Could you please let me try to be of help to you or to her?"

"It's no good, Bob," I told him. "It ain't any good. You ain't the sort of a man who could help a woman like her."

He was humble enough, but he had his pride, and now he bit his lip. He said: "I want to do what I can, partner, if you'll only tell me what it is that I can do."

"Nothing, Bob," I said, very sad. "I see that there's nothing that you can do. You could never settle down and live quietly, keeping out of the sight of folks."

"Why couldn't I?" asked Bob, getting excited. "Would you please tell me why I couldn't be quiet?"

"Oh, I know you, Bob," I said, "pretty near as well as I know myself. Yes, maybe better even. What you want to do is to be out there on the hills, galloping along and living wild and free and fine. It would be poison to you to settle down and be quiet. . . ."

Said the kid, fairly stuttering with eagerness: "You don't know me, chief. Dog-gone it, I tell you that you don't know me. Gallop around over the hills? Live wild and free? Why, chief, do you think that it's any pleasure to me to be herded around the mountains like a wolf? No, only it's my fate to be an outcast, hounded by enemies, surrounded by hate, walled in by venom. . . ."

He stopped for a minute. There was such tears of self-pity in his eyes that he couldn't go on for a while. He had kidded himself into a great state of mind. He was all worked up. When he got that way, sometimes he would open up and talk like sixty. He would talk as good as you could find in a book. Mostly his speeches used to come out of some of the yarns that he used to read, I think.

I had to bite my tongue to keep from laughing in his face, but I asked: "You don't mean it, Bob. You don't really mean that it's distasteful to you, living high and free and wild, the way that you do?"

"No," said the kid, sighing. "Living doomed and desolate though I do, my secret yearning is for some quiet corner of the world . . . a house of peace, and a little garden where I could work with hoe and spade."

Here he got so choked with sorrow for himself that he had to stop again and let off steam. The idea of him ever turning his hand to a cottage and a hoe made me smile inside—but, after all, anything was possible for that kid, if the right sort of suggestion was only used on him.

"I see how it is," I said, keeping my face fairly straight. "And it gives me a lot more hope that maybe you could help her. Except that it would be terribly hard. Mind you, I would try the job myself, but she wouldn't let me. She wouldn't let me sacrifice myself for her. She's that fine, Bob. She would do some terrible wild thing if she thought that she was messing up my life."

Bob blinked and swallowed the idea on the wing, so to speak.

"I see," he said, "that she must be a wonderful woman."

"She is," I said, "different from any woman that I ever met, or that I ever heard of." Which was exactly the truth, as you'll agree with me before you've heard the finish about Mabel. "But," I continued, "to take care of her, you would have to actually take the terrible danger of finding a way of living right here in the middle of this here town. The idea of a horrible risk like that . . . why, it makes me sick to think of it even. It would mean living . . . say, in the barn behind her house, and keeping yourself out of the sight of everybody as long as the sun was shining, and only sneaking out at night like a wild tiger right in the middle of the town."

Terrible? I could see that Bob Nelson was almost swooning with happiness to think of tackling such a job.

"Chief," he said, "even if it's dangerous, I would like to tackle. . . ."

I raised my hand. "Don't talk to me about it, because the more that I think about it, the more I see that it would be sort of suicide for you to attempt it. Too many men are out gunning for you. And if they saw you . . . well, you might get away, but that would be an end of the protection that poor . . . I can't tell her name, though."

"Chief," gasped out Bob, "I beg you to tell me!"

"No, no," I told him, "I wouldn't dream of it. Why, youngster, this here is a harder thing than I've ever heard of before. Not you nor any man could ever do it."

He was foaming now with despair and enthusiasm. "Bart, I want to beg a little favor of you."

"Bob," I said, pretending not to understand, "of course I would do anything that I could for you."

He said: "Tell me the name of the girl."

"It's not fair, trapping me like that?" I said. "But I suppose that I've got to live up to my promise to you. Her name is Maybelle Rand."

"Chief," he said, "if you won't send me to her, I'll go myself and offer myself to guard her."

I swallowed a smile again. "Bob," I told him, "I like your nerve, I got to admit. But before you ring into this game, you've got to know what you're to guard her from."

"Aye," he said. "That's it."

"I . . . you'll have to ask her yourself," I said. "And let her tell you in her own words what the danger is, because I can't do it half so well. And here, Bob, is a picture of her."

I had held back that photograph for the last minute, and now I passed it across to Bob Nelson.

Well, he wasn't of age, and until a man gets along toward thirty, he has a weakness for girlishness—and again after he's fifty. The only period when he's fairly safe is between thirty and fifty. Bob had never paid much attention to girls. So you can see how it was that Mabel could step into his mind without any competition to give her a run for her money. I sized the situation up for a while, watching poor young Bob simply turn groggy with wonder as he stared at that snapshot.

Then I said: "I'm going to keep you right here in this room until tomorrow night. And then I'm going to take you to see Maybelle."

VI

Keeping Bob inside four walls was like keeping a royal Bengal tiger in a hen coop. He was wanting to rip loose every minute. He was always pretending humility and gentleness—but the fighting devil that had always been pretty strong in that youngster had been given a thorough cultivating during the past months, when he was free to roam up and down the range as he would.

I had to watch him like a hawk all the time that he was with me, and, in the middle of the next afternoon, I made him swear not to budge out of the room while I was gone—then I started for Mabel.

She had a house on the edge of town that her husband had fixed up for her after he decided that he couldn't leave her with his folks on their ranch. When I sauntered up to her door, the piano was rattling and Mabel's voice was chirping out a rag tune.

When she came to the door and found me there, she brought me right in and introduced me to a tall young chap with a brown face that was never got except prospecting or punching cows. He'd come into money lately. He had an emerald stickpin that looked like a big green eye in the middle of his red necktie. And he had a wallet that looked like a football in the throat of an ostrich.

I forget what his name was. She sashayed into the room, saying: "Here's my lawyer come to talk business to me, dearie. You run along, and don't stand on the corner with your hat off, because there's sunstroke in the air. So long."

The big guy backed out the door and gave me a dangerous look while he was passing out.

"You're kind of rough on that gent," I said to Mabel. "He knows that I'm no lawyer."

"What difference does it make, foolish?" asked Mabel. "He's the kind that likes to be handled rough. Anything to get him out of his trance. He's had a rush of dollars to the head and he can't think straight. Now sit down and tell me about Bob Nelson. I've been dreaming about him in the middle of the day."

"That's because he's coming to see you tonight," I told her.

She was a good deal surprised by that, and so I went ahead and told her when Bob had showed up, and how.

"Just crazy," said Mabel. "But what'll I tell him is the danger when you bring him around tonight? I'm in no danger from anything."

"You work that up yourself," I said. "If this is a partnership job, Mabel, I've done more than my fifty percent, already. Now you do your part. The thing for you to do is to look young and get a pair of wings. He says he can see already that you're one of the most wonderful women in the world. He won't see much of you. Just his idea of you."

"I've got to prune down the slang," said Mabel, "and talking English is a terrible strain. Does the poor fish have to live in my barn while he protects me from things that ain't?"

"It's the only way," I explained to her. "I've got him all heated up about the idea. Now, Mabel, when you get that young madman out there in the barn, the thing for you to do is to imagine that you got a wild hawk in your hand. You got to teach him to come when you whistle. You got to get him tamed. And when it comes to working out the saving of him, we'll do that together. Main thing for you is to keep him put safe. If he keeps on rampaging around, sticking up stages and what not, he'll be ripening himself for the gallows in no time."

She agreed that was the thing to do.

I had a couple of other people to see, and it was already the warm evening of the day, and the town was settling down—as much as Porter's Pass ever settled down—when I started back for the hotel. The sprinklers was whizzing and swishing on the front lawns of the houses that I passed, and the householders was out in their shirt sleeves, hollering their opinions about weather and politics to their neighbors. Everything was peaceful until I got pretty close to the hotel, and then there was a sudden yipping of men, half scared and half mad, and the barking of Colts, deep and hoarse.

When I come around the corner, keeping close to the building, I saw half a dozen gents in the vacant lot next to the hotel slipping around and shooting at shadows.

"Where did he go?" they was yelling. "He went behind that tree."

"No, he started straight back for the hotel."

"You lie! He ducked out onto the street."

"He headed for behind the blacksmith shop!"

I hung around until they had quieted down a mite, and then I found out what had been happening.

The deputy sheriff, Barker, had been just standing there, talking to some of the boys, telling them that they had got to quiet down because he was gonna bring law and order into that town of Porter's Pass, if he had to kill himself doing it. The boys agreed that it was time for the old town to turn over a new page, but they suggested that the first thing for him to do was to get out on the trail and run down Bob Nelson.

The deputy sheriff agreed that that was a fine idea, but he said that he had already worked himself ragged on the trail of Bob Nelson after the stage hold-up. All he could figure out was that Bob was headed right straight back for Porter's Pass itself, and, when he came to that point, he decided to give up the search altogether for the time being. Because, as he pointed out, it was madness to imagine that even Bob Nelson would dare to try to hide himself in Porter's Pass.

He said that he would get Bob before long, though, and he said that the chief trouble with the other folks who had ridden out to get Bob was that they were licked and ready to be bluffed out before they ever got within shooting distance of the kid. Barker wasn't going to be bluffed.

It was the blacksmith that told me this stuff, talking behind his hand. He was a hard one, that blacksmith, but he didn't want his opinions to get aired.

"They got about that far in their yarning, and the boys was beginning to agree to everything that this here Barker said," said the blacksmith, "when, dog-gone me, if a shadow didn't drop out of the branches of that fir tree yonder, and right into the bunch of them. It started a flock of trouble, because that shadow had the action of a wildcat and the shape of a man. It landed right on poor Barker, first of all, and squashed him flat. Then it flickered around for about ten seconds, and everything that it touched went flat. Just about the time that the guns began to chatter, the shadow disappeared, and the boys have been milling around ever since trying to locate it."

Now, before that story was half told, a chilly idea had begun to percolate into my brain and send a shiver clean down the length of my spine. I said to the blacksmith: "Who could it have been? Some drunk having a party all by himself?"

"Drunk?" the blacksmith said, grinning sidewise at me. "Well, no drunk that I've ever seen was half as fast on his feet or hit half as hard with his fists. But my idea is that the shadow that dropped on those boobs and flattened them out was Bob Nelson."

It was my idea, too, of course.

I separated myself from the blacksmith as soon as I could and I slid into the hotel and up to my room. The whole town was beginning to wake up all over again, and men were hunting everywhere for the fellow that had played the joke on the deputy sheriff and his gang of pals. Most of the people that I met in the lobby of the hotel swore that the shadow must have been wearing brass knuckles. Well, I knew something about the strength in the hands and the shoulders of Bob, and there was something so foolish and childish and useless about the whole proceeding that I could have sworn that it was Bob and nobody else.

When I got up to the room, whatever doubts I had were put to rest. There I found Bob, walking up and down with a long, soft, easy stride, like a cat when it figures that a mouse is probably behind the next door.

When I popped in, Bob whirled around on me as though he expected that I might be the mouse. The lamp wasn't lighted. I could hardly see him, but his satisfaction sort of lighted up the room for me. He was as happy as a kid with a whole Christmas tree to itself.

"I thought that you'd be having a sleep, Bob," I said, "or cleaning your guns, or something like that."

"I slept myself out," said Bob, "and I'd finished cleaning my guns . . . when I decided that a little air wouldn't do me any harm. So I just went out for a little walk."

"Bob," I said, "you swore to me that you wouldn't leave this room until I got back to it, didn't you?" It knocked him all in a heap, as the saying is.

"Old-timer," he said, "I'm terribly sorry. I just forgot all about it."

"Maybe you'll explain how come that you forgot," I said, pretty stern, "and maybe you'll explain, too, what all of this shooting has been about? And finally, maybe you'll tell me how it comes that a gent that acts the way that you've been doing the first day that you're put on your good behavior, is going to be able to play soft and low and take care of a poor, lonely girl like. . . ."

He was repentant. He fairly crawled to get back into my good opinion. He said that as he sat there at the window, he could hear them talking. And it was a little irritating to him. He didn't intend to make any trouble. But he wanted to see them closer, and so he leaned out of the window and eased himself into the big fir tree that stood next to the wall—and after that—well, the temptation was too great.

I went to the window and looked out. The tip of the nearest branch of that tree was six feet away. How could anything but a bird or a monkey get into the tree at that distance?

Well, I don't know to this day.

VII

I waited about half an hour, and during that time some of the furor died away in the town. They were still hunting for the stranger who had broken up Barker's little party, but they weren't hunting with half so much vim, when I said to Bob: "Now, son, I'm going to go down to the street and turn up to the right. In about five minutes, I'll be at the second corner and I'll wait there for a minute or two. After that, I'll expect that you'll be watching and following me, though how you'll get there I leave to you."

That didn't seem to upset him at all. I went down into the lobby and there I found big Barker. He was a mess, there was a big cut under one eye, and his nose looked like a toy red balloon moored to his face and about ready to rise. He was pretty hot and he was telling the men down there that he was sure that the man who had done those things to him had got into the hotel. Barker intended to search the place. In the meantime, he told what a cowardly thing it had been—for a man to drop out of a tree on top of him.

Nobody dared to smile, because Barker was a known man. But I went out onto the street, and heard a fellow in a corner of the room saying softly: "It looks more like the work of Nelson than of any other man that I know."

It looked like Bob Nelson to them, and that was the reason that Porter's Pass was so worked up over a mere fist fight. That town hated Bob Nelson. The very fact that he was so decent in his very crimes was a thing that made the town hate him more than ever. There were a full twenty real bad men in Porter's Pass. The history of the town read like a few pages out of a jail record. But if Porter's Pass had never done any other thing, it had always made itself respected as a fighting community. Here was a fellow who came along and made a mock of them, and started to work first on the outskirts of the town with a stage hold-up—and then came in and beat up their leading citizens with his bare hands—half a dozen of them at a time. No wonder Porter's Pass was angry. Any other town might have been for a smaller provocation than this.

When I got to the second street crossing, I waited for a minute, making a cigarette. Then I went slowly on again. When I came to the house of Mabel Rand, I stood again just inside of the big hedge that circled the yard. There wasn't a sound from the house. Its face was black, except for a single lighted window on the first floor. The smell of the wet lawn and the sound of the sprinkler, which was still spinning with a hushing murmur in a distant corner of the yard, made me feel like I had come back to a real home.

It was Mabel's work, of course. She knew how to play a part. If she had to turn a whole house and lot into part of her stage, why, she could do it. I had no doubt about that.

There was a soft, cat-like step crossing the sidewalk, and here was Bob Nelson beside me.

"Sorry I'm late," he whispered. "But a fellow saw me down the street and started to hold me up."

"Good heavens, Bob, what did you do?"

"It wouldn't do to have any noise. I knew that might spoil everything. Besides, I knew that you were pretty mad at me because I'd . . . er . . . had a little party earlier in the evening. So I tied this chap up and left him there with a gag between his teeth. I'm terribly sorry that I'm late."

That was like Bob. He took himself and his ways for granted. He was the only living human being that could.

I took him up to the front door, but he wasn't in any rush. He kept whispering: "Wait a minute, Bart. I want you to brush me off. I'm pretty dusty."

After I had knocked at the front door, there was no answer, except that the light went out in the front room.

The kid grabbed me by the shoulder. "Look," he whispered to me. "You've frightened her."

"Go on," I said, "what's there to frighten her in a knock at her front door?"

I rapped again. After a while, there was a rustle in the hall, and then, as I knocked a third time, the door was pulled open about a quarter of an inch.

"Who is there?" said a whisper, very shaky.

"Bart Chambers," I said, swallowing a grin.

She was slick, was Mabel, but I never imagined that she would stack the cards like this.

When she heard my voice and name, she jerked the door open wide. "Oh," said Mabel, "a friend."

She was revealed, as they say in the papers, all dressed up in white, with her hands clasped at her breast, breathing hard and fast.

"Were you scared, Mabel?" I asked.

"Oh, Bart . . . dear Bart," she said. "Thank heaven that it is only you . . . I thought . . . I thought. . . . No . . . no, I can't say it."

The little cat. She was going it a bit strong. I was afraid that even the kid would begin to see through this.

I said: "I've brought a friend to see you, Mabel."

"A friend of yours, Bart, will be my friend, too, I trust and pray."

Dog-gone her, where did she pick up words like that? It was just plain book talk, near as bad as Bob Nelson's own kind.

"But I must get a light," she said. "When I first heard you come, I thought that the lamp might give an enemy light to. . . ." She left that unfinished and went scuttling off down the hall with her dress whispering around her.

The kid grabbed me by the shoulder. "Bart," he said, "how terrible. Who would think it? A woman afraid of what men may do to her . . . afraid . . . that they'll see her. Oh, I'd like to do ten murders on the strength of this."

"Leave go of my arm," I said to him. "Leave go of me before your fingers scrape the bone. Maybe you will do ten murders before you're through with it."

She got a lamp lighted and come out into the black hall and held the lamp up above her head so's we could see our way—and see her, too. She was worth seeing, I got to admit—all dressed in white. She had no color on her except a red rose bud and the whole green stem pinned across her breast, diagonal. She had that yellow hair of hers done into a pigtail that snaked down her back, and the lamplight flared on it, turning it into gold. I have always figured that there is as much in the way that a pretty woman holds herself as there is in her beauty alone. If a girl has a beautiful face, she's got to have a beautiful way, too, or else she'll never show it off. She's got to learn to stand up in the eye of the world as much as to say: "Here I come. Now is your chance for a good look at me, boys. Don't miss me, because I'm worth seeing."

I mean, they don't have to be artful other ways. But I've seen fourteen-year-old girls—yes, and little kids hardly more'n able to toddle—that had that same air. They know that there is something dog-goned neat about them, and they want the world to stand off and take a good look at them.

Well, I hardly need to say that Mabel had this air. She kept it in her pocket most of the time, but tonight she had taken it out and she wore it like a light in her face. I hardly looked at her; I kept my eye fixed on the kid, and dog-gone me if it wasn't almost sad, he was so hard hit. He stood there and he gaped at her as though she had been a fairy, and he a five-year-old kid.

She led us into the living room, and I had to support the kid. He was so weak and shaken that he was trembling. I don't think he could have budged from the spot where she first hit him like a thunderbolt.

I pressed a mite ahead of him, saying to Mabel: "Loosen up a mite, will you? You've got him paralyzed."

Well, she turned around, with one of her hands resting on the table in the light of the lamp. Usually she was pretty brown, because she loved the outdoors, and she wasn't particular about a hat. That was how come that the sun had faded a good deal of the gold out of her hair. But tonight she had put the gold right back into that hair, and she had gummed up her hands and face and neck with powder so that they looked crystal-white—but not a bit floury, the way that some girls do themselves. She sure looked shrinking and delicate and so dog-goned tender that she would melt in your mouth, so to speak.

"Mabel," I said, "I want you to know my friend, Jerry Burns. Jerry, this is Mabel Rand."

Of course, I couldn't right out and introduce him by his outlawed name.

When I spoke Mabel's married name, she caught up both hands quick to her face, and she stood there sort of swaying for a minute at the side of the table.

"Oh, Bart! Oh, Bart!" she exclaimed with a break in her voice. "Do I have to take that name . . . even to your friends?"

When she covered up her face and registered pain, the kid reached her in one jump. He didn't know what to do. He wanted to help her; he wanted to support her; he wanted to show her that names didn't make any difference to him. He wanted to make it clear to her that even if her name was mud, it wouldn't keep him from knowing how beautiful and clean and good and wonderful she was. He stood about first on one foot and then on the other foot like the worst young jackass in the world. Then he would look at me, as much as to say: "Tell me what to do. Tell me what to do."

I didn't know myself. I only leaned close to Mabel and whispered: "You're laying this stuff on pretty thick."

She whispered right back: "The poor boob is eating it up. Don't tell me what to do. I know him like I was his mammy."

Then she looked up and put down her hands; her eyes was all teary and bright and sad, and her lips was trembling. With her head a little on one side, she went up and held out her hand toward him a little ways, like she was afraid that maybe she wasn't good enough to shake hands with him, and she said: "I don't know that you can wish to . . . wish to. . . ." She was choked, she was.

What did the kid do? Oh, he done something out of a book, of course, because it was a lot too good an opportunity for him to miss. He dropped on one knee and took her hand in his and raised it to his lips. It nearly floored me. Mabel was as cool as marble; there was no nerves added when the stuff that she was made of was first mixed up. But even Mabel was a little staggered by this.

She blinked and she said to me with her lips: "What sort of a fish is this?"

Right on top of that, she had to look down and catch her hand away from him and stand back and be all confused and startled and embarrassed. She done it fine, and the kid got up, looking like the boy on the burning deck. Well, it was just sickening. It was like a moving picture close-up. I couldn't stand it. I stood back behind the kid and made a face at her.

She only gives me a horrible sugar-and-water smile as she said: "Dear Bart, how kind and good you are to me. Have you brought another friend into my life?"

VIII

I suppose that she had a right to do the job in her own way, but all the same it was pretty hard on me, as you can see for yourself. I stood it as well as I could, but then I says to Mabel: "I want you and Burns to have a chance for a good talk. I'll go out on the verandah in front . . . and watch in the dark." I said it real dangerous.

"Oh," said Mabel, "you always think of everything." She ran along with me, real girlish, toward the door, saying: "You big fish, are you gonna leave me here with this tub of cold water, while you sit outside and listen? You'll have bad dreams for this, Bart Chambers!"

Well, sir, I was so glad to be out of that room and all of the fooling that was going on inside of it that I hardly knew what to do. I walked up and down the front lawn for the length of time that it took me to smoke one cigarette.

Then I heard the piano begin, very soft and light, and what do you think she was playing? Some go-get-'em tune like she knew how to reel out? No, sir, that little devil was singing "The Last Rose of Summer," so dog-goned sad and pathetic that it pretty near choked me—and not just with laughing, either.

Well, after I had finished my cigarette, I walked up onto the verandah to see how the show was coming along, and what did I see? There was the kid sitting at the table with his face dropped in both hands, and yonder was Mabel Crofter leaning back in the couch, wringing her hands a good deal, keeping her eyes closed and her brows lifted—real cinema-like. Now and then the kid jerked up his head and grabbed his heart and gave himself a look at her. That would knock him in all in a heap, then, and he would start in again and hold his head. It was pretty ridiculous. Yet I had to admire Mabel. I had been wondering how she would cover up her slangy talk and her slangy way, but when I seen her that evening she was pure actress and nothing else at all.

Suddenly the kid jumped up. He was facing the window direct, and so I could tell pretty clear what he said, which was: "Don't tell me any more. I don't want to hear. It . . . it just makes me sick." He looked like it did, too.

She went on: "I want you to know. It . . . it would kill me to have you as a friend unless you knew all the terrible truth about me. And . . . and . . . you must know that I have been married three times."

"Three times!" the kid exclaimed, turning simply white. I got a little pale myself. It looked to me as though Mabel had chucked her cards right out through the window and thrown away a fine winning hand.

She said: "Yes. The first time was because my poor father was growing weak with sickness. . . ."

I remembered old Crofter. That old tough devil never had a sick day in his life, unless you was to count the heartaches that his daughter give him.

"And I found a man who wanted to marry me . . . who promised to give my poor father everything that. . . ."

"No, no!" yelled the kid.

She bowed her head.

"You didn't!" said the kid.

"I married him," said the girl.

The kid locked his hands above his head and went through the room in one or two strides, very grand, and he turned around and come back through it again.

It struck me sort of queer. Here were two fakers. Only, one of them was unconscious and didn't know that he was faking. The girl was just on a stage and having a wonderful good time out of it.

"And then . . . I discovered that he . . . that he didn't keep all his promises, Mister Burns."

"The lying, cowardly, traitorous sneak!" cried the kid. "Oh, heaven, to have been there!"

He meant it, well enough, and, while he paced up and down the room, Mabel turned her head toward the window and shook it at me, as much as to say: "This kid is nitroglycerine, and I don't want him to explode."

"And then . . . after he was gone . . . ," she went on.

"Dead?" asked the kid gloomily.

"Divorced," said Mabel very resigned.

"Ah," said the kid, "he is still living . . . and then . . . ?"

You could see what he meant. It was written all over his face in letters a mile high. When he got the first chance, he would turn that divorced man into a divorced corpse.

"And then," went on Mabel, "I was left alone. My father was dead. My husband was gone. . . ."

"And no alimony for you?" cried the kid.

I was surprised that he knew as much as that even; Mabel seemed a little taken back, too.

She said: "Oh, Mister Burns, do you think that I could take money . . . or even a crust of bread from a man that I didn't love?"

Confound her, how did she dare to say such lies as that, when all the kid had to ask her was: where did she get the house and the clothes that she was living in right at that minute? Of course, no question as low and common and full of sense as that would ever come into the kid's brain. You could depend upon him being solid bone from the ears up.

He was smashed all to bits, you might say, for having seemed to suspect that she could do anything as low and terribly indecent as take alimony from a divorced husband. I happened to remember that divorce case. There was a lot of sympathy for that poor devil that got Mabel first. It made it funny to hear her go on.

"Well," said Mabel, "if that had been the only time. But then . . . but then . . . there was another, Mister Burns."

"Yes," said the kid. He sat down and set his bulldog jaw and got ready to endure more torture. He got it, too. She didn't leave none of his expectations unfulfilled, I can tell you.

She said: "He seemed a poor, haggard, dying man. He had no money. When I met Jeffrey Young, I thought that he would die within a month. The doctors and his friends thought so, too. Chiefly, they said, because he had nothing that could interest him. There was nothing to hold his mind and his hopes. He was a sad case, Mister Burns, I thought."

I could remember Jeffrey Young. And I don't suppose that he had many interests more than most men, outside of running a string of race horses on the Southern tracks, and running a salmon fishery on the mouth of the Columbia for half the year. Outside of those things, and running a set of three houses, in three different parts of the country, Jeffrey didn't have very much to fill his mind. He did look like a sick man, but he was just a mite tougher than leather.

Before he got through with running through my mind and my memory, I could hear the girl sashaying through to the finish of how she had married that lying Jeffrey out of the kindness of her heart, and then he had turned out to be no invalid at all, but just a mean, low. . . .

"I can't stand any more," said the kid. "Don't tell me any more. I'm . . . I'm going mad, Missus Rand. . . ."

"Please! Please!" cried Mabel, covering up her face again. "Not that name!"

The kid was knocked fairly woozy.

"And then the third man," Mabel picked up, "married me and gave me the name which I loathe and dread . . . and, after he married me, he learned to hate me."

"Hate you?" gasped out the kid in an amazed voice.

"Yes."

"It's not possible," said Bob Nelson.

"Ah, yes, Mister Burns," said Mabel. "Because some men think that a wife should take part even in the wretched swindling games which their money. . . ."

"Lady," said the kid, just white with sickness and disgust and sympathy, "please tell me in one word . . . what it is that you are afraid of? Is it this husband of yours?"

"Yes," said Mabel, "of him and of his men."

It was a terrible shock to me. I thought that I had warned her that, no matter what she said, she had to keep away from bringing any living man into the danger of the kid. It looked to me as though she had already gone too far in talking about two of her husbands. But now she was getting right down to cases, and I had a pretty uncomfortable feeling, for a minute, wondering if she really intended to bamboozle the boy into going out on the warpath?

It didn't seem like Mabel. Yet here was the kid turned into a wild man, begging her to tell him where he could find that husband of hers. I was afraid to hear her answer.

"Ah, dear friend, dear friend," Mabel said. "I see what you mean. You would rush out and find him and strike him down, like a true knight. But, no, I could never again be happy if I felt that any man had been caused to die for my sake. No matter what harms have been done to me," Mabel said, looking up to the ceiling, "and no matter how much he pours his scorn and rage and slander around me, I had much rather die myself than have harm come for my sake upon any other living creature."

It was pretty strong stuff, but the kid swallowed it without getting a raw throat. He was a regular boa constrictor when it came to taking down a lie whole and digesting it quick.

But, oh, what a neat gag this was. To whip up the kid with one hand and to rein him in with the other. I had to laugh, but I had to admire that girl for the

champion liar of the entire whole world, which I
guess that you'll agree with me when you hear how
she worked out the rest of the case against poor old
Arthur Rand.

IX

I can't go on telling you how she pulled the wool
over the eyes of that poor young idiot, because it
makes me blush for being a man—to think how any
woman could hoodwink one of the same species
that I belong to. I just tell you in general what she
said to him, which was that Arthur Rand, not being
able to use her for his crooked ends, decided that
he would get rid of her. You would think that the
kid would speak up and ask what was the crooked
ends that Rand intended to use her for. What sort of
crookedness was it—confidence game, or what?

No, sir, he didn't ask any question as sensible
as that. The mere idea of asking a question never
entered his poor brain. All he done was to rage and
groan when she revealed the "wickedness" of poor
Rand.

"I want to tell you, Mister . . . ," she commenced.

And then he broke in: "My real name is Nelson.
Bob Nelson, I'm called. I can't hear you calling me
by that made-up thing that Bart gave me."

Mabel done that real well, I have to admit. She let
out a little squeal and got the table and the couch
between her and Bob in a flash. There she stood,
apparently scared to death. "Are you the terrible
bandit? Are you the outlaw?" asked Mabel, seeming
to want to squeeze her way through a crack in
the wall.

It was a fine thing to see Bob fold his arms and look grand and calm. He was pretty white, he was so hot. "They've given me such a reputation, then?" he asked. "Even the women are afraid of me?"

She done a quick step around the end of the couch again, saying: "No, Mister Nelson! No, no! I don't care what they say about you. I know how men can lie. And they lie about you, as they've lied about me . . . swearing my reputation away. Swearing yours away. And you're good . . . and kind . . . and true . . . and worthy of being the friend of dear Bart Chambers."

Bah! The smile on his face was like salvation come to a sinner.

"Thank heaven," Bob said, very deep and humble. "I thought that this was the end of everything, perhaps. I really thought that this was the end of everything. You . . . you seemed to be a thousand miles away from me."

"No," said Mabel, "this is what draws us close together. We have both been wronged by the world. But, oh, Bob Nelson, how I pity you . . . that a life like yours should be wasted . . . when you are so young . . . so good . . . so true . . . so gentle . . . so kind."

"Don't talk about me!" gasped out Bob Nelson. "I don't exist except to help you, if heaven will let me."

She shook her head, very sad and sweet. "You might go to find him," said Mabel. "And how could I ever close my eyes in peace, if I knew that any man had come to harm through me? No, let him go his own way. Except . . . that I do humbly pray that I may be shielded from some murderer's hand."

"Murder!" cried the kid. "Murder! I knew that there would be something like that before it was done. Do you tell me that is what keeps you so frightened in this house . . . so frightened that you dare not kindle even a lamp? Do you tell me that you are so hounded with fear that your devilish husband is sending back villains to attempt your life?"

"Ah," said Mabel, "you are so wonderful. The very things that I would not have you guess for the whole world, you know at a glance. Oh, Mister Nelson, I have never met a man so brilliant!"

Bob was not too excited about her to be a little pleased by these remarks about himself. He allowed that if he had been able to see through this deal, it was because he could scent scoundrelism a long distance off. Then he said: "But from now on, you're not to be without some protection. Day and night, I want you to know that there will be someone watching over you, someone with a strong hand will be near you, to keep you safe, dear lady."

Mabel had dropped back on the couch and looked at him from a great distance, so to speak.

"Oh, Mister Nelson," she said, "I hardly dare to guess what you mean. I hardly dare. I have no right. But do you know what I shall feel tonight?"

"Tell me?" asked Bob.

"I shall feel," said Mabel, "as though your strong arms were around me, warding me from danger, keeping me safe."

Bob Nelson pretty near swooned.

Then she told him that she was tired with happiness and that she would have to go to bed, and Bob went out of that house and foamed away into the darkness like a running horse. He was just as enthusiastic as a small kid with a new game to play. But there was this mighty important difference—the playing of Bob Nelson was done with a .45 Colt and a real hunting knife and a pair of the hardest fists that ever cracked a jaw bone.

I went in to have a chat with Mabel and I found her happy but pretty tired. She sat down on the couch and kicked off her little silver slippers.

"My feet are spreading as I get older," said Mabel. She stuck out a foot no bigger than a minute. "I shall have enlarged joints and chilblains," said Mabel, "if I have to keep up this game with the kid very much longer. It was hard work, and I'm fagged out. Oh, how fagged I am. Tell me how good I was, Bartie, because I'm ready for a little applause."

"Where did you get that lingo?" I asked. "Where did you learn to talk like a book?"

"My husbands educated me," said Mabel. "They done a good job, too. No trouble for me to put on a high polish that you can see your face in. The kid is full of fancy stuff, too."

"Well," I said, "I'll tell you one thing . . . you're gonna lead a lonely life. You better put up a sign . . . 'Beware of the Dog.' Because when some of your men friends come around here, they'll step into trouble up to their necks."

"How do you mean?"

"I mean that you've told the poor fish that you're expecting to be murdered, and, when a stray man comes this way, you can lay to it that Bob will be watching for him."

"I didn't think of that!" exclaimed Mabel.

"You didn't think of a lot of things," I said. "And among the rest, you didn't think what would happen if he finds out where Rand has gone."

"Well? What if he does?"

"There'll be a dead Arthur Rand, that's all, if he does find out," I told her.

"A dead Arthur Rand?" Mabel laughed. "Why, Bart, Arthur Rand is a man, and a real one. If he met up with this kid, he would turn Bob Nelson over his knee, give him a spanking, and send him away again with a good lesson."

That explained everything, of course. She hadn't appreciated the facts.

"Maybelle," I said, to sort of break the ground, "will you please tell me how the kid got a reputation like this, if he's not a dangerous fighter?"

"Sure I'll tell you," said Mabel. "Every gent that wants to step out and wear a mask and a Colt gets a reputation. He sticks his miserable little gun in the face of a dozen men, and the dozen men just curl up and throw up their hands and beg him not to kill them. I've met up with some of these desperadoes before, and they're all bunk."

She was so sure, that I was sort of paralyzed. At last I said: "Have you heard what happened this evening?"

She hadn't.

I said: "Do you know Barker?"

"That brute?" she said. "Yes, I know him."

"Is he any mamma's darling, or is he a fighting fool?"

She gave a little shudder. "I saw him beat up two men with his bare hands one day. I shall never forget it. He's not a man, but a gorilla."

"All right," I said, "I agree about Barker. Now lemme tell you what happened. The kid got tired of staying in my room this evening. He eased himself out of the window into a tree that it would break my neck to try to reach. And then he dropped on top of Barker and five others that were talking underneath the tree about the best way to capture Bob Nelson. He made a mess of Barker. He turned the rest of them upside down. And when I came back to the hotel . . . well, you saw him for yourself. Not a mark on him."

She thought that I was joking at first, but when I stayed grave, it began to sink in on her.

"Heavens," said Mabel. "Is he as much of a man as all of that?"

"That's only an index finger pointing the correct way," I said. "That's what he can do with his hands. But usually he don't feel at home with his bare hands. He has to have something in his fingers, you know, and, when it happens to be a gun, he don't miss, Mabel . . . not him."

She was more excited than before now. "Bart, Bart," she said, "you're telling me that the kid is a real man?"

"I'm telling you that," I said. "And I'm telling you that I know Arthur Rand, but if this kid ever goes on his trail, he'll kill poor Arthur. And killing ain't what you want for Arthur, I suppose? Killing ain't the same as alimony, old-timer."

She only stared at me. She was pretty hard hit. "Heavens above," said Mabel. "I haven't any malice toward Arthur. But why didn't you tell me some of these things before?"

"Because I thought that the first time that you met the kid you'd only take a trick or two, and not try to play out the whole game. Mabel," I said, "the thing for you to do is to wrap the kid up in cotton batting and keep him from the air. Because news about Arthur Rand is going to bring about a little man-size murder."

X

When I got back to the hotel, there was no Bob Nelson. There was only a note from him on my table.

Dear Bart:

I wanted to wait here for you and tell you what had happened. But I can't wait. All I can say is that I have found the most wonderful woman in the world, and that she has permitted me to try to defend her from some of her troubles. I thank heaven and you, Bart, for bringing me in her path, and I pray that I may be able to undo some of the terrible wrongs which she has suffered from the world. Oh, Bart, what I've learned has made me despise all men, including myself. She is a sacred angel—and she has been treated like a dog.

Good bye, Bart, for a little while. I intend to do or to die.

Affectionately,
Bob

There he was, off in a cloud of glory to his work, and there was I in the hotel, chuckling over my pipe and then hoping a humble hope that maybe the salvation of the kid might be worked out of this deal. If only Mabel would play the game right, and not lose her head, and if only the kid didn't learn where to find Arthur Rand. That was the main pinch, and I take a little credit to myself for seeing that much in the distance.

I knew that Mabel would put the soft pedal on the brutalities of Arthur Rand, for a time, but she had given the kid such an overdose of poison on the subject of Rand at the first meeting, that I knew it would crowd his system for a long time.

I had a good sleep that night, and then I waked up in the morning to find that there was a new sensation that made poor Bob Nelson look like a tallow candle by the side of a comet of the first magnitude.

This was the time of the Garm murders—too dog-goned awful and blood-curdling to be repeated here. What paralyzed me and everybody else at the time was the knowledge of Garm. I'd seen Wully Garm myself, not once, but half a dozen times. He was a plain half-wit, never had done any harm in his life. He was as good a shepherd as a man would ask for, and that was the work that he stuck to.

How he should have got his grudge against the old man that hired him, I don't know. I've always held that Garm's mind just slowly turned from imbecility to insanity. First, he had no more mind than a brute, and then the mind that grew up in him became an addled thing, with a devilish leaning toward mischief.

So the first murder came, and, after he had the taste of blood, the others followed as he roved. What made him so frightful hard to catch was his being able to live like a beast. He could walk through a mountain storm that would have killed an ordinary man. Besides, he had no nerves. When he drew his bead on a target, nothing in the way of mercy ever come between him and the pulling of the trigger. He shot to kill, and he didn't miss, because shooting a man was no more to him than shooting a pig.

Bad as Porter's Pass was, it was stirred up by the news about Garm. It sent out its contingent to join in the hunt the next day, and I went back to the ranch from which I had been away longer than I really had any right. I had a busy ten days following that, and all that I heard from Porter's Pass was two letters from Mabel.

The first one came at the end of about a week. It ran like this:

Dear Bart:

The wild man is turning out pretty good. He still acts like I was something on top of an altar, and it is very funny to be treated not like a woman, but like a sort of thing made out of china. I might as well be an image, so far as the kid is concerned. He comes to see me every evening after dark. And he tells me that I'm the greatest woman in the world, and bunk like that. It's a scream.

He has fixed himself up in a little room in the top of the barn, a sort of an attic, right under the roof. I've been up to see it today, and it's quite snug. He begged for a picture of mine, and I gave him a couple—he certainly deserves them.

He's just like a child, Bart. I feel like an old woman when I'm around him and I have to fight like a demon all the time to remember that I'm only a girl about his age. That's the way I dressed the first evening that I saw him and that's the way that I should never have dressed for him. However, that milk is spilled, and there's no use crying about it.

This lonely life isn't at all bad with him around. Only, I wish that he would treat me as though I were flesh and blood, instead of a statue.

I've gotten to such a point that I can drill into
him my ideas about the life of an outlaw, and,
of course, I make those ideas pretty strenuous.
I tell him that it's a crime for a young man to
throw himself away and I point out the fact
that outlawry, if nothing else, is what makes
him skulk like a whipped puppy instead of
being able to come to see me in the open day.
He seems to see the point of that remark, and
I really believe that the noble free life of a two-
gun man is not such hot stuff in his eyes as it
was when I first saw him.

So long, Bart.
Maybelle

That was just the sort of a letter that I had wished
for. Well, I read that letter once a day. Three days after
it came, there was another in the mail from Mabel. It
was shorter and pretty near as exciting as the first one.
It said:

Dear Bartie:
Come quick. I have a grand idea that I want to
talk over with you. I think that I have a scheme
by which the kid can get out of outlawry and back
onto his feet again. It's mighty simple. The best of it
is that the same talents that made him a successful
bandit may be the means of making him over into
an acceptable member of society once more. Hurry
and come to me at once. I can't wait to talk it over
with you.

Well, I wanted to hurry, but cows are cows, and I had
some work waiting for me on the ranch that had to

be done first. It was two days before I could make the long trek to Porter's Pass, but, when I made my start, I didn't hitch a span to a wagon. I just threw a saddle on the fastest horse on the ranch, that I borrowed from Tod Hunter's string, and then I made the road smoke all the way from the ranch to Porter's Pass, wondering every minute if the delay was going to make it too late for Mabel to work her fine new plan. I didn't stop worrying until I pulled up in front of her house and saw the smile on her face when she opened the door to me.

There was still time—that much was plain.

XI

You would have liked to see Mabel the way that she was that day, full of pep and snap, and smiling. She hooked her arm through mine and she led me into her house and sat me down, saying to me: "What would you say, Bartie, to making this Bob Nelson a plumb-free man, without the shadow of the law over his poor head?"

I just closed my eyes. "Mabel," I said, "don't I pray every day that he'll have a chance to get back again where he was when he first came to work for me?"

"I think that I've hit on the way to put him right," she said.

I said: "You mentioned something in your letter about using the same means for setting him right that was used for setting him wrong . . . a fast hoss and a pair of Colts. Did you really mean that, Mabel?"

She didn't seem to hear me. She was sitting there, looking past me, with her eyes screwed up, trying to get a distant shot into the future.

"He's able to handle most other men, isn't he?" asked Mabel.

"Like they was children."

"And after all," Mabel said, "nothing ventured, nothing won. He's got to take one big chance. But the first thing is a trip for you to see the governor."

"Me? The governor?" I said. "That would be a treat to him, to have a chance to sit down and talk to me, wouldn't it?"

"You ain't funny, Bart," said Mabel, very cold. "You're just silly, y'understand?"

Well, I couldn't believe that I was hearing her straight, because not a word of that lingo sounded a bit like the Mabel Crofter that I knew, who was such a good pal and square-shooter.

She left me flabbergasted, and then she went on: "You're going to go to the governor, however, as fast as you can get. When you arrive there, you're going to break in and see him, if you have to kill a couple of flunkies to get at him. When you see him, you're going to get five minutes of his listening time, if you have to take it at the point of your Colt. And you're going to say to him . . . 'Boss, do you want to be a mighty popular governor down in my neck of the woods?' And when he says 'yes,' you're going to say to him. . . ."

Well, I won't tell you here what it was that Mabel suggested to me. It was a rank thing to try on the governor of a state, and at first I said that it wouldn't work at all. She insisted until I gave in, and after that the more that I thought about the deal, the more I felt that it might work.

I had a thirty mile cross-country ride to get me to the right railroad to run to the capital of the state. I made that ride on a fresh hoss that I borrowed from Mabel, and then I sat up all night, bumping over a mountain roadbed in a day coach that was filled with dagos that had got themselves all filled up with vino. Funny thing how long it will last those fellows. Of course, they got themselves as chuck-a-block as a lot of blotters dipped in water. And every time anything happens, it just squeezes some more noise and good nature out of them. Those dagos didn't mind the jolting of that car. When the brakes went on with a wham, piling up half a dozen of them at one end of the coach, they just picked themselves up, laughing, starting out with a new song. They knew all the songs that there was in the world outside of the English language, and they sang them so good that you wouldn't believe it. They kept it up to the crack of dawn. Then, just as they began to sober up enough to fall asleep, the train pulled in at the capital town.

I wouldn't've had the heads that those muckers would own by the time that they got to the end of that day's trip and the mines where they was to start working right away.

After I got out, I had my eye full of the city right away. I have been to Denver, but that's just too big to understand. It's like a world all by itself. It would take you a year, just to memorize the names of the streets, and even then you wouldn't know half of them. You could go around and eat in a different place—as a hotel or a restaurant—every day pretty near for a year.

Denver, as I say, is too big to understand. The state capital had only about 25,000, which you'll agree is a whopping big town. It had streetcars and pavements and electric lights and shops with wax models in the windows, and businessmen that wore rubber-heeled shoes and bright polishes, and high-stepping hosses— pretty near everything that you could ever wish to see.

I'll tell you, you could hope to learn to understand a town like that, if you was to live the biggest part of your life in it.

I was terrible interested, and, when I went up to the big white-stone building where the governor's office was, I hardly minded it when they told me that I would have to have an appointment made with his secretary before I could talk to him. I went in to see his secretary, which was a young man that smiled a good deal, but didn't seem to mean much. He hoped that he would see me again, but he didn't give me much hope that I would see the governor, who he said was suffering a lot from having shaken so many hands the week before at a reception. He kept right on talking until he talked me out of his office, and I went back and wandered around the town again.

Altogether, I was pretty well satisfied that there was only one way to manage, and that was to break in on the old governor when he wasn't expecting me.

I walked around to his house, that afternoon, until I had a pretty good idea of the lay of the land. I seen a man polishing the brass on the front door, where there was a hook-nosed knocker and such trumpery all around, y'understand? I told him that it was a mighty big house and that it must be a fine thing to work in such a big place. He said that it was, but that, if I was looking for a job, it was no good, because there was a waiting list. I said I was sorry to hear that because I had heard it was fine to work for such a kind-hearted man as the governor.

He replied: "Where did you hear that? The chief is made out of horse hide and iron. That's all. He's so mean that he won't even mind the sunshine in the morning, and he sleeps on the east side of the house with the blinds all up."

That was a good deal to learn. That night I waited around in the back garden of the house for the light to flash on in that big set of windows on the second floor. However, I didn't have to do no porch climbing, after all.

Just before midnight, the governor and his wife came out for a breath of fresh air, as they put it. They walked up and down, with the moon on their silvery hair. What would you think that important folks like that would talk about? Important things, of course. Well, you would've been surprised.

"What an old bore the judge is," said the governor.

"Would you mind not walking so fast?" said the governoress.

"Are your feet sore from those infernal tight shoes?" asked the governor.

"My shoes are not tight," she said. "Heavens . . . at my age I hope that vanity. . . ."

"Stuff!" he said. "There are a lot of queer things about you, Lizzie, but nothing quite so queer as your ideas about yourself. The trouble with women is that. . . ."

"Harry," she said, "I've sat on platforms and listened to your silly speeches, but I won't listen to them in my own back yard. I'm going inside for a little peace."

"*Humph!*" exclaimed the governor. And he let her go in.

Well, there you are. There was a couple of great ones. The newspapers always printed pictures of the governor and his wife with their two grandchildren on their laps, and their growed-up sons and daughters standing, grouped around, trying to look like they didn't know that they was in the papers. Thousands of votes, the size of that family got for the governor. Because you take a big family man like that, people take it for granted that he hasn't got such a lot of fancy brains, you know. It looks solid and simple. You even feel a little superior to him, and a little pity for him.

The governor threw away his cigarette as soon as his wife was gone inside of the house, and he got out an old black pipe, whittled up some plug, stuffed that pipe, and lighted it up. I tell you that pipe was a snorter, even out there in the open air. I got a lot more respect for the governor right away. He walked up and down with a frown on his forehead, the moon on his face. I got a whiff of his pipe smoke, and it brought a sneeze ripping out of me before I could do anything to control it. The governor turned around with a grunt, and there was me stepping out of the shrubbery behind him.

He made a grab at his hip pocket and gave a little squeal of excitement, more like a pig than a governor, but I made free to grab his right wrist.

"Chief," I said, "let's talk it over friendly. I don't mean you no harm at all."

He was as cool as the devil, after the first fluster. "I don't think you do," he said. "But why are you back here like a sneak thief?"

"Because your secretary says that you're engaged until the end of the year."

"Bless him," said the governor. "The tonnage of lying that he's able to get through in a lie would sink an ocean liner. Well, sir, what do you want of me, now that you have me? I only make one bargain with you . . . that you don't keep me here more than ten minutes."

XII

That was a pretty fair bargain. Ten minutes was really enough for me to tell my yarn in, and, as I accepted, the governor pulled out his watch and wound it, looking me in the face.

"Now," he said, "what do you want?"

"I'm here," I began, "to make a bargain for an outlawed man."

The governor was pleased right away. He dropped the watch into his vest pocket and put his hands on his hips. He looked a square-shooter. "Who's your man?"

"Bob Nelson."

The governor shook his head. "You're aiming too high," he said. "I don't mind being held up for the sake of some common or garden criminal. I have a lot of sympathy with the crooks. Every honest man ought to have, if he's taken enough fair looks into his own heart. But in the meantime, what I want to know is . . . how could I strike any sort of a bargain with a desperado who has been making fools out of my sheriffs, laughing at our posses, and cramming the newspapers with accounts that make the law and the governor of the state look very foolish indeed? No, sir, you can't talk to me about a fellow like Nelson. I have an almost personal grudge against him. I don't mind saying that I feel a record like his is a blot on the record that I have made as an officer upholding the law with my whole strength."

That was pretty much of a facer for me, but I wasn't to be beaten off at the very beginning. I said: "Your honor, you were under twenty once."

"Don't talk to me like a judge," said the governor, grinning. "Yes, I was under twenty once. What follows from that?"

"Nothing, except that you know that when a man is under twenty, he's apt to be a good deal of a fool."

The governor grinned.

"D'you know that Bob Nelson was under twenty when he started?" I asked.

"I know that some of these rascally gunfighters are precocious, but that doesn't incline me to be more merciful. What is your name?"

"Bart Chambers."

"Chambers," said the governor, "I've never heard your name before, but you've got a clean pair of eyes in your head and you ought to know that a gunfighter is a detestable cur, as a rule. He spends his life practicing with his weapons, instead of working honestly. And when he can think of nothing else to do, he starts out and finds himself a fight. What chance would I have against a real gunfighter? I can't hit the side of a barn with a revolver, and I'm inclined to thank heaven for it. Rifles are meant to bring down game, but revolvers bag nothing but human beings . . . and I wish that the sale of them were prohibited by a most stringent law, by heaven."

It was my luck to run into a governor for our state who was so red hot against desperadoes and gunfighters.

"Well, sir," I said, "I want to ask you to remember in the first place that you can't count the time that you talk out of my ten minutes."

He wasn't offended. He chuckled and nodded. "I guess I've been on the stump again," he said. "It's a bad habit that we politicians have. We can't think except in headlines. Go on, Mister Chambers."

He was a real good one, was that governor. The sort that you wouldn't mind having in camp, even in winter. You could lay to it that he would lift his share of the work.

I said: "You got to make a distinction between a gunfighter and a man who shoots straight."

"Perhaps, perhaps," he said. "But what are you driving at?"

"Well," I said, "I want you to notice that the kid . . . I mean, Bob Nelson . . . shoots so dog-goned straight that he hasn't killed a man yet."

"Hold on! He's wanted for murder!" cried the governor.

"That was a sneaking head-hunter . . . a no-good swine," I said. "No district attorney in the state would dare to try him for that. The jury would wind up by voting the kid their thanks, I tell you. No, I want to get a pardon for the other fracases, but I'd as soon see him step to the tune for that killing."

The governor was pretty interested, by this time. "Are you an uncle of Nelson's?" he asked.

Then I opened up and told him the story. As fast as I could, but even at that the story didn't fit into any short space of time. I tell you, I left out nothing, from the first time that I met the kid up to the time that I said good bye to Mabel. The governor listened like a good sort.

"I'd like to help that boy. I'd . . . I'd like to have a talk with him, even. But . . . show me a loophole through which I can step with any dignity and pardon him?" he said.

"I'm going to make you a loophole," I said. "This Bob Nelson isn't the only critter that's roaming around in this here state and messing up the face of the law and cramming the newspapers."

"It's true," he said.

"Now," I said, "suppose that I get Missus Rand to take this job up with the kid and to tell him that he has to make his peace with the law and to start him after one of these crooks . . . these real crooks, that shoot to kill every time they get their fur up? If he brings in one of those bad men, dead or alive, will you write him a pardon?"

He considered this thing up and down. "It's illegal," he said.

"But natural."

"Tell me," he said, "is this the girl's idea?"

"Yes, every word of it. I wouldn't have the nerve to think out a whole idea like that."

"*Humph,*" he said. "You go back and tell her to go ahead. If your man Nelson can land Green, the counterfeiter, or that scoundrelly kidnapper, Wilson, or, of course, the abysmal brute, Wully Garm, I'll sign a pardon for this Bob Nelson. Will that suit you?"

I said that it would—that it would suit me all over, and I couldn't help throwing in that it would make me and a lot of other honest men the friends of that governor for life.

"Humph!" he exclaimed. "Now about that girl. What's to become of her?"

"She'll have her divorce and be free in a little while," I said, "and then she can go on making business for the lawyers, I suppose."

"Perhaps," he said. "But I wonder if mothering this Bob Nelson may not make everything else pretty dull for her?"

I had never thought of that and I told the governor that the whole thing was just a joke.

"A joke?" he asked. "Now let me tell you, Chambers, that you're old enough to know that women have no sense of humor . . . inside their own affairs. They're too serious, even the best of them, and you put that in your pipe and smoke it for a while, will you? But as for this business, you've taken an hour of my time, not ten minutes. Good night, Chambers. Heaven be with you and the boy . . . I wish you all the luck in the world."

He was such a straight-shooter, so simple and so fine that it just brought the tears to my eyes. I shook hands with him, and then I went to find a hotel.

The next morning, I was driving south, as fast as a train would carry me, and that same night I was in the house of Mabel again. What would you think that I walked in on?

Well, it was Bob Nelson sitting in a corner of the room with his mustaches more waxed out than ever. The girl had a book under her arm when she opened the door to me and led me in.

"Hello," I said, after I'd shaken hands with Bob. "Are the pair of you back in school? What's the book?"

"The most wonderful book in the world," said Mabel. "It's all about Tristram and Lancelot and Arthur and Guinevere, and the rest of 'em. They were a gay lot of high steppers, Bartie! Sit down while I read you about. . . ."

"Have you been reading aloud?" I asked.

"Yes," she said, "and never had such a. . . ."

I just stood there and wondered at her, because I knew that the only reading that she ever cottoned onto was the ads in the fashion magazines, and such-like things. Here she was sober enough to do knitting and wear glasses.

I cut in on that reading and pulled her to one side. "It's fixed," I said. "Garm . . . or Wilson . . . or Green, the counterfeiter, dead or alive. Garm doesn't count, of course. Don't sic the kid after him, because Garm is too dangerous even for the kid. But if he fetches in either of the other pair, dead or alive, there's a pardon waiting for him in the governor's office. You understand?"

"Thank heaven!" cried Mabel. "Then he's saved."

"There's only one dead gunfighter between him and another even start," I said.

I left her to work up the idea with the kid in her own way, because there was something about this bartering of one life for another that I didn't like particularly, as you may understand for yourself.

It had been a rough, long trip, and an anxious one. I was mighty glad to hit the hay that night. The next day I sashayed out to the ranch without even stopping to call on Mabel. I didn't have to. There had been something close and chummy in the air of that room the night before that made me know that what one of them wanted, the other would be sure to try to do.

All the way out to the ranch I kept remembering what the governor had said—that the kid wasn't the only one to be thought of in this game—that Mabel counted, too, and counted pretty big. Perhaps he was right—how right he was, I never guessed till the end.

XIII

What happened was what we might have known beforehand, if we had used any sense. When she turned him loose, the kid, like a hawk, sighted the biggest quarry and went after it.

He had Wilson and Green, big enough quarry for any man, you would say, but the kid had a different opinion. I got part of the history from Bob himself, and part from others. The rest of it you could deduce from what was known.

Before Mabel got through with him that night, there didn't seem anything strange in bringing in one man to stand for him—turning over one outlaw to take the place of the kid's own danger. He was off in the dark before morning, riding hard, but the direction that he picked out was not that in which Green or Wilson had been seen last. He galloped for the region where the brute, Wully Garm, was last seen.

Even Bob must have felt some fear while he was riding on that trail. He wouldn't've been human, if he hadn't. But he got into the mountains just after the worst of all of Garm's crimes had been committed—I mean the murder of the three Chippendales in their ranch house. No reason for that killing. Wully was simply running amuck, now, and killing for the sake of the slaughter.

Well, Bob Nelson followed the trail of Garm, hard and fast, and he came on the fourth day from the Chippendale house in sight of the body of a deer. The way that deer had been butchered was so rough, showing such a strong hand that the kid made up his mind on the spot that Wully Garm must have done that work. Having done that work, it occurred to Bob that Wully would probably have eaten his fill and gone into the woods somewhere pretty near to sleep off his meal.

Bob was a great hand at following a trail. Under some fallen leaves he picked up the mark of a great, sprawling foot, and in ten minutes of careful work he came into the sound of a heavily breathing creature.

Then he stepped out into a little clearing and in the shadow at one side of it he had his first view of Garm.

It must have been a horrible thing to see that great, loose-lipped face even when it was quiet in sleep. Bob told me afterward that the face was not really quiet, but working a little all of the time—the jowls quivering, or the big lips twitching a bit, or the fleshy brow being disturbed into a wrinkle. It was just the way that a wild dog acts by the fire—jerking open an eye, every now and then, and looking around out of his sleep with a start. He was a vast bundle of loose nerves.

There was Wully Garm, found at last—the whole two and a half shapeless hundredweight of him. I think that if I'd been the lucky fellow who made that discovery, I should have put a bullet through his head while he lay there and never let him see the light of the stars again.

Even the bravest man wouldn't have wanted to do anything bolder than to tie the hands of the giant while he was sleeping. That wouldn't suit Bob. He sat down on a rock and waited while the moon rose and shone bright over the trees.

At last there was a grunt and a snort, and the sleeper was awake, and rolling to his knees. He wasn't confused; he was too near to the brute to have his brain numbed by sleeping. Like a wolf, the moment he opened his eyes, he was himself. He reached for his revolver, his rifle, his knife.

They were all gone, of course. The kid had had the sense to see to that. Bob stood up facing the big, squat beast of a man, and he said: "Garm, I've come to take you back to jail. Will you go along quietly?"

Garm showed his yellow, pointed teeth.

Imagine asking Garm that!

"Do you hear me?" asked Bob, with a shudder going through him, I suppose, as he saw the brute stand up on its hind legs and snarl at him.

"I hear you," said Garm. "But I'm not going. If I got to be murdered, I'll be murdered here."

"Murder?" said the kid, and I can see how his head would go up and his lip curl. "Murder? There's to be no murder, Wully Garm. We'll fight it out fair and square in any way that you want to mention."

Of coarse Garm wouldn't believe him. When he finally got the idea through his head, he went almost crazy with joy, and reached out his long arms and his great, thick, wriggling fingers.

"No guns . . . no knives . . . hands!" cried Garm, and his mouth gaped with a wolf's grin. "Hands, hands!"

What did Bob do? He simply threw aside guns and knives and rifle and all, and he stood out to the giant with his bare hands.

I'm glad that I didn't see that fight. It must have been too horrible—not like man and man, but like an eagle and a bear, say, with Garm the bear, and the kid the eagle.

The kid tried to close with his man and grapple. I suppose he felt that the only real knightly thing was to do just exactly as Garm did. The instant that those great fingers closed on him, he knew his mistake.

I knew that the kid could turn himself into a greased snake, when he wanted to get away from anyone. I'd seen him do it at the ranch, when half a dozen of the boys tried to get him down, but he would have died this time, if, as he twisted about, his shirt hadn't torn to shreds and so let him, half disrobed, out of the hands of Garm.

Garm rushed, fairly trembling with joy, running on his great, crooked, thick legs. He caught at the thin air and got a blind pair of slashing punches across the face. The kid stood off and began to box. He slammed Garm with both hands until his arms ached and he couldn't put the big fellow down. But he cut the face of Garm simply to ribbons, and the pain addled whatever little wits there were left to big Wully Garm.

I suppose that he would have been sure to win out in this sort of fighting, if he had just waited long and patiently enough. Although the cutting hands of the kid might hurt and sting him, they couldn't do him any real harm, any more than the talons of an eagle harm a bear.

Wully couldn't stand the gaff. Finally he reached down and caught up a rock the size of half a man's body and heaved it at the kid. One corner of it brushed his head and knocked him flat—and Garm rushed in to finish his job.

He rushed in, but here the luck was against him, just as he was aiming to finish the fight in grand style by falling on the kid and choking the life out of him with one mangling grip of his big hands. He made a mistake, because the spot where the kid dropped, half stunned, was where he had shied his guns when he shed them in standing up to face the challenge of Wully Garm. When the active hand of the kid fell on the cold steel of his Colt, there was a flash of light let into his brain. Or maybe that hand of his acted almost automatically, it had been so well trained by Bob Nelson for hour after hour, and for day after day.

As Wully threw himself through the air at the kid, the hand of Bob Nelson flicked out faster than the tongue of a snake, and it came back carrying a .45 that barked right into the hideous face of Garm.

Afterward, Bob lay for a time, sick and done for. He managed to pull himself together finally, for, although exhausted, except for that scratch along his head he wasn't badly hurt. When he was rested, he went back to his horse and rode on down to the nearest town.

"Is there an officer of the law in this place?" the kid asked.

The gent that had met up with him said that there was, because a deputy sheriff had just come up there from Porter's Pass on the trail of Wully Garm, and right now he was at the hotel. To the hotel went Bob and walked straight in. It made a pretty good picture, and I'll never forgive my luck for not giving me a chance to see it.

There stood Bob Nelson, and yonder stood Barker, whose face was still swollen and purple and out of shape from the beating that the kid had given him not so terribly long before.

Barker let out a bellow and grabbed out two Colts, and gents who were there at the time say that his hands shook a lot. He was so excited, he probably couldn't've hit the side of the wall, let alone Bob Nelson.

However, Bob hadn't come there to find more trouble. He just smiled at Barker and said: "I've come to surrender myself, Barker, and to tell you that your chase of Garm is ended."

"Ended?" asked Barker, fairly paralyzed, of course. "Has the brute fallen over a cliff?"

"More or less," said the kid. "I'll tell you where to find him laid out."

XIV

When Barker came tearing back to Porter's Pass, like a conquering hero, with Bob Nelson along with him, he timed his entry so as to make it about noon, when everybody would come out into the streets and see him go by with his rifle balanced across the pommel of his saddle. Bob was all covered with irons and guarded by gents with naked guns, riding behind. Barker got a lot of cheers for that bit of work. People sort of overlooked the fact that Bob had come in and given himself up. When that was suggested, Barker allowed that Bob had been scared into surrendering, because he knew that he, Barker, was on the trail.

Anyway, there wasn't a long time left for Barker to lick his chops. The papers were all full of the news the next morning, and the message was telegraphed through to Porter's Pass that evening.

It was all full of "whereases," extreme legal. It set out that since Bob had only one death laid to him, and that being the death of another man in bad odor with the law, since he had voluntarily submitted to arrest, showing a willingness to stand his trial and submit to punishment for his crimes, and most of all because he had done a lot for the people of the mountains by killing the murderer, Wully Garm, the governor felt that young Nelson was the sort of stuff out of which a good citizen could be made with a little care. Above all, it was because Bob had found out that he was not as strong as the law.

Well, that wasn't a popular message in the town of Porter's Pass. Maybe there was a lot to be said on the side of Bob Nelson, but Porter's Pass wanted the pleasure of having the trial and the hanging of a famous man to its credit and right in its midst. Certainly there was one man that didn't flourish on the news that the kid was to be turned loose.

That was Barker. He developed business in the far corner of the county right away, and he rode off the morning that the kid was released. Everyone knew it was because Barker had been talking a little bit too freely, and he didn't want to meet up with Bob and have the kid ask him some pointblank questions.

Anyway, there was only one important thing to me. I come hiking into town as fast as I could whack the miles out of a tough-mouthed mustang, and I headed straight for the house of Mabel Rand, because I figured for sure that the kid would go there as soon as he got loose from the jail.

I found Mabel, but Bob hadn't come, as yet. She was so excited that she was shaking. She was half laughing and half crying, and I shook hands with her hard enough to break bones.

"Mabel," I said, "I don't give a hang what some folks hold against you. You've done such a good job of the kid that it would outbalance all the rest. I want to say that. . . ."

She wasn't even interested in praise. She just broke in hollering: "But he ought to be here! He ought to be here! Why doesn't he come, Bart? Why doesn't he come?" She was actually walking up and down and wringing her hands—and her the coolest-headed girl that ever stepped.

I remembered then for the hundredth time what the governor had said.

"Mabel," I said to her, "d'you mean to tell me that you've gone off your balance about this youngster . . . this kid, Bob?"

"Bah!" cried Mabel. "You make me tired, Bart Chambers. Who brought that kid to me? I'm flesh and blood, ain't I? I'm human, ain't I? And wouldn't anything human go crazy about him?"

It knocked me dizzy. "All right," I said. "But you'll get over it quick enough. You'll get over it easy. You've got over things like this before."

She laughed in my face. "You don't know nothing, dearie. The rest were all pikers or meal tickets or something, but this kid is the real thing. Get over it? I'll be dead and buried before I'm over it, Bart."

"You're really in love at last?"

I never would have believed it of her. She was a good pal and fine company, and all of that. But when it came to love—why, it didn't seem to be in her. It was something that she knew about and looked at from a distance and could always laugh at.

Now here she was leaning up against the wall with her hands over her heart and her head back and her eyes closed.

She said through her stiff lips: "Love him? Yes. I love him. And always have from the first moment that I saw him."

"You laughed when you first saw him," I reminded her.

"I laughed for happiness, because I knew that he was real. I want to fill up his life. And I'll make him happy. Bart, I'll pour out my heart like water for him. I'd want to die for him. I love him and love him and love him! It'll kill me unless he comes soon. Go find him, Bart. Quick, quick . . . because he'd be here with me before this if something serious hadn't happened. Go, Bart . . . go quick!"

She just pushed me out of the house, and I went down toward the hotel, feeling pretty groggy. I still couldn't believe it. I still couldn't believe that Mabel had lost her head about my man, least of all about a youngster like Bob—not just five years younger than she was, but fifty years younger. If he lived to be half a century older, he would never be as old as she was, because he didn't have the kind of a mind that got old. He would stay young, half foolish, likable, and silly and grand and proud and star-gazing all his life, but Mabel was born wise and had got wiser and wiser. There was nothing that she couldn't see through—except this one thing—love. Or blindness, you might call it. Because that's what love seems to be.

When I got downtown, I asked for Bob Nelson, and the boys just laughed at me.

"He's gone hunting for Barker," they said. "He just pulled out of town, bound west on the train. And Barker rode off in the same direction."

That was a wild bit of news to me.

I couldn't understand it. I knew that Bob got ideas quick, and that he acted on them quicker. But it never entered my head that he would leave Porter's Pass before he had seen me and Mabel, and all for the sake of getting even with a no-account fellow like Barker. No, I wiped Barker off the books. There just had to be some other reason.

I got one, too, mighty quick. When I asked how he happened to start so soon, Bosco Jones, that run the hotel, told me that the kid had heard somebody mention Arthur Rand's ranch and Bob had turned around and said: "Where's Arthur Rand now?"

"In Nevada," said the cowpuncher, "in Carson City."

"Are you sure?" asked Bob.

"Ain't I just mailed a letter to him?" said the cowpuncher. "As sure as I'm working for him."

The first thing that you know, he had ripped out the name of the hotel where Arthur Rand was staying.

Well, when I heard that, I knew. The westbound train might go in the same direction that Barker had ridden out of town that morning, but it also went on a long distance past the place where Barker was riding for. It went on to Carson City. And I knew the reason. The worst pile of danger that ever had come toward Arthur

Rand was headed for him now, and, unless he got help, he would be finished before another twenty-four hours had passed.

You could see how the kid figured everything. He owed his return to a free life out of fear of the law to the wise ideas of Mabel, and before he even so much as went to her to thank her for what her brains had done for him, he was going to manage to pay her back, if he could. And how could he pay her back? Why, by making her as free as he was, and by removing the gent that was slandering her and hiring rascals to make her life a torment. By killing Arthur Rand he would be doing a good deed for the world and he would be repaying the girl that he loved—worshiped, would be the better name. Mabel, as a woman, hardly entered the mind of the kid. She stepped in as a goddess.

I did three things quick. I wrote down the street address of Rand in Carson City, just as I had got it from the hotelkeeper. Then I hiked to the telegraph office and wired to Rand:

> Watch yourself. Keep under cover. You are running into danger of your life.

For the third thing, I started to find Mabel. She might be able to suggest something.

She didn't need a pair of opera glasses to read the importance of the news that I was bringing her. She knew right away that it was likely to be the beginning of the end—although of what sort of an end, she couldn't guess, of course.

"If he kills Rand, Bob is no better than a dead man himself," she said, scared white. "Because Arthur Rand is no common man, and his killing would make a terrible stir. Bart, you and me start for Carson City, and we start right now! Oh, I wish that I'd never been born. But how could I ever of guessed . . . ?"

It wasn't like her to talk like that. But I didn't stop to ask questions or to wonder at things like that. I hot-footed it to the station, and there I got some good news—that, if we waited an hour more, we'd get an express that would hike overland and arrive at Carson City that night about eleven o'clock—a whole hour ahead of the jerkwater local that the kid was traveling on.

I busted back to Mabel with that news, and you can bet that when the Overland pulled out of Porter's Pass that afternoon she may have had a lot more important people aboard of her, but she didn't have no more anxious ones than us.

XV

We was right on time, and the way that we rolled along and clicked off the miles with the spinning wheels chuckling along under the train was a caution. Yellow dust clouds flurried up past the windows on one side, and white smoke scooped down on the other side. You couldn't open a window on one side without getting your eyes and nose and neck and lungs all full of fine Nevada sand. You couldn't open a window on the other side without getting a cloud of smoke, which is worse than sand.

All that we could do was to sit there and stifle and turn red and get mean and start hating the whole world and each other most of all. That was the way that the trip started, but, really, we didn't care much about the heat down in our hearts. All that we minded was the swift, smooth, steady way in which the miles was rattling out behind us.

All the afternoon we done fine, and during that time we climbed most of the grades, but in the evening—it was twilight at the time—we had a stop.

"There's no station," Mabel said, shaking all over. "Go out and see what's happened, Bart."

I went and found out what was wrong—a hot box.

"It'll be all right," I said to Mabel when I went back inside. "They'll get this thing fixed up, and, as soon as they do, we'll snake along so fast that it'll make your head swim, I tell you."

That was what I hoped, but my hopes didn't pan out. For three hours we crawled. I'm not going to write about those three hours. Mabel had more nerve and more courage than any man or woman that I've ever known, but that nerve petered out here. She couldn't stand the gaff, and I watched her lying with her head back against the seat, looking half sick and half ready to be hysterical, very pale of cheek and red of nose. She wasn't pretty; she was homely. She was homely as the devil that afternoon. The wonderful thing was that I knew one glimpse of the kid would make her even prettier than ever.

I got to wondering, too. Even if the kid did marry her—after her divorce—he might do worse. She would never stop loving him till she was in her grave. She had said that, and I knew that it was true.

At last they made a change, and we started to make up time. But there wasn't much use. We got in ten minutes past midnight. Maybe the local had been delayed, too.

I jumped for the porter and shook half his wits out of his head, but he stammered out that the local had come in right on the stroke of midnight. And that was that.

We got a cab and went rushing toward the hotel, with me sticking my head out of the window and cussing that driver and telling him that his hosses was going to sleep between steps. We got to the hotel, and at the desk the night clerk told me that Mr. Rand had left the hotel two days before, because he expected to be in Carson City some time, and had rented a little cottage out on the outskirts of the town.

"Has a young chap been here . . . about ten minutes ago?" I asked.

"Yes," he said, "and he went on.

"Gimme the address of the Rand house . . . life or death," I said.

I got it and I made one jump to the door of the hotel and one more into the cab.

Then we started out again, just as fast as those bosses could wing it along the streets. We sounded like a cavalry charge. The echoes came flying and spattering around our ears. We got to the house. I was out before the cab was stopped, and Mabel was right there beside me, and running.

There was a dark streak of young poplar trees, and behind them there was a little pink and blue stucco house—more like a girl would pick out than what a big, roughneck rancher like Arthur Rand would be expected to want.

"It's quiet . . . there's no noise," said Mabel.

I heard the last of that dying out behind me as I started sprinting. I cleared the hedge right in my stride like a hurdler. I made one jump to the middle of the lawn—and then I pulled up short, because right in front of me was the shadowy form of a man. It was Bob, and he was calmly smoking a cigarette while he waited for the return of Arthur Rand. That Bob had already made sure that Rand was not in the house, I could tell by Bob's manner.

I felt a twitch at my coat and turned in time to see Mabel. She just stood there for a moment, and then she began to sway a little. I caught her in my arms just as she fainted dead away.

Bob Nelson carried her into the house and put her on the bed of Rand. Mabel had saved Bob from himself, and as he leaned over the girl's body there was a century of tenderness in him.

As I watched Bob Nelson at that moment, I saw

what would happen. He would marry Mabel. Then he would have a dream made to order for him by someone else, and he would live in the middle of that dream perfectly happy.

Rifle Pass

As early as 1917, Frederick Faust had been publishing stories in *Argosy*. By 1935, when "Rifle Pass" was published, *Argosy* had become a substantial market for his fiction, with twelve of his stories, both short and serial length, appearing that year. This story was published in the February 9th issue, and is concerned with the family fracture between Sheriff Thomas Weller and his son, Dick, whose courage is tested when he is deputized and sent out to capture the outlaw, Harry Sanford.

I

The sheriff said: "There was a Weller at sea when the *Constitution* sunk the *Guerrière*. There was a Weller at the taking of Mexico City. There was a Weller under Sheridan and another under Mosby. There was a Weller that died with Custer. And I've been sheriff of this country for twenty years. Not that I rank with the rest of the family. But I've kept on riding, and I've never turned my back. And now the Wellers come down to you . . . to you . . . and there's not another man in the family. You're the last. And you spend your time playing cards, thrumming on a damned guitar, making love to girls, and lazying around the ranch smoking cigarettes."

He pulled a long, sleek Colt .45 with an eight-inch barrel from the holster. "Take this," he directed.

Young Dick Weller took the revolver without rising from his position of perfect leisure in the verandah hammock. He had the long, sleek, easy lines of a mountain lion and a smile that was the most good-natured and disarming that a man could wear. He used that smile on his father now, but it had no effect on the iron-gray sheriff. Thomas Weller had become a sheriff, twenty years before, in order to carry on the bold tradition of public service in the Weller family and also because his huge holdings of land and cattle made it necessary for him to keep a close eye upon law and order. For twenty years he had struggled, and after all his ten wounds and his many battles he could only say that he had succeeded in part. Five years before, Papa Lermond, that prematurely bald young son of a lightning flash and the devil, had appeared on the horizon, and since that day the rustling of cattle had increased, to say nothing of stage and even train hold-ups. Ranches were raided constantly. In the three big towns there had been three big bank robberies. And the people who had looked up to Sheriff Tom Weller for twenty years were beginning to murmur against him more than a little.

"This gun," said the idle son, who was to inherit all the wealth of the family and the family's unstained name, handling the long Colt for a moment, "has a good feel. Nice balance to this gun, Dad."

"Look yonder," said the sheriff. "You see that pair of crows on the fence, there? Knock them off it. Sit up and try your luck."

"I'll try my luck lying down," said Dick Weller, and, swaying the gun to the side, he flicked the hammer twice with his thumb. One crow disappeared from the top of its post, leaving a puff of black feathers hanging in the air. The other shining bird left some feathers behind it, also, but rose with a startled squawking, then dipped toward the ground to gather more speed, quickly. It kept on dipping, however. The revolver spoke the third time from the leisurely hand of Dick Weller, and the black crow skidded along the ground, turning over and over. It lay still. Only the wind fluttered the red-stained feathers.

"Shoots high and to the right," said young Dick Weller. "I wouldn't have it for a gift."

The sheriff narrowed his eyes. He was still staring at the two dead birds, but he seemed to be seeing his own thoughts, farther away than the dim horizon. "Get your own guns, then," he said. "Saddle your own horse, the best you've got, and go get Harry Sanford for me. I appoint you deputy sheriff for this job."

"All right," said the son. "But who's Harry Sanford?"

"He's the right-hand man of Papa Lermond." Rifle Pass

"Why go after Lermond's right hand? Why not go after Lermond himself?" asked the son.

"Why not go after the blue in the sky?" demanded the sheriff. "What I been doing for five years except trying to get Lermond? Do what I tell you, and do it fast."

"Yeah. But tell me where this Sanford hangs out, and what sort of a looking *hombre* he is," answered Dick Weller.

"He's big. Dark as a Mexican. Last seen down near San Jacinto on the river."

"What's he done recently?"

"Raised hell all over the map. Some crooks run off the cattle from his ranch and now he seems to think that the world owes him a livin'."

"Dad," said Dick Weller, "you know where he is and what he looks like. Why don't you give this job to Hughie Jacobs or Walt Miller, or one of the other deputies that's all set to make himself a big reputation?"

"You . . . ," said the sheriff, "you don't need any reputation, eh?"

"I'd rather take it easy till there's some excitement around," answered Dick Weller.

"You know what you're going to be?" said the sheriff. "You're going to be a disgrace to the family name. There's plenty of people right now that say you haven't the nerve to be a man."

"People will always be talking," said Dick Weller.

"Get up and out of that hammock and go get your horse and guns!" shouted the older Weller. "I don't want to see you back under my roof till you've put young Sanford in jail! Understand?"

"Well," answered Dick Weller, "that sounds pretty serious, I must say." He sat up slowly in the hammock. "I don't come back till I'm carrying the bear meat. Is that it? I come back with blood on my hands, or I don't come at all?"

"Say it any way you please," said the sheriff. "I'd rather see you dead than talked about the way people do now."

"All right," said Dick Weller. "I'd better go and make a reputation for myself."

San Jacinto was a mere junk heap of a town—mud walls with whitewash daubed over the adobe bricks. The white rubbed off near the ground and the occasional rains washed away small portions of the walls. The streets were deep in dust, which made them comfortable resting places for the pigs, dusting baths for the chickens, and playgrounds for the children. The back yards of the little houses contained grape vines; the front yards contained hitching racks. San Jacinto produced, every evening, a certain number of tortillas and *frijoles*, a certain amount of wretchedly empty bellies, and a certain amount of song.

Dick Weller, riding down the street with his guitar, thrummed the instrument and made a contribution to the song. People came to the doorways and gave him their Mexican smiles, which are the most brilliant in the world—more white and less pink than the smile of the Negro.

He waited until he saw a girl in one of those doorways, the young body silhouetted slenderly against the lamp shine from inside the hut. Then he stopped his horse, lifted his sombrero, swept it through a liberal arc in the greatness of his courtesy.

"*Señorita*," he said, "I am looking for a *compadre* of mine, Harry Sanford. Where shall I find him?"

The gruff voice of a man growled: "María, be still!"

But she answered: "What harm could come from such a *caballero*? *Señor*, you will find him in the cabin there on that side, in the house at the far end of the street, against the river."

"And where shall I find you, my lady?" he asked. "In the heart of what song, lovely María?"

Dick Weller rode on, while the girl in fact sent her pretty laughter after him, and he heard a man growling: "That music is smooth enough . . . I could sharpen a knife on it!"

Down to the end of the village passed Dick Weller before he dismounted and went on foot to the little house at the edge of the river.

The sunset lay like bright, flowing oils on the slack of the river, and the damp coolness passed gratefully into the air. Climbing vines shrouded the small house to distinguish it from all the rest in the adjoining town; one light shone through a window, but the man of the place still sat outside to enjoy the evening, his chair tipped back against the wall as tall Dick Weller stepped around the corner of the house.

"Mister Harry Sanford, I presume?" said Dick Weller, a gun in his hand. But the gun was held low, hardly higher than the hip, and perhaps it was this casual position of the revolver that made Harry Sanford try his luck in a desperate chance. He leaned slightly to the left and snatched a sawed-off shotgun that stood against the wall beside him.

The thumb of Weller caressed the hammer of his gun without actually firing the shot. Instead, he stepped a little closer and with a whip-snap movement of his left arm drove the hard fist against the chin of Sanford. The other spilled loosely back against the wall. He would have fallen from the chair if Weller had not clicked a pair of handcuffs over his wrists and held him up by the chain that linked them.

Sanford, recovering himself, groaned heavily. Flying footfalls and the whisking of skirts brought a dark beauty of a girl into the doorway, exclaiming: "Harry? Anything wrong?" Then the sight of the gun and the handcuffs stopped her, staggered her against the side of the door.

"Wife?" said Weller.

"Sister," said Sanford. "What are you?"

"Hmm," murmured Weller. "Sister? Get up and go inside."

Sanford rose. "You could have drilled me clean," he commented. "Who are you?"

"Dick Weller. Come along, Harry."

They passed into the shack. There were only two rooms. A mist and hissing of cookery came from the kitchen door, and by the table, on which plates were laid out and knives and forks, stood the girl. Her face was sun-darkened with fear.

"Listen, sister," said Dick Weller, "why not lay the table for three?" And he took from his pocket the key that unlocked the handcuffs.

II

Back in the little moldy hotel of San Jacinto, that night, Dick Weller wrote what was for him a long, carefully written letter:

Dear Dad:

Bad luck! Harry Sanford got away. The pair of handcuffs I have with me are still empty. All I can give you is a description of the sister of the criminal.

Name: Muriel. Height: about five feet six. Weight: about right. Eyes: blue. Hair: black as a crow's wing, n.b. with the same shine in it. Forehead: broad. Nose: straight and small. Mouth: delightful. Cheeks: dimpled. Chin: perfect. Throat: divine. Voice: like a song. Should she be arrested for complicity, malice aforethought, or anything like that?

I wait here in San Jacinto for your orders respecting her.

Your obedient son,
Richard

As Dick Weller was finishing this careful report in his room at the hotel, he heard the trampling of many hoofs down the street, the sounds muffled by the deep, soft dust. He heard the jingle of spurs and went to the window in the hope of beholding an array of bright Mexican caballeros, always a sight to fill any eyes. But what he saw, instead, was a procession of four riders who guarded a handcuffed prisoner with naked

guns. The leader of the procession was that human
bloodhound, Hugh Jacobs. The sight of his starved
face—for famine seemed to live in the heart of the
man—sent a shudder through Dick Weller. There was
only one reason why Hugh Jacobs served the law. It
was because he liked to shoot at bigger game than bear
and deer.

The same ray of broad, soft, yellow lamplight that
had struck on the face of Hugh Jacobs drifted, in turn,
over the features of the prisoner, and Weller saw the
dark, handsome fellow he had met that evening at
sunset—Harry Sanford.

The trail that Hugh Jacobs followed with his prisoner
and the escort led up from the river bottom through a
rough trail that was thickly bordered, here and there,
by growths of tall brush. The horses went rather slowly
because they had covered a good deal of ground on
this day, and because the night was still and hot. When
they reached the height of the trail among the hills,
a movement of air was sure to make breathing more
easy. In the meantime, the unseen dust rose in clouds
and turned their throats dry.

Harry Sanford was saying: "The sheriff's been after
me for a long time. He'll be proud of you, Jacobs. What
sort of a fellow is the sheriff?"

"He's all right," said Jacobs.

"He has a son. What about Dick Weller?"

"No good," said the blunt Jacobs.

"I've heard he's quite a man," answered the prisoner.
"You've heard wrong. Shut up now. I've done enough
talkin' to last me."

They toiled up another bend of the trail, the
formidable Hugh Jacobs always in the lead with a
rifle balanced across his saddle bow, and then two
men riding side-by-side with the prisoner. The fourth

member of the group formed the rearguard. They were urging their horses a little more rapidly, now, in the hope of coming suddenly on the better air, and they had a thin sickle of a moon to give them light.

It painted black shadows under the rocks, but that light did not penetrate a thick copse at the right of the trail. Hugh Jacobs was just beside this thicket when a rider burst out from it, with his horse on the spur, as suddenly as a bird from a cloud. The length of revolver barrel clanged on the hard side of the head of Jacobs, but, as he pitched from the saddle, he yelled: "Dick Weller . . . turned crook . . . !"

Hugh Jacobs, landing half stunned, picked up his fallen rifle and was about to use it when he saw that the rider who had dropped on them so suddenly had tumbled all three of his chosen men aside and was now fleeing at full speed, with the rescued prisoner beside him.

The deputy sheriff, waiting until he had a chance to shoot without endangering one of his own men, opened up a fusillade. But his hand was just a trifle unsteady and the moonlight was more than a trifle obscure. The result was that he was pumping lead into thin air, and very well knew it. His three men, following the example of their leader, did not pursue the fugitives. They merely sat still in their saddles and emptied their rifles.

And then the pair had disappeared among the big rocks of the lower valley and only the heat and ring of distant hoofs floated vaguely back to the ears of Hugh Jacobs.

Pursuit was not a useful thing. The horses of his own men were tired out; those of the fugitives were comparatively fresh and of a good quality, also. Rage burned the heart of Jacobs till his whole soul was dry.

184 Max Brand®

"Did I hear you sing out that that crook was the sheriff's son?" asked one of the men.

"You heard right," said Jacobs.

"He wore a black mask, Hughie," said another.

"The jump of his hoss moved the mask up . . . I seen him fair and square as he come bustin' at me out of the trees. It was the son of Weller, right enough. And . . . by God, I hope he hangs for it! I hope I have the pleasure of pullin' on the rope that chokes him."

"But wait a minute, Hughie. Why would a gent like that want to spoil his old man's work?"

"Because he's a damned worthless, useless good for nothing, and that kind, they always take more pleasure out of doin' one wrong than out of doin' ten rights."

It was on the next day that the sheriff sat in his office glowering at a letter that informed him that Muriel Sanford, sister of the criminal, was five feet six, her weight about right, her eyes blue, hair black and shining as a crow's wing, mouth delightful, cheeks dimpled, throat divine, and voice like a song. He had just said "Bah!" two or three times and crumpled the paper to hurl it into the waste basket beside his spur-scarred desk when his leading deputy, the formidable Hugh Jacobs, burst into the room with a purple lump on his forehead.

"Where's Sanford?" demanded the sheriff.

"I had him, and he's gone," said Jacobs. "Your fine, high-priced son that got all the book education, he jumped us on the trail and set Sanford loose!"

"Hold on . . . ," gasped the sheriff. "Jumped you on the trail . . . but there were four of you, Jacobs!"

Hugh Jacobs swallowed. He took a long breath and blew it out again with an audible wheeze before he was able to say: "Was I gonna shoot your own son, Weller?"

"You'd shoot the two of us, or the two of anybody, if you had a safe chance," said the sheriff truthfully. "What happened?"

"I been to the paper and told them all about it. I reckon that you'll be able to read it this evenin'," said Jacobs. He raised a long, bony forefinger. "I'm gonna foller him till I have it out with him," he said.

"You won't have far to go," said the sheriff. And he spoke with a white and hard-set face. "It's the first disgrace to the Weller name, and it's going to be the last one. Find Sanford's sister . . . Dick won't be far away."

"If I go hunting him, I go with guns," said the deputy savagely.

"Yes," said the sheriff, whiter than ever, but his eyes burning. "There's only one law in this country and it goes for everybody in the land. My God, I wish he'd been born dead. He'll pour shame over ten generations of honest men that wore the name before him."

The papers did the thing justice, if not honor, by devoting big headlines to the tale. The three leading papers of the three leading towns in the county had not handled news as hot as this for a long time and they spread themselves.

Some of the space was taken up at the expense of Deputy Sheriff Jacobs, who was very well known and cordially hated. And the outstanding fact was that Jacobs and three of his picked men had been swept aside so that the prisoner could be free.

Instantly young Weller became "the notorious desperado, Dick Weller."

Motives had to be found for this delivery, and of course the deep editorial brains surmised that there must have been a long connection between the two men.

Dick Weller was probably desperate. A hidden career of crime was about to be exposed. He dared not wait for the moment when Sanford was compelled to answer the questioning of a district attorney. The result was the onslaught which overpowered Deputy Sheriff Jacobs and three picked men.

There was the usual dripping verbiage on the editorial pages: *Dishonorable son of an honest father—an old and esteemed name smudged forever.*

But Dick Weller, as he rode down a mountain trail thrumming his guitar, lifted his head and sang with a cheerfulness that set the valley ringing. He had read those newspapers and laughed at them because he could not help feeling that a man's act is no worse than the purpose that inspired it, and, if it was evil to love such a girl as Muriel Sanford, this was too strange a world for his understanding. As for the depth of trouble to which he had committed himself, it never entered his mind. That was why he sang so loudly and so long as he descended the mountain trail.

The cabin, when he saw it, was to him like a smiling face, and the bright flash of the stream that curved about it, whitening with speed along the mountainside, made him laugh aloud, interrupting his singing.

For Muriel Sanford was in that cabin, he was sure. He sent his mustang ahead at a strong gallop, with never a glance behind him, but even if he had paused to scan every boulder, every shrub, he hardly could have spotted the cadaverous face of Deputy Sheriff Hugh Jacobs or the dozen men who received his covert signal to close in on the little house.

III

When Dick Weller came closer to the cabin, he began to sing a song about the foolish world that built roads to Rome, whereas for him all roads led to Muriel. The girl came laughing into the doorway, to greet him. The wind gave the old blue calico dress line and grace about her.

Dick Weller dismounted, stripped bridle and saddle from the mustang, and picked from the saddle the limp bodies of four long-legged jack rabbits.

"But you had no rifle!" exclaimed the girl, taking that solid weight of fresh meat.

"No rifle?" exclaimed a big man, who loomed inside the shack. "Shootin' rabbits with a Colt?" He came glaring at Weller as though at a liar.

"This is Martin Tully," said the girl. "He knows that you're Dick Weller."

"How are you, Martin?" said Weller, shaking hands. "I've heard a lot about you."

"Have you?" said Martin Tully, still staring from the dead rabbits to the hunter who carried no rifle.

"Oh, I've heard quite a lot," went on Weller. "You're a member of Papa Lermond's gang, aren't you?"

"Pa Lermond and I get along pretty good," growled Tully. "What else you heard about me?" He stood leering with vanity.

The girl had gone toward the stove and with swift hands began to cut up the rabbits.

"I've heard about the killing of Porky Morgan, and

the cutting up of the Donald brothers, and the stealing of the Crispin horse, and the murder of those two fellows in the Second National the other day at Buffalo Crossing. . . ."

"Murder?" said Martin Tully.

The girl started and whirled half around.

Dick Weller continued to smile. "What else would you call it?" he asked. He hung his hat on a nail, poured some water into a basin, and began to wash his face and hands thoroughly. But he still wore his guns.

"Murder you call it, eh?" said Martin Tully. "What would you do if a fool stood up and sassed you back? You with no time on your hands? But . . . how'd you get these rabbits? You never hit four jack rabbits in one morning with a Colt."

"I tell you how I do it," said Dick Weller. "I sing them a song first, and, when they hear me sing, they have to stick their ears up and listen, and, while they're listening, I just walk up and shoot them through the head."

"The head?" growled Martin.

"Otherwise, a Forty-Five-caliber slug wastes too much meat," said Weller.

Martin Tully, staring at the rabbits, saw that in fact each of them was shot through the head, the big slugs making frightful wounds.

"You sing to 'em, do you?" he murmured.

"I always sing before I shoot," said Dick Weller. "It makes things die happy."

"Men, for instance?" growled Tully.

"Why not?" Weller asked, with his bright smile. "Look at little Tommy Tucker, who sang for his supper."

"What?" exclaimed Tully suspiciously.

"Dick," ordered the girl, "you be good."

"And bring in a pail of water? I shall," he said. He took the pail and held it over the wash basin that he had just emptied, and said: "There's enough water here to wash one side of your face, Tully. You want it, don't you?"

"Hey, what you mean by that?" asked Tully, making a stride forward.

"I mean that Muriel will lend you the soap. She's a bighearted girl."

He emptied the water into the basin and went singing through the doorway. Down to the spring he went, unknowing of six rifles that were leveled at him from convenient range.

But the range was not close enough to suit Deputy Sheriff Hugh Jacobs, who already had the smack and taste of sweet death against his palate. He held fire, and the others did not dare to shoot first. Hugh Jacobs was waiting hungrily for the day when he would be able to walk into the office of Sheriff Weller and say: "I put in a good week's work. I've just killed your son." He could say that safely and gloat in silence. That moment, he felt, would feed in him the malice of a lifetime.

So Hugh Jacobs held his fire and Dick Weller returned safely to the cabin. As he neared it, he heard the growling voice of Martin Tully saying: "I dunno that I'll stand it."

Weller went in. "Here's enough water for both sides of your face and half your neck, Martin. Help yourself. I love to carry water in a good cause."

Martin Tully had a face that was almost exactly square. A slit of a mouth divided it almost exactly in half, because the chin of Martin was very large and his forehead was very low. This slit widened to the ears in a grin of rage.

"Are you maybe kidding me?" he demanded. "And

what was that about murder, a while back? Murder was the word you used, kid."

"It's a term that means, for instance, walking up behind a man, leveling a gun, and shooting him through the back. You've done that, Mister Murderer Martin."

"Martin! Dick!" exclaimed the frightened girl.

But Dick, standing cheerfully erect near the door, began to sing, very softly:

> A crop-eared mule
> And a one-legged stool,
> An unpainted shack,
> A chimney up the back. . . .

Martin Tully, leaning his wide shoulders forward, stood in a perfect attitude to charge with his fists, or to snatch out a gun. But the song seemed to charm him. His face, which had altered in color a trifle, relaxed some of its fierceness. He ran the red tip of his tongue across his dry lips, and then straightened.

"You're one of these funny kind of birds, eh?" he said. "Well, I guess you're all right. And I'm bringin' word to you from the chief . . . from Pa Lermond. He thinks that maybe he could use you, and he's willin' to see you."

"Tell Lermond," said Dick Weller, "that, when I see him, it will be with a gun in my hand. I hope he lasts till I get my own bullets in him."

"Tell him what?" gasped Martin Tully.

"Tell him I hope to sing the last song he'll ever hear."

"I will tell him that, by God, and I'll start for him now!" exclaimed Tully in a rage. "You may be drunk and you may be crazy, but Lermond is gonna hear the words exactly the way you spoke them!"

"Thanks," said Weller, and watched the big fellow catch up a sombrero and stamp out of the shack.

"Wait . . . Dick, you can't send a message like that to Lermond!" exclaimed the girl. "I'll call him back!"

"Don't do it," commanded Weller. "I've seen all that I can stand of him. I may be living outside the law, but I'm not rubbing elbows with murder."

The pounding of the hoofs of a horse began near the cabin and rushed away from it.

The girl, from the doorway, looked anxiously after the rider. Neither she nor big Tully could realize how many trigger fingers were itching to shoot at the fugitive, waiting in vain for the deputy sheriff to commence the firing. But Hugh Jacobs was not wasting ammunition.

There was only one target at which he cared to shoot, on this day, and his gun was consecrated to that high purpose alone.

Inside the shack the girl turned back to her cookery. She was very worried. "Suppose that Lermond gets this news," she said. "He'll never rest until he has you at some advantage, Dick." He merely answered: "If I thought that Lermond didn't hate me, I'd hate myself. Where's Harry?"

"He rode over to Crystal Creek."

"For what?"

She drew a great breath. "I don't know," she said.

"You're doing a lot of fast guessing, though," said Weller. "Has he gone because we're broke again?"

"I don't dare to think, Dick," answered the girl.

"If we have to have more money," said Dick Weller, "it's time for me to contribute my share."

"You must not!" she exclaimed. "You've never broken the law, yet. You can't begin. If you do a single wrong thing, it will break my heart, Dick."

"I've done enough to make them want me . . . wearing guns while they come," he told her.

"That was for the sake of poor Harry," said the girl. "When I think what we've drawn you down to. . . ."

"Hush," said Weller. "I did it for myself. And I'm proud of it, not ashamed. I'm not worrying about Dick Weller. I'm worrying about you. What's becoming of your life, out here in calico and cooking jack rabbit and canned tomatoes for a pair of tramps like Harry and me? You ought to be trying on engagement rings and refusing them because the diamonds are too small."

"Sit down here, Dick," said the girl, smiling up at him. "While you're eating, you can't say so many foolish things."

"There's one foolish thing that I've been planning to say to you," Weller said as he pulled back a chair and sat down. He leaned forward eagerly. "Know what it is, Muriel?" he asked.

"I know what it is," she answered. She shook her head at him. "I'm the hundredth girl, I suppose."

"Hundredth? What do you mean?" he asked.

"I mean that . . . why, Dick, you're famous for loving girls and leaving them. I *do* love you, but not that way. You're the straightest and the cleanest fellow I've ever known, but. . . ."

He had jumped up to protest, and, as he moved, a rifle *clanged* close to the house.

Deputy Sheriff Hugh Jacobs had drawn a sure bead on a man seated quietly in a chair. He could not believe the trigger finger and the sure eye that told him the target suddenly had jumped away from his shot, and now he raised his voice with a great shout: "Close in! Close in!"

Answering voices ringed the cabin around on every side.

IV

Listening to those shouts, tall Dick Weller said: "That's old sawdust Jacobs come for me. So long, Muriel. I'm going out to have a talk with him."

She used both hands to catch one of his. "If you move a step from the door, I'll go with you. Listen, Dick, if they hurt you, they've hurt you for my sake and Harry's. Wait till he comes back. He'll be here by the evening."

"There are a dozen of them, at least," Weller answered calmly. "Harry couldn't raise this siege."

"Hey! Weller!" sang out a long-drawn, nasal voice.

"Hello, Hughie!" answered Dick Weller. "I've been missing you, old sawdust! How's the place where your marrow ought to be, old buzzard?"

He stood close to the door, smiling as he talked. And the girl, throwing herself into a chair, buried her face in her arms.

"I hear you, Weller!" called Hugh Jacobs. "Are you gonna come out and surrender?"

"I could surrender to anybody but you, Hughie. I couldn't knuckle under to a carrion-eater like you."

A brief, wild yell of rage answered this taunt, but a dim sound of laughter came from other places near the shack. "If you don't surrender, send the gal out of that shack!" shouted Jacobs.

"You hear that, beautiful?" asked Weller. "You've got to leave the shack."

"I won't stir from it. They can't drag me away from you," she answered.

"She says that she won't go, Hughie. Will you send in a man to take her away by force? I'll promise not to salt him down with lead while he's doing the job."

"You think that I'd trust the word of a thing like you?" asked the deputy sheriff. "If she won't come out, and come quick, I'm gonna have the boys open up, and we'll comb that shack high and low, Weller."

"You hear me, Hughie? Are you half the man that people think you are, or do you really prefer, as most of us know, to shoot your game from behind?"

"Who says that I shoot from behind?" yelled the deputy. "We all know about the case of Tim Hoolihan in El Paso," said Weller.

"You lie!" shouted Jacobs. "He turned to run. I couldn't help shootin' as he turned to run!"

"Is that so? What about Jake Marberry, down on the Little Big Horn?"

"I never shot him from behind!"

"That's what you say. The rest of us know the truth."

"You lie, and lie, and lie!" yelled the deputy.

"There was Stan Wilder, too, and Vince Gresham. All shot in the back, you murdering crow!"

"I tell you . . . by God," cried the deputy, choked with wrath and with virtue, "I shot them all fair and square, fightin'! Nobody can say. . . ."

"You old sawdust liar," said Dick Weller. "You know that you were never in your life in a fair fight."

"Are you gone clean crazy?" shouted the deputy. "Didn't a hundred men see me face Jack Western?"

"After you got the bartender to put dope in his beer," said Dick Weller.

"If you stand out here, fair and square, I'll prove what I can do on you!" screamed the maddened deputy.

"You wouldn't dare. The moment that I stepped out you'd tip the wink and have one of your own men shoot me from behind. That's all you understand . . . murder! Murder!"

Turning toward the girl, Dick Weller laughed a little, silently. And the girl stared at him with eyes that were empty of everything but wonder.

"I swear to God A'mighty!" raved the deputy, "that if you step out of that door, I'll meet you fair and square, and we'll shoot when somebody hollers a signal. Dick Weller, if you got half the makin's of a man in you, you'll come out here and take your chance with me!"

"I'm coming now!" called Weller.

Before the girl could cry out, he had issued boldly from the doorway.

In fact, she tried to follow, but utter terror made her knees fail under her.

Dick Weller was walking calmly from the house, smiling, his hat well on the back of his head. "Where are you, sawdust?" he asked. "Where are you, old August heat? Where's Cactus Hughie? Where's the king snake? Where's Mister Shot-In-The-Back Jacobs?"

The deputy sheriff appeared suddenly from beside a great rock near the well. He had jammed his sombrero far down over his head, and he stood like a blue crane, his shoulders bunched and his head thrusting forward at the end of his long neck.

"All right, Hughie," Weller said, walking steadily toward him, "what sort of a trick is there in this job? How many of your men have been tipped to sink lead in me?"

"Not one . . . you rotten liar!" screamed Hughie Jacobs. "There ain't a man of them that don't know, if he shoots on his own account, he's gonna have it out with me afterwards."

"And what would that mean to any of them?" asked Weller. "They all laugh at you, Hughie, just as I laugh."

He began to sing, actually laughing through the words:

> Here is the beanstalk and castle, alack!
> Where shall I find my bonny boy, Jack?

"Take this to hell with you!" yelled Jacobs, and snatched out his gun.

Weller leaped sidewise like a frightened cat and fired at the flash of the steel in the sunlight. His own draw was so lightning fast that the advantage of the first move was quite stolen from the deputy sheriff. And the bullet, striking true by something far more than chance, knocked the heavy Colt out of the hand of Jacobs and flung it back against his body.

The deputy stared for an instant at his numbed, empty fingers, then snatched up the fallen weapon with his left hand. He should have been dead long before he leaned for the gun, and he knew it. He was expecting the shock of a .45-caliber slug through flesh and bones, tearing its way, every split second of this time of expectation. But the bullet did not come; the gun did not speak. Instead, a shadow flashed past him, skidding rapidly over the ground, and, as he half straightened, the gun in his hand, he saw tall Dick Weller, racing like a deer, dodging from sight among the great boulders down the gulley.

The whole of the posse was up now, and firing at the fugitive, shouting with excitement. But the deputy cried: "The hosses! He'll get to the hosses! Run, for God's sake! And shoot straight . . . straight . . . !"

He himself set the example. But it was not because he had any hope of overtaking the flying feet of the fugitive; it was merely that he hoped, running to this side and then to that, that he might get a clean chance at Weller.

Twice and again he had a glimpse and used it for a shot, but each time he knew, with the instinct of the perfect marksman, that he had missed his target by a scant inch or two.

There was another hope—that Chuck Thomas, worthy and proven fighter who had been left behind the shoulder of the hill in charge of the horses a mile away, might hear the rattling of the guns and come out to meet the runner, rifle in hand. Chuck was not a fellow to miss his shot. He was not a fellow to give up a chance at a fight for money or for fun.

In fact, Chuck did finally hear that distant uproar, and, coming up from behind the tree where he held the long line of the horses, their reins all tied together, he got on top of a low rock and shaded his eyes with his hands to stare. He could make out figures swarming down the gulley; he could see the quick flashing of the sun on naked weapons, but he failed to look much nearer at hand, where a man ducked in behind some screening boulders and slipped swiftly down upon him. All that Chuck knew was, at last, a leaping shadow behind him, and, as he whirled, he received a crushing blow that sent him staggering. He was not actually put down, but he discovered, as his senses cleared, that his rifle had been caught from the ground, his revolver had been snatched from its holster.

He, with empty hands, while the rest of his comrades came up beside him, heard the slow drumming of hoofs, increasing rapidly in cadence. And then, sweeping rapidly up the slope beyond, he saw the whole line of the posse's horses being led away at full gallop by a single rider.

V

On the whole, we can stand anything but laughter; and Hugh Jacobs could endure mirth less than any other man. When he saw, in the little four-page newspapers of those country towns, the full details of the escape of desperado, Dick Weller, when he discovered that the entire countryside was laughing heartily, even editorially, at the discomfiture of the celebrated manhunter, Hugh Jacobs, the heart of the deputy was consumed by fire.

He was pursued by only one dream—the lovely vision of tall Dick Weller staggering while the bullets of Jacobs smashed into that young body.

Some of his posse had pointed out that it was strange that Weller had taken such a chance as to run by the deputy instead of shooting him down and making the break through the cordon sure. As it was, Weller had played tag with death—and had almost been caught.

Jacobs would answer to this: "Weller is a cool kind of a rat . . . but that day he was rattled. He didn't do no thinkin'. He just started to run for his life when he seen me reach for my gun, because he knew that I was as good with the left hand as with the right, pretty nigh. That's the reason of it."

But, in his soul, he knew that this was not true. It had been on the part of Weller the magnanimity of the truly chivalrous spirit that will not strike at a disarmed and helpless figure. And this thought, instead of easing the burning pain of the deputy sheriff, made his heart ache all the more and made him yearn more than ever to cast his coils about the fugitive.

Even terrible Papa Lermond no longer received the attention that followed this new and startling outlaw. People spoke of him everywhere, and, when they spoke, they laughed. They always laughed. And why not?

The stories came in by the score. Here he had stopped for breakfast and scrupulously paid down 50¢ for ham and eggs. There he had appeared and courteously begged of an old rancher for a look at the last newspaper. Yonder he showed his head again at a school picnic, high in the hills, and played leapfrog with the youngsters. A harmless man, it seemed, except when he encountered Barney Ginnis.

Barney was a celebrity in his own right, and had built up as black a reputation as any two men would need to get them through life. Behind him were clustered strange tales of dead men and the plunder of mines; to him were attributed half a dozen hold-ups of stages, and on his list were a dozen dead men. But there was never the actual damning proof that the law demands.

Then the story came in that Barney Ginnis, badly wounded, had been brought to the door of a doctor's house in a small village and left in the doctor's hands by a tall man who answered the description of Dick Weller, and who borrowed the doctor's guitar and sang to his own accompaniment before he left. Men said that this surely had been Dick Weller, but Barney Ginnis lay on his back, slowly recovering his life and strength and would not speak a word to explain his "accident."

What actually had happened was as follows:

Barney Ginnis sat in front of his shack smoking a pipe and content with the world because he had in his pantry a saddle of venison, in his locker plenty of guns and ammunition, and in his heart the consciousness that he would never have to lift a hand again in labor so long as he lived. He looked upon the world with a grim amusement when he thought of how he had plundered it and yet the clumsy hand of the law had allowed him to slip from its vengeance time after time.

The brain of Barney Ginnis was as swift, direct, unhesitating as the forepaw of a wildcat. He could not appreciate subtleties that led to the loss of advantages.

Down the trail just above him came a rider who thrummed a guitar and whose gay voice proclaimed in song that kings have their thrones and misers their gold, the sky has its sun and rivers their sunlight, but he scorned them all because his lady filled his heart.

The tall rider with smiling eyes and a sun-browned face halted near Ginnis and said cheerfully: "How are things, Barney?"

Barney looked at the stranger and said nothing. He was not unpleased by the young stranger, but he was so in the habit of being a churl that he could not change on the spur of the moment. He merely pulled on his pipe and looked away from the stranger toward a broad, flat-topped rock that lay near the spring that bubbled from the ground not far from the cabin.

"No news is always good news," said the stranger cheerfully. "And as long as things are like this with you, I'd as soon tell you why I came. I want to borrow five or ten thousand dollars from you, Barney."

Even the rock-like calm of Barney was shaken by this remark. First he fingered the sawed-off shotgun, best of friends, which stood beside him, but then his wonder burst forth in the words: "Hey, whaddya mean?"

"Why," said the stranger, "you know how it is." And then he sang in his pleasant voice:

> Sharper than the tiger's eye
> In the tooth of poverty,
> Poverty is colder thrice
> Than the winter's face of ice.

Barney Ginnis said nothing. The man was not mad, he decided. But speech was not Barney's habit.

"That's why," explained the rider, "I've come to ask you for a loan."

"What sort of security?" Barney asked finally. Not because he expected to have any faith in the answer, but because he wanted to prolong this queer conversation, the queerest in which he had ever been a partner.

The stranger answered, thrumming his guitar and singing:

> Craven hearts are never loath
> To give lying words and oath,
> Singing birds are in the hedge
> And their music is my pledge.

"Take your blather down the trail," said Barney. "I've had enough of it."

"If I can't sing money out of you," said the other, "I'll have to shoot it out." And he slung the guitar behind his saddle. "Well, I'll be damned," Barney said frankly.

He caught, not at the shotgun, but at the revolver that was to him as important as life and soul. But the hand of the rider flashed sudden steel and a heavy bullet smashed into the body of Barney. The impact knocked him backwards against the wall of the shack. Still there was fight in him, but, instead of shooting into the sprawling body, the stranger leaped from his horse like a cat, kicked the gun out of the hand with which Barney was trying to lift it, and then stood back thoughtfully.

"Sorry, Barney," he said. "I sang for my supper and you should have been generous."

"What's your name?" asked Barney.

"Dick Weller."

"Ah? You're him?" said Barney. He was comforted. He had dreamed, for a moment, that he was dying at the hand of a nameless man.

"Now, Barney," said Weller, "we can make a bargain."

"Yeah? Can we?" answered Barney Ginnis.

"I can leave you here to bleed to death," Weller said calmly, "and bleeding to death is an easy way for you to die. And while you're dying, I can hunt for your hidden money. Or else you can tell me where the money is, and then I'll pack you to the town and leave you on the doctor's front porch. How does that sound to you?"

Barney looked down to the blood that pulsed from his body. He was not afraid of death, and neither did he wish to throw away life. "How would I be able to trust you?" he said.

"Look twice at me and you'll know that I do what I say."

"You'll find the money under the bread box inside," said Barney.

"Thanks," said the other, and stepped into the shack.

Everything was very neat, for no old maid is as precise as an old sourdough. There was a tin box to keep bread fresh and moist. Under it, Weller found a thin sheaf of greenbacks—$100 or more. He put this in his pocket and came outside again.

"That's a starter," he said. "Where's the rest?"

"There ain't any more," said Barney.

"All right," remarked Weller, and sat down to roll and light a cigarette. "There's no great hurry, except that you're bleeding to death."

Barney Ginnis looked again at the blood that pulsed out of his breast. "Lift the flat stone by the spring."

So Weller went to the spring and heaved until he had raised up the big, flat stone. Under it he found a small hollow, filled by a package that was wrapped in tarpaulin. He took the tarpaulin by the edge, and, as he lifted, the package unrolled and spilled on the ground—four thick sheaves of paper money in brown wrappers.

"Good boy, Barney," said Dick Weller. "I knew that you and I would get on together." He sang:

> One blink of your bonny blue een,
> One sound of the lark in your voice,
> Of all that I ever had seen,
> There was Barney alone for my choice.

"I hope you rot half a grain a day in hellfire," said Barney Ginnis, and coughed red.

"We'll have to look into this," said Weller. "If doctors can save you, they're going to have their chance."

He got cloth from the house, made a packing of powder-dry dust to stop the bleeding, and bandaged the breast of Barney. "How do you feel, old son," asked Weller when he had lifted Barney to the saddle of his horse.

"Shut your mug, and get on," gasped Barney.

They went on, slowly, toward the village. Even when the lights of it gleamed in the distance, Barney was sure that the life would all have run out of him before ever he came to the town. And still he kept his grip on the pommel of the saddle and set his teeth hard against the black poison of despair.

So he was surprised when, actually, Dick Weller helped him from the saddle and then, with astonishing strength, carried the bulk of Ginnis up the path to the porch of the doctor's house and knocked at the door.

Footfalls came at once, and Weller, leaning over the wounded man, said: "There they come, old-timer. They'll fix you up. You're a pretty game old devil, and, when I ride past your shack again, I'm going to put back half of what I've taken from under the big flat stone by the spring."

Perhaps that was why Barney, when they found him lying bleeding and silent, nevertheless wore a faint ghost of a grin on his iron face.

VI

Dick Weller knew where to find Harry and Muriel Sanford, but the way to them was not easy. Outraged authorities had put a price on his head by this time, not because of things he had done, but because of crimes that could not be traced to malefactors and that were, therefore, shifted in blame to the head of that singing, careless, laughing desperado. Besides, Dick Weller was in no great rush. It was true that he wanted to get Muriel and Harry out of the country and that he now had over $40,000 in his pocket to foot the bill, even after restoring half the loot to the tarpaulin under the big flat rock, but since he had no means of accomplishing his purpose, it was pleasant to loiter along the way.

Also, to gain the reward in cash and the greater reward of having put down such a famous man, posses had started out from all sorts of towns and were combing the range for him. No less than three times he almost ran into the coils.

That gave the indefatigable deputy sheriff, Hugh Jacobs, the time necessary to prepare to strike again. It was not for Weller that he struck, directly, but, as he confided to the gray-faced sheriff: "I've spotted Harry Sanford and his sister again, I think . . . and, if I can grab them, I'll have Dick dead before long."

The sheriff said nothing, because there was nothing for him to say. If some people were a little sorry for the terrible plight in which he found himself with a wifeless and a childless life stretching ahead of him, there were always others to say, with the poisonous cruelty of the casual man: "It must be Weller's own fault. A man gets out of his family what he puts into it. If you put nothing but cash into the raising of your son, you'll reap nothing but trouble in the long run."

So Hugh Jacobs went across country with his dozen picked men, all of them fellows who had been made fools of in that first great attempt to capture Dick Weller, three of them men who had twice before been baffled by the outlaw. For Hugh Jacobs knew perfectly well that there is only one way to use a beaten man, and that is to give him a chance to take his revenge.

The result was that his dozen followers were ready to lay down their lives, if they could have a chance to strike one hard blow at famous Dick Weller.

The hint that had reached the ears of the deputy sheriff was that Harry Sanford and his sister, who so devotedly refused to leave the outlaw, were somewhere on the bank of the Tulomay River. So he went up the river as cautiously as a hunting cat and there, sure enough, he found Sanford and Muriel. They had the two covered with a dozen rifles in no time, while Sanford was busily cutting up a fat stag that he had just brought into camp. With the red unwashed from his hands he was tied against a tree and gagged. Muriel Sanford was tied, also.

Deputy Sheriff Jacobs, licking his dry lips with savory satisfaction, said: "They've seen Dick Weller hither, and they've seen him yon, but we'll sure find him dodgin' into this here camp before long. So set tight and don't you make no noise."

However, as the hours of that afternoon wore on, and the evening came, Sanford was ungagged for a time, allowed to eat, and then fastened once more in his place.

The deputy said to him: "When he comes nigh the camp, is he likely to holler out to make sure that everything's all right?" But the other said nothing.

"He's sure likely to send in a holler," said the deputy. "And if you'll sing out that everything is all right, I'll tell you what I'll do. I'll turn you and your sister loose. The point is, Sanford, that the law wants you pretty bad, but not the way it aches to lay hold of that rat of a Dick Weller."

Sanford laughed in his face, and the deputy, in a fury, struck Sanford a back-handed blow across the mouth that brought a stream of blood.

It was too bad that the deputy had drawn that blood. It was a thing that he would live to think about in other days.

However, before he had the man gagged again, he said to him: "You oughta see that your partner can't last it out. It ain't only the law that's ag'in' him, but it's your own people. You know how I got the tip that I might find you here? Right through the men of Papa Lermond. Know that? They figgered that they didn't want to hurt you, but they sure wanted to get rid of that Dick Weller. There ain't but few that wouldn't be happy if that varmint was dead."

However, since the prisoner would not make conversation even on this point, Jacobs gloomily gave him up as a bad cause and had him well gagged again.

He could trust to fear to keep the mouth of the girl closed, he felt. He had said to her: "If a sound comes and you yell out, I'm gonna bash your face in with the heel of my gun. Understand? I'm gonna spoil the pretty face for you."

This was enough, thought the deputy, to close the throat of any girl with a handsome face.

Now the camp grew very still, for, with the sunset, instead of turning in, the thirteen watchers sharpened their eyes and prayed for the moonlight to brighten. The moon was in fact not far above the tops of the trees when, from the black bluff on the farther side of the little river, a singing voice and the thrumming of a guitar floated down to the hushed camp.

> The boulevards are pretty gay
> But I prefer the homeward way,
> The city lights are sort of pale,
> But stars are on the old mule trail.

The treetops thickly fenced away the view of the top of the bluff, but to every mind that listened to the song came the picture of the tall, familiar figure, with the guitar held in the cradle of one arm.

And then the needle-sharp voice of the girl screamed: "Dick, keep . . . !"

The leather-hard palm of the deputy sheriff was clapped over her mouth so hard that her head was struck violently back against the tree on which her shoulders rested. She turned limp.

"I gotta mind," said the whisper of Hughie Jacobs, "I gotta mind to wring your damn' little neck for you . . . I gotta mind to. . . ."

There was a soft rustling of the brush and Hal Perkins loomed, panting: "I seen him clear, right up ag'in' the moonlight in the sky. I seen him as clear as a lamp. I might've brung him down with one shot, but moonlight makes mean shootin'."

"The question is . . . has the gal scared him away?" asked the deputy sheriff. "Damn her, has she scared him off?"

"No, after she sung out, he waited there a minute, and then rode up the bluff. He didn't ride back into the back lands . . . he didn't start away fast."

"He's comin' down to investigate," said the deputy sheriff. "Where can a hoss cross this here man's river?"

"Fifty yards up is the ford," said Perkins.

"Hal, you gonna be worth your weight in gold to all of us. There ain't no other ford?"

"Not a one."

"I mean to say, you sure they ain't no place where a hoss could get across inside of a coupla miles of here?"

"Listen, chief," said Hal Perkins, "I been raised around here, and I know. The old Tulomay, she runs like a flight of arrows all the way, inside of steep banks, like there is down here. But up there, fifty yards, she pools out, like you seen her. She's four times as broad and as shallow there, and she don't run her current so fast. There ain't no other place where a hoss can cross her. No, not inside of ten miles."

"Good," said the deputy sheriff. "Then he's comin' down the far bluff, and he's sure gonna cross at that ford. Now, I ask you, how could that *hombre* get away from the thirteen of us, when he comes across that there ford in the full moonlight, him ridin' slow on a hoss and our rifles ready? I ask you, how?"

"There ain't no way," agreed several thoughtful voices.

"Hal, you done fine," said the sheriff. "Now, you stay on here and see that this couple don't get the gags out of their mouths. I put a mean one inside the jaws of that girl . . . I half hope that it'll choke her, and maybe it will. Mind that the hosses don't start to neighin', neither. If they start up a chorus, he'll sure know that there's a crowd on hand waitin' for him."

Hal Perkins was so eager to be in on the keener "fun" of ambushing the lone rider that it required a stiff word or two from Hughie Jacobs to quiet him, and then the party of a dozen men went up the bank of the stream.

Before them the ford stretched wide, the water fairly quiet except for the shadowy current that swept through the center of it. Overhead the moon showered a deadly brightness, throwing out the black images of the trees only a little distance on the silver of the Tulomay.

Deputy Sheriff Jacobs, putting each man securely inside covert, rubbed his hands as he sank into his own chosen place. He had, at last, set a trap from which there could be no escaping. Now, clearly in view for an instant, a rider appeared against the skyline at the top of the opposite bluff.

He was only in view for a single instant, since the horse pitched at once down the steep slope and against the darkness of that background was practically invisible.

They heard, also, the thrumming of the guitar, and then the voice of the singer as he raised his song even on the steepness of that slope.

"He don't suspect nothin'," murmured the deputy sheriff to his nearest companion.

"He didn't understand nothin'," said the other. "There wasn't enough words for him to find out. That's all there was to it."

"Aye, that's all there was to it," said the deputy. "My hand it sure worked fast on that mouth of hers . . . and it sure worked hard, too. Damn her, I wished I'd broke her neck."

After a time the deputy muttered: "But seems to me like we'd oughta see him comin' out through the trees before this."

"Likely he's got down and tightened up his cinches before he takes his hoss into the ford. A lot of hosses get kind of tricky in cold water, like this here."

"Aye," said Hugh Jacobs. "Aye, and that's likely. But still . . . by this time it looks to me like there was time for him to have come through the brush and cinch up his saddle, too."

"Time always seems slow when you're watchin' something," answered his companion.

High above them an owl checked its stoop and shot up into the sky again.

VII

On the farther shore, a little back from the bank, Dick Weller stood in the stirrups and looked through a gap in the brush. The outcry he had heard from the girl had not gone unheeded. It had startled him like a knife thrust—that broken cry, and then the silence.

He had to get back to the camp quickly, because there was a riot of fear in his thoughts. And there seemed only one way of going. That was why he had ridden straight over the bluff and down toward the ford. If men were watching for him, they would look in that direction. If they saw him once against the sky, they would certainly wait a long time before they grew suspicious.

As he stared across the dazzling white of the stream toward the mysterious darkness of the trees on the farther bank, he saw an owl stoop, then veer up suddenly, swing to the side, and finally slide away on hurrying wings across the treetops. It had seen something that interrupted the entire course of its intended hunting. That was enough for the hair-trigger wits of Dick Weller. He smiled a little, and instantly tethered his mustang and left it.

The guitar was what he hated to desert. He touched it with a caressing hand before he laid it away in the branches of a tall bush. Then he took off his boots, tied them and his revolver around his neck, and slid instantly into the current.

A horse could not ford that darting stream with a man's weight on its back. And even Dick Weller, swimming like a fish, found himself unable to make headway in the middle of the stream. He had to abandon gun and boots before he could bite into the shadowy rough middle of the Tulomay. But once past that icy center of danger, he was quickly on the farther side, and waded up the bank.

He paused to wring or slick the water out of his clothes. Then, in bare feet that served him as well as eyes could serve another man, he made his way soundlessly up the bank. There was no campfire to greet him with its yellow eye glancing through the brush, and that was strange, also, because certainly his song from the edge of the bluff had been heard.

Like a cat he went testing the ground with his bare toes before he entrusted his weight to it. So, brushing gently through the trees, he came upon that long-remembered scene of two figures tightly bound against trees, their mouths stuffed with gags, while a tall fellow slouched back and forth with a rifle over his arm and spurs *jangling* faintly on his heels.

Now and again Hal Perkins stopped and erected his head a trifle. He had turned, his back to the place where Dick Weller waited, when he repeated this attitude of intent listening, but his ears were not good enough to tell him of the leap of the barefooted man. The crook of Weller's right arm clamped around the throat of Perkins and jerked him flat on his back. By the time he staggered to his feet again, the muzzle of his own rifle was against his breast. And before him there was a dripping figure with very bright eyes and a smile.

Gradually he realized that it was Dick Weller.

"Cut the two of them loose," said Dick Weller. "I'll watch you, partner, while you do the work."

And Hal Jenkins, in a trance of fear, obeyed. Afterwards he sat obediently while a rope was wound about him and he was gagged and bound in the place of Harry Sanford.

Still, enchanted by fear as he was, he was able to remember, afterwards, certain valuable details. For one thing, he remembered that the girl, when she was free from her bonds, began to cry a little, and then stamped her foot and gripped her hands to make herself stop. He remembered that Dick Weller leaned as though to kiss her and that she said—"No, Dick!"—after which he straightened again without a word. He remembered that Dick Weller said to Sanford: "How did that blood come on your face?"

"Hughie Jacobs whacked me," said Sanford.

Weller had said quietly: "I thought that I'd have to kill Jacobs. I know it now. I swear to God. . . ."

"Stop it, Dick!" broke in the girl. "And quickly, quickly, before they come back. . . ."

They got the horses together. Then, after they had mounted—counting the extras there were nearly twenty horses in that long line—Weller said: "I've had to give up another banjo, and I'm damned mad about that. Muriel, help me with that song about the sorrel horse and the old gray mare, will you?"

The girl laughed a little, softly. But, when the song was raised, she carried a part of it, still laughing, and a pretty picture she made with her laughter and her singing in the moonlight.

It was this song that came like a disaster to the ears of Hughie Jacobs and his men.

> I'm gonna leave my home,
> I'm goin' to love to roam,
> I'm goin' away-ay-ay,
> I've found my day-ay-ay!

Two blows are better than ten that land on the same spot. And Hughie Jacobs had been hit twice on the same spot—hard. He had gone out by himself alone, many a time, and brought back his man. Now he had gone out twice with numbers and failed. And his lean face was convulsed with agony when he read the comments in the county newspapers.

> Amusement or habit?
> Deputy Sheriff misses man,
> Loses all horses again.

The account that followed had its stinging moments, also. It said, in one portion:

When the desperado, Dick Weller, is out of horseflesh and doesn't feel like paying good money for new mounts, he never worries a great deal. He simply waits for Deputy Sheriff Hugh Jacobs and a strong posse to overtake him. Then he laughs at the deputy sheriff, takes possession of the horses, and rides happily on his way.

When asked about this, Mr. Jacobs could say nothing. We agree with him that there is hardly anything to say.

So ran the newspapers.

But Sheriff Tom Weller had something else to say. He announced it in print. *Various attempts have been made to apprehend the well-known criminal, Richard Weller. I have made up my mind to go out and take him or never to return.*

When people read that comment, they looked at one another. Then Charlie Street, one of the most prosperous ranchers of the county, stopped the sheriff on the street and said: "Tom, are you gonna light out after your own son?"

"I've swore an oath to uphold the law," said the pale sheriff.

"God A'mighty won't encourage you none," said Charlie Street, and went on his way.

In fact, most men felt that there were frightful calamities in the air when blood was ready to fight against itself. But the grim sheriff rode out with six chosen men and struck for the trail of his son.

That was the time when Papa Lermond came down on the Western Limited, stopped the train, overturned the first two coaches, caused the death of eleven passengers, and escaped with a quarter of a million. Other posses quickly started on that trail, but the sheriff remained quietly at work on the task in hand.

He set a trap at Bison City and it barely failed to close on Dick Weller. He prepared his meshes on the trail between Haley and Four Rivers, but was eluded again. He rode at night into the cow camp of Steve Marshal only to find that the man he wanted had ridden away half an hour before.

Commenting on these failures, the county newspapers said: *Sheriff Tom Weller has failed again in his pursuit of his son, while Papa Lermond runs loose and free. Sheriff Weller only misses his son by a few minutes each time. But he keeps on missing. This is very strange. Perhaps the voters of this county will notice the strangeness of it at the next election.*

This was the talk that was in the air far and wide, as well as in the newspapers, when Dick Weller sat over his portion of a saddle of venison that had been roasted in a Dutch oven and said to Muriel Sanford: "You know, Muriel, that I've been riding this trail for quite a while, but now my father is on it. What about cutting all of this and going away with me? What about marriage?"

But the girl said: "Dick, you're the best I've ever known. You're so good that you even can persuade yourself that you want me."

"You mean that I don't mean it?" asked Dick Weller.

She smiled at him curiously, sadly. "You know you don't," she said. "But you've saved the Sanfords so many times that you begin to think that they must be worth saving."

"Wait a minute," said Dick Weller. "Does that mean you really are not interested? Does that mean I'm barking up the wrong tree?"

She nodded. "I'll never marry a man outside the law," she said.

"I'm glad to know it," Weller said soberly, and said no more on the subject.

"Muriel, you're talking through your hat," said dark, handsome Harry Sanford. "Do you realize what you're saying? This is Dick that's talking to you."

"I realize everything," she said. She realized it so well that she was awake, late that night, when she heard a little crackling of twigs, as though underfoot, and instantly roused herself. Then, far off against the dimness of the moonlit sky, she saw the faint outline of a rider who sat singularly straight in the saddle.

The moment she saw that figure, she recognized it, and started running in pursuit, crying out: "Dick! Dick!" But the rider went on, far beyond earshot.

When she came back within the range of the ghostly light of the red embers of the campfire, she saw a tag of paper pinned under a splinter of a log by the place, and, when she took the paper, she read:

Dear Muriel,
   If I can't interest you outside the law, I'm going back inside.

                                                    Dick

Under the note, pinned by the same strong splinter, there was a thick stack of greenbacks.

And on that same night, just as the light of the dawn was beginning, the man who mounted watch at the mountain camp of Sheriff Tom Weller saw a rider come vaguely out of the horizon and head toward the camp.

"Who goes there?" he challenged.

"What's this? Part of the United States Army?" came the answer.

To which the sheriff's man very properly answered: "A damned sight better than the best part of that army. Who are you, *hombre*?"

"Looking for Sheriff Weller."

"Who's been stealin' your cows?" asked the sentinel.

Then he saw, by firelight more than the radiance of dawn, the face of the rider who was approaching him. He jerked his rifle to his shoulder.

But Dick Weller merely said—"Don't be a damn' fool."—and rode on in to the fire. There he dismounted, threw the reins of his horse, and kicked together the embers of the fire. "Got any chuck around here?" he asked. "I'm hungry. By the way," he added, "do something more for me, will you?"

"What's that?" asked the sentinel, staring hard at the fugitive, but still looking down the sights of his rifle.

"You might wake the sheriff up and tell him that he's captured that desperado . . . you know the one that I mean . . . that desperado, Dick Weller."

VIII

The sheriff traveled for three days, slowly, carefully, through the mountains, with handcuffs on the wrists of his son. And for three days the sheriff's chief deputy, Hughie Jacobs, never took his eyes from the prisoner, never left his side by day or by night. Hughie Jacobs was perfectly silent most of the time, because he was receiving more through the eyes than his ears could ever tell him. He was seeing, daily, hourly, momently the perfect vision of his greatest enemy, the man who had disgraced him, locked inside handcuffs, helpless. He had been present at the surrender of Dick Weller—that was enough to wipe out the blots on his record. There was only one ghost to spoil his happiness and that was the question: Why had Dick Weller surrendered?

The question grew always more and more important.

Now when the sheriff found his son in his hands, he could remember old formulas according to which he had handled other cases of captured criminals in the past, and according to these formulas he tried to handle the case of Dick.

For instance, when he sat down beside his son and said: "Now, Dick, whatever you say is likely to be used against you, but I'd like to ask you a few questions."

"Blaze away," said the son. And he turned his bright, thoughtful eyes on his father.

"On the Eleventh of August, were you in Tucson?"

"Yes," answered Dick.

"Were you in Tucson, and present at the death of Doc Manly and Joe Price?"

"Oh, sure," said Dick Weller.

The sheriff closed his eyes for an instant. Then he said: "Is it true that on that day and date, seeing the two men, you walked up behind them and fired a bullet into the back of each, because of which wounds they died instantly?"

"Why should I have killed a pair of fellows I never saw before?" asked the prisoner.

"I ask you the question."

"All right. Write down that I killed them."

The sheriff closed his eyes again for a moment. Then he nodded and wrote down the answer that meant that his son would hang. He consulted a list and asked: "Did you meet Stewart Liscomb on the trail between Pine Wood and Red Stone and shoot him dead?"

"Stewart Liscomb? What did he look like?"

"I don't know," said the sheriff.

"Neither do I. But I suppose I may have killed him."

"Did you, on August Nineteenth," said the sheriff, "feloniously and with purpose to kill, attack Jim Stevens in the Bar One Saloon in Little Bank?"

"I suppose so," said the son.

The sheriff jerked up his head. "How did you get from Pine Wood to Little Bank inside of two days," asked the older Weller, "without a bird big enough to carry you?"

"I don't know," said the son.

"Are you telling me the truth or are you lying?" asked the sheriff.

"I'm making things easier for the law," said Dick Weller. "I never killed a man in my life."

At this, the sheriff shut up his notebook with a slam, and growled: "Why, don't you say so, then?"

"Why should I say so?" said Dick. "Nothing I say will be believed unless I confess. You and the rest have made up your minds that I'm no good."

"I never made up my mind to that," said the sheriff.

"You've thought so for years," said Dick Weller. "You tried me at cowpunching and fence-building and mining and timbering, before you washed your hands of me."

"I never washed my hands of you."

"That's not true. From the day I came back from school, you were ready to suspect me of everything. I'd looked inside a few books, and you knew that they must have ruined me . . . so you said."

"Dick, you can say what you please and I'm not able to contradict you."

"The truth is always hard to contradict. Let me tell you another thing. The reason that I never wanted to lift a hand was because you kept the doubt in your eyes whenever you looked at me."

"You are the last of the Wellers," said the sheriff.

"Damn the Wellers," said the son. "I'm sick of hearing about them. Because you're proud of the family, you would have sent me to hell. I was too lazy to suit you. The only reason you wanted me on earth was because you didn't want the straight line of the old blood to die out!"

"Nonsense," said the sheriff.

"Be honest. I'm telling the truth."

"You've shown your blood," said the sheriff slowly. "You showed it the moment that you got off by yourself. I sent you to arrest a criminal. You preferred to rescue him from the hands of honest men."

"Honest like Hughie Jacobs, you mean?"

"I mean that."

"I haven't any regrets," said the son.

"I know that," the father said bitterly. "I can see the happiness in your face, Dick. Danger for its own sake or for the sake of the money you can get out of it. And that's why it's better to put you in jail. Better to keep you behind the bars for life than to have you endanger the lives of other people with your freedom."

"I'm not asking for your pity," said Dick Weller.

The sheriff turned away and his heart was ashes in him. He had no other children, no other relatives. He could see his estate dissolving among the hands of many men and the name of the Wellers clouded and lost in a final disgrace.

They entered Rifle Pass, which, straight as the barrel of a gun, cleaves through the mountains, a chasm so long and so narrow that, from one end, the gap at the farther side appears hardly larger than the spot of brilliancy seen through the sights of a rifle. The rocks seemed as hard as metal. They have a steel sheen, and the cliffs rise to such a height that one feels a nervous sense of being shut away from the sky, a half-buried feeling. The bottom of this gorge is somewhat furrowed by the action of the water that cuts the entire gap, working at leisure for a few million years. But that soft chiseling has ended. There is no water at all in Rifle Pass except the few pools that remain standing for a time after melting snow has trickled down into the gorge. And on this hot day the rocks glowed as though they had been through a furnace and there was not a sign of a drop of water anywhere.

However, Rifle Pass was a convenience because in its short length it carried one through the mountains without having to spend weary leagues of effort among the rough lands above timberline, and the hoofs of the horses, as though they wanted to escape quickly from this sleek piece of hellfire and hot rock, began to jangle the echoes with redoubled speed as they pushed on down the gap. They were well past the center of the gorge when something spatted and hissed on the polished face of a rock near Dick Weller.

He saw, or thought he saw, a thin streak of light appear on the stone. Then the long, distant ringing of a rifle report came swinging down, dim in the thinness of the mountain air.

A sudden fusillade followed. The air was alive with bullets. A swift slash with a red-hot knife slithered across the ribs of Dick Weller beside his heart. But he was the only one hit as the party made for the only shelter. That was a single cluster of great boulders that lay in a heaped circle of confusion near the center of Rifle Pass. Looking up, one could see a great section bitten out of the south wall of the pass, and here the monstrous fragment had loosened and fallen into the gorge. The cliff was so high that the niche in it did not appear very huge, but in fact the individual boulders were tons of weight. And the sheriff's party quickly scattered here and flung themselves out of the saddle.

The place was intolerable instantly. That heat, which was bad enough in the open, was now frightful. The boulders, offering more surface to the sun, had soaked up its heat and now were giving it back into the frightful strength of the noonday. The air quivered with the hot radiations. Instantly sweat sprang out on the bodies of the tough mustangs and thirst struck the roof of every man's throat.

From the edge of the lip rock, down the valley, a thin sound of cheering reached them. It was echoed from the west end of Rifle Pass, a certain proof that both ends of the gorge were blocked. And there the posse would have to stick like so many fish in an oven.

There had been no water on the upgrade leading to the pass. Canteens were nearly all empty—except that of lean Hugh Jacobs. The heat sucked moisture with terrible suddenness out of the bodies of the men.

The great red blotch that stained the side of Dick Weller seemed a trifling thing. The pain from the wound was nothing compared to the torment that he suffered instantly from the oven in which they were placed. It was the concentrated essence of Death Valley. The men began to fumble at their throats at once and look wildly at one another.

Even the wise sheriff could give them no comfort.

They knew and he knew what had happened. He had hunted men for twenty years, and now men were hunting him, and they had him cornered. He was as good as dead, and the rest would go down with him. This, in silence, stared out of the eyes of them all.

The sheriff went to Dick Weller and bent to examine the wound, but Dick said coldly: "It's a scratch. The bleeding won't be bad. And we'll all be cooked brown before I die of the bullet, Father."

It seemed true enough.

After sunset the light of a high moon would gild that valley with silver and expose the fugitives to rifle fire, if they attempted to escape. They were as thoroughly caught in the trap as though chains held them. They could live through this day. On the morrow they would begin to go insane with thirst.

Dick Weller sang softly:

> Oh, were you ever in Lonesome Town,
> Where the men are red and the gals are
>   brown,
> And sow-belly's all that they will cook,
> And every day has a Sunday look?

"Quit your damn' noise," said Deputy Hugh Jacobs.

"All right," said Dick Weller, "but I'll tell you what, old son. I'm the only man who can show you fellows the one way out of this corner."

IX

The sheriff, rebuffed by his son, had stepped back and looked at Dick with a singular sadness. But now he said: "You have a brain, Dick. What's your scheme?"

"Take the handcuffs off me," said Dick Weller.

"Yeah, I thought that would be the first part of the idea," sneered Hughie Jacobs, thrusting out his head on his long crane's neck.

"Then put me on my horse," said Dick Weller, "and let me cut loose out of this. I'll go down the valley like a rocket and the rest of you filling the air with bullets as though you didn't want me to escape."

"I wouldn't be wasting bullets on the air," said Hugh Jacobs.

"Be still!" commanded the sheriff. "Let him talk out his idea. What next, Dick?"

"Why, the crooks down there, whoever they are, will be glad to see another crook who's managed to slip away from the sheriff. They'll see the blood on my side to prove that you fellows really were shooting to kill. Isn't that easy?"

"Yeah, easy for you," said the deputy sheriff. "But what does it do for us?"

"When I get my chance, I start a ruction down there among them. I get into a fight with somebody, say. And while that fight lasts, there won't be much attention put on the rest of you here. Understand?

Then you can make a straight charge to get out of the valley. Isn't that clear?"

"You'd start a fight with a whole gang like that? Even you ain't that kind of a fool," declared the deputy.

"All right," said Dick Weller. "Vote on it, you *hombres*. You're all dead men, anyway. I know I'm offering you a damned thin chance, but isn't it better than nothing at all?"

Hugh Jacobs said: "Sheriff, you ain't gonna let this kind of a crooked deal go through, are you?"

"I'm going to ask for votes," said the sheriff. "Speak up, men."

There was perfectly equal division. Hugh Jacobs expressed the opinion of the dissenters when he said: "It would sure eat the heart out of me to think of this here crook gettin' off free while the rest of us stay here and stew in the hell broth that he led us into."

With that equal vote announced, the sheriff had the decision in his own hands. He sat on one of those burning rocks with the sweat pouring down his reddened face and thought making his eyes dim. At last he said: "Dick, there's one chance in a hundred that you're a real Weller down in your heart. There's one chance in a thousand that you might do what you promise. There's one chance in ten thousand that we might be able to use you, and get away. Well . . . even a small chance like that ought not to be thrown away. I'm going to set you free."

A howl came from the deputy sheriff at this, but the other men agreed that it was probably the best thing to do. So the handcuffs were unlocked, the prisoner given a gun, and the sheriff stood beside the horse on which his son was sitting.

"Dick," he said, "I'm beaten. I can't understand you or the things you've done, but it's not likely that we'll see each other again, after this. Will you shake hands?"

Dick Weller, looking down into that grim face, burst into a sudden rage. "Not till there's been more blood," he said. "Not until there's been enough blood spilled to wash our hands clean. So long, everybody. Remember to raise a yell and start shooting."

Hugh Jacobs began to shout: "It's against the law! It's against everything. It's a damned outrage and . . . !"

But Dick, with a wave of his hand, suddenly spurred the dripping mustang out of that oven-like enclosure and sent it darting down the floor of the pass.

Two or three rifles crackled instantly from the eastern end of Rifle Pass. But this shooting ceased as a yell went up from the rock heap and the guns of the posse commenced their clangor.

The noise of the shooting was real enough, but none of the bullets at first came anywhere near Dick Weller. It was only after a moment, the horse running at full speed, that he heard and almost felt the whiff of a bullet past his head. Another bullet almost brushed his right shoulder. Then the hat was twitched at lightly, and he knew that a slug had clicked through the crown.

He understood. Hughie Jacobs, in an agony as the man he hated began to escape, could not help shooting near the mark, snuffing the candle, as it were. It was beautiful and delicate shooting that he did, and if perhaps his rifle actually hit the bull's-eye—well, it would just be one of those accidents.

But the sprinting horse swept Dick Weller rapidly out of easy range, and he made the mustang dash up the steep slope toward that low, outjutting shoulder of rock that commanded the length of Rifle Pass. Here were the men who had bottled up the sheriff.

Weller, rounding the top of the shoulder and bursting through the broken rocks of the ledge, saw, on the narrow plateau, a dozen men who were waving their hands and shouting for him. But among them he spotted two at the first glance that chilled his blood. One was the wide, evil face of Martin Tully. One was the sleek bald head of a fellow who had prematurely lost his hair.

He had fallen into the midst of brigands, indeed, for he had come upon the band of the coldest-blooded slayer of them all—Papa Lermond and his crew of evil-doers. He saw all of this at the first glance, and one single note of hope and of happiness—that was big Harry Sanford, who came running to him, shouting with joy.

They were still yelling down there in the nest of rocks as Dick Weller dismounted. He shook hands with Harry Sanford heartily and heard Sanford murmur: "It's Lermond. Look out. He's poison. But I had to get him on this job. There was nobody else to turn the trick for us."

Sanford, then, was the man who had brought so many of the law-abiding into terrible danger? For the sake of Dick Weller, who had freely given himself up?

There was no time to ponder the thing in detail. Martin Tully and the great Papa Lermond were both coming up to him.

"You're Dick Weller, eh?" said the outlaw. "Nicked bad in the side, there?"

"Scratch," said Weller.

The other made no offer to shake hands. But the rest of the crowd gathered around with great interest to stare at the newcomer. They were men of all kinds, and their clothes were as various as their faces. There was even a pale-faced fellow with a derby hat on his head and the tip of his nose fried crimson by that Western sun. The rest of his outfit, horribly grease-stained and soiled, was a blue suit that had once appeared natty enough, no doubt. He must have been a new recruit. He was not more than eighteen and in profile looked like a snub-nosed, smiling, cheerful boy. Only in the full face was the danger seen in him, a callous cruelty glittering out of his eyes.

He was merely an outstanding element in that group of the followers of Papa Lermond. For all were dangerous, and all were a little strange, down to the short, bow-legged man who walked with a limp and carried on his hip not a revolver, but a rifle with the barrel sawed off until it was little longer than the barrel of a revolver. A terrible rifle that was, a repeater that hurled a .44-caliber bullet, a thing to smash in the forehead of an elephant.

These were the men who blocked the end of the valley. And what hope could the man with the sheriff have against such enemies as these? No hope whatever, to be sure. No hope, because one of these scoundrels was equal to any two men in the posse, except the sheriff and that dried-up buzzard of a fighting man, Hugh Jacobs. But one thing made the little blockaded group in Rifle Pass a danger, and that was the reputation of the sheriff for twenty years of success and because he wore that invincible name of Weller.

Papa Lermond said: "Your old man is going to catch hell, it looks like."

"He's already in hell," answered the son.

"Yeah, and maybe he is." Lermond grinned. "Now I wanna tie myself to some facts about you, kid. I've been hearing things from a lot of people about you, and the things I hear from Sanford are fine, and the things I hear from big Tully, here, ain't no good. Which can I believe?"

"How can anything but a lot of noise come out of a mug like Tully's?" asked Dick Weller. He laughed as he spoke, and all the while he watched the right hand of Tully, which shuddered to get at a gun, but which did not quite dare to make the final gesture.

"What's the matter?" asked Lermond of Tully. "Has this kid got you bluffed, Tully?"

"I could swaller ten like him," declared Tully.

"Yeah? I guess you're afraid that he'd stick in your throat," remarked the great Lermond. He smiled on Dick Weller.

He had the strangest face that Weller had ever seen. It was like the face of a Negro, with a white skin drawn over it. The features were as the African—the nose was blunted and rounded over; the pull of the lips was very wide when he smiled. He had a sallow complexion and there were a million small holes, like needle scars, stuck into his face. Yet he was not as repulsive as an accurate addition of all his features might indicate. There was a strange sort of good nature about his expression, and he seemed always smiling or about to smile. Only a knowledge of the things he had done could finish the picture, and Dick Weller knew enough to turn even his flesh cold.

"The main thing that I want to know," said Lermond, "is what my friend here, my old friend Tully, tells me . . . that you said you'd rather be damned than join up with Papa Lermond. Is that the straight of it?"

Weller took in a good breath. He had the lie ready on his lips, and the smile to go with it. To fight Tully—oh, that was one thing, but to fight Papa Lermond, that was quite another. He would have to get out of this crisis unless he wished to die, because no man of all those who had faced Lermond in combat ever had succeeded in putting him down with a bullet.

It was a lie, therefore, that was forming on the lips of Dick Weller, but, before it could be uttered, a great spirit of detestation and scorn rushed over him and forced from his lips: "I'd rather be tied to a mangy dog than tied to you, Lermond!"

X

The mere sense that those words had been spoken worked like lightning in the brain of Weller, dazzling his eyes. He noted that the smile of Lermond had not faltered, and then he was aware that it was not a smile at all, but simply a savage grin like that of a hunting cat. There was no more than a cat's mercy in it. He shifted his glance a little from the face of the great outlaw, and, as his eye roved down the valley, he was amazed to see a small and compact body of riders going up Rifle Pass—at a walk!

He could not believe what he saw—and then he understood.

The wise sheriff, hoping that the arrival of his son might absorb all the attention of the outlaws for a time, had chosen the moment of that arrival to lead his men out from the rocks and advance—without noise, in the hope that thus he might be able to come within charging distance.

Well, that was because he did not know that Papa Lermond was up here—Papa Lermond and all the rest of these handpicked murderers. Yet a grim admiration for the rancher and sheriff came over his mind, and with that admiration there was a sudden, fierce warming of all his blood with pride. That man, yonder, was his father. Their blood was identical. And only a few moments before he had refused, savagely, to shake the hand of Sheriff Weller. . . .

Lermond was saying: "All right, kid. You have to get it in the eye, eh?"

"I get it!" exclaimed Dick Weller, in a transport of the enthusiasm that had just come over him. "I get it! Lermond, I'm going to blot you out if you ever lift a hand at me."

The boy in the derby hat laughed aloud. "Listen to him," he said. "Buck up, chief, and let me have him. I want him. I need him." He began to curse Dick Weller with a soft persuasiveness of voice, inviting him to go to any number of strange regions.

The chief cut suddenly through this tirade. "Shut up, Banjo," he said.

The boy was instantly still, but the green devil remained in his eyes.

"I'm glad it's this way," said Lermond. "I want to get the taste of the Wellers right deep down in my throat. I wouldn't make a meal of the two of them in one bite. I'd rather have them in two swallers." He raised his left hand. The enchanted circle of his men stood in a frozen attitude of suspense.

Then Dick Weller took stock of the things around him. There was poor Sanford, first of all. Harry Sanford was a good fellow. He was white with the agony of the moment, but would he have the courage to come to the help of his friend in such a crisis? To expect that was to expect the superhuman. No. Sanford's hand would be held by terrible fear.

And what other escape was there? A mere jumble of small rocks lay scattered, here single stones and there ragged heaps of them that had rolled down from the higher section of the cliff and, in fact, were overlooked by that height. But if Dick Weller could get to one of those heaps, he might be able to keep up the battle until his father and his men came charging to the sound of the guns and, so, manage to turn the tide of the fighting. . . . Well, it was not a real summing up of chances. It was merely the last ghost of a chance.

Lermond was saying: "This ain't gonna be any murder. Ready, kid?"

"Ready," said Dick Weller.

"When you want to, just say . . . 'Shoot,' Lin, will you?"

"Sure," said big, hairy-faced Lin.

So Weller faced the great man and waited. He knew instantly that the signal would not be given at once. No, Lin and the rest would want to see him reacting under the acid test.

The silence dragged out. And those seconds were priceless to the group of men who, now out of the sight of Dick, were still pressing on toward the east end of the valley.

It seemed to Weller that the knowledge of their coming was a sort of inward strength. And if he died—well, he would be dying in a cause that was not yet quite lost.

He looked steadily at the great Lermond. There was nothing extraordinary about the fellow's appearance except that Negroid face—and the hands. Such hands Dick had never seen, the fingers long and thin as the claws of a bird. They were flexing and extending slowly now. And the sight of them, for some reason, convinced Weller that he had not a mortal chance. In those lean fingers there was lodged an inhuman speed that he was certain he could not rival. The battle was lost before it began, unless he could think of some counter measure. What counter measure could there be? What could conquer speed in such a battle as this?

Surety! That was the only way. To whip out his gun fast enough, but not with any attempt at a lightning draw that might enable the fast performer to throw in the first shot but generally prevented him from striking a vital place. He, Weller, must take no chance of sending his bullet wrong. He must shoot straight into that body. That meant that, first, he must stand fire. It was a horrible prospect. The heavy .45-caliber slug of lead, fired pointblank, was capable of knocking a man flat if it struck his body a solid blow. But he, Weller, must not be knocked flat. He must endure, and then shoot.

"Shoot!" shouted the sudden voice of Lin.

The hand of Lermond convulsed. It disappeared with the speed of the draw. There was only the flash of the appearing Colt, like a glint of sunshine on water. And then a roaring explosion and a sledge-hammer stroke through the left shoulder of Weller, jerking him around.

It pulled him sidewise, but it did not even stagger his prepared and stiffened body. His own gun, held just above the height of his hip, spat fire. Lermond, still pouring bullets from his weapon, but pouring them wildly, pitched sidewise to the ground. In the stunned instant of paralysis that followed among the gang, Weller turned and leaped for the rocks.

One figure moved after him, swift as thought. In his haste he tripped and rolled on a loose stone, pitching forward. But powerful hands seized him and jerked him ahead into the shelter of the nearest heap of rocks.

The first bullets came flying at the same instant, a humming shower, spattering on the faces of the stones, and then Weller was aware that it was Harry Sanford who crouched beside him, not idle, but lifting weighty rocks and piling them to increase the strength of their breastwork. Behind the bullets there arose a storm of wild, savage yelling.

"Are you done in, Dick?" asked Sanford as he worked.

The left arm of Weller lay helplessly beneath him. The numbness of the shock had prevented pain, for the moment, but that agony was commencing now. Yet he could have laughed at the pain. Dying was the simplest thing in the world, when there was a proved friend at his side, a greater friend than ever his expectations had hoped. Dying was simple, also, if a man were a Weller, fighting on the right side of the law.

"Harry!" he exclaimed. "I feel good enough to dance." Then he heard the voice of the great Lermond yelling out orders.

"Lin and Tom, get over there to the left and flank 'em! Josh . . . Parkin . . . Danny . . . crawl down that hollow and blast hell out of 'em from behind!"

There was a steady fire maintained, all this while. Two big slugs, hitting the last stone that Sanford was putting in place, knocked it right out of his hands and dropped it on the ground. The gang yelled with delight and redoubled their fire. Would any of them take the trouble to turn and look into Rifle Pass while all of this was going on?

Weller, edging to the side, wriggling like a snake because he could put the weight of his body on his knees and right elbow only, gained the side of the little breastwork that Sanford was piling. Behind the rocks that lay just ahead, as he peered through a chink, he saw just the humped back of a man running with head down from cover to cover. Weller put a bullet neatly through the hump and saw the man straighten suddenly, flinging out both arms.

That was Lin. He would never give a signal for another gunfight. He would never have a chance to clean that hairy face of his with a razor. Standing there like that, other men of the gang yelled to him to get down, but Lin, silent, his arms still extended, swayed slowly back, then snapped, it seemed, like an overweighted bough of a fruit tree and fell over the edge of the boulder, where he lay motionlessly. His back had been broken by the bullet, perhaps.

Lermond was crying: "They've got Lin! They're going to sweat in hell for that. Here . . . carry me up that rock so that I can get a shot or two in. Buff and Charlie, carry me up there!"

Sanford, ceasing his building work that was raising a rude protection all around them, suddenly began to fire rapidly. A wild, howling screech came out of the valley beneath them in answer, a terrible and endless cry of agony.

"Where?" said Weller.

"Through the belly," said Sanford.

"My God . . . the poor devil," said Weller.

"Aye," said Sanford. "I wish that I'd put the slug through his heart, instead. Look out!"

For a bullet cut through a small gap in the wall and slashed Sanford's shirt sleeve open, just drawing one pinpoint of blood from the flesh.

Another shot crunched through a barely visible crack and whirred past the face of Weller.

"That's Lermond," said Sanford. "Nobody on God's earth but Lermond could shoot like that. And God help us now."

Peering through the crevices between the rocks, Weller made out a spitting revolver that played from between two boulders up the slope; from such an angle that the weapon raked down over the breastwork of Sanford. The next shot knocked the heel off the boot of Weller's right foot.

Sanford began to fire toward the hollow again. "Missed! Missed! Missed!" he kept grunting with every shot. And then: "Winged him that time."

From the left more guns opened suddenly. It was the weakest part of the breastwork, and the bullets were sure to find a mark sooner or later, but still Weller gave no heed to the marksmen in that direction. Instead, he concentrated on those two boulders up the hills and the gun that flashed from behind them now and then. It did not appear in the same place each time. The wounded man was lifting his weapon now to the right and now to the left, showing never any more than his hand and wrist, and these only for the barest instant.

And Weller, waiting, holding his fire, trained his revolver patiently on the spot to the right where the gun of Lermond had appeared before. Small black spots began to dance before the eyes of Weller. There was a hollow nausea of agony filling his body. But he told himself that he could not miss because he dared not miss.

Distinctly, beside him, he heard the heavy thud of a bullet smashing into the flesh of Sanford. He heard the crunch of the slug against a bone. But he would not relax his fixed vigil.

There—it winked again, the quick gun of Lermond, and Weller tried that delicate target instantly.

The answer was amazing. Up from behind the rock sprang Lermond with crimson from his body wound plainly visible all over his breast. His right arm dangled, scattering blood. But in his left hand he carried a revolver and with it he charged straight down the slope toward the breastwork!

Another very strange thing happened then. From behind the boulders leaped the half comical figure of Banjo, with the derby hat atilt on his head, and rushed after his chief, shouting out to Lermond to come back—to drop to the ground.

And Lermond dropped, with a bullet from Weller's gun straight between his eyes.

Once, twice, and again, with his second gun Weller fired and emptied the weapon. He knew that all those bullets must have driven into the body of Banjo in vital places, but still he came on. Now, his revolver emptied, Weller groaned to Sanford: "Pass me a gun . . . or stop that devil. . . ."

And then he saw that Sanford lay flat on his face, still, and his gun must have fallen under his body.

There was no help from that true partner; there was no time to roll the inert body of Sanford over and try to get at a weapon, for now the insanely contorted face of Banjo was close to the breastwork.

He was leaping over it. He was screeching out insults, as he aimed his gun down at Weller. Once and again he fired—and neither of the shots reached home. For Banjo was staggering. The lips were still stretched for screaming, but no sound came from them. His head fell over on his shoulder and he sank gradually to the ground.

He must have been dead before he reached it, his whole body slumping suddenly forward at the end, and now he lay crumpled and small and still. He had died as he had lived, half beast and half hero.

From all sides the firing had stopped, for the moment. There was a wild shouting of despair and rage as the crew of the great Lermond realized that their chief was dead at last.

Bullets would follow again, before long. And Weller, picking up the fallen gun of Banjo, gritted his teeth as he saw that it was empty.

This was the end.

He shook Sanford by the shoulder. "Wake up . . . Harry!" he called.

The wounded man lifted a wild face from the ground. "Coming . . . coming, Dick," he whispered.

"Wake up," said Dick Weller. "We've lived together and now it's time for us to die together. We're done for. Stand up with me, and we'll take it like men, instead of being chewed up piecemeal while we lie here."

He had barely said that when he heard a sudden ringing of hoofs and over the edge of the slope he saw sombreroed heads and shoulders, and then horses and armed riders sweeping over the crest. They looked gigantically large to Weller as he watched that charge, with the gallant sheriff in the forefront. No, not actually in the lead. For a long, lean, dry figure, bent far forward over the saddle, holding the reins in his teeth and a gun in either hand, was pushing his mustang past that of the older sheriff.

That was strange Hugh Jacobs. And when he saw that wild figure, Weller closed his eyes. "It's going to be all right, Harry," he said, and let his tormented body and brain sink into unconsciousness.

It was, in fact, very much all right. Lermond's men had lost their leader and the cream of their fighting force. Now a rush of equal numbers charging in on their flank with all the advantage of the ground was too much for them. They got up and tried to run for their horses—and that was how they were shot down until the remnant fell on their knees and howled for mercy.

Dick Weller knew all of this later, a great deal later.

He did not recall anything of the trip back to town, when he was carried on a stretcher between two horses. He remembered nothing of the jolts and the jars along the way. He knew nothing at all until, a number of days later, he found himself looking up at the high, white, cool ceiling of a room and turned his head, bewildered, to find that he was at home.

When he looked again, he saw the rigid profile of Harry Sanford in an adjoining bed, his eyes closed, but the folded sheet lifted above his breast by a regular breathing, and between the beds sat Muriel Sanford with her weary head fallen upon one shoulder, asleep, also, but smiling in her sleep. One of her hands lay on the bed of Dick, palm up. She seemed to Dick more beautiful than an angel from heaven, and more merciful.

She was not the only watcher by the beds of the wounded. On the other side sat a man with a gray, stern face and relentless eyes. It was Hugh Jacobs.

When Dick looked up at him, Jacobs attempted to smile, and his face seemed to crack to pieces. He leaned far forward. "Know me, kid?" he whispered.

"Yes," murmured Dick Weller. "I remember you sailing into the Lermond gang as though they had only paper bullets in their guns."

"You remember that?" said Jacobs. "Well, kid, I remember you lyin' like dead with the dead men in front of you. I remember that I was a fool of a man-killin' crook that. . . ."

"Hush," said Dick Weller, smiling. "You'll wake up Muriel."

"Aye"—Jacobs grinned—"and I wouldn't do that. It's her that pulled you through. No man could've done it. No man could've picked up what was left of your life . . . there was so damn' little of it. But she found it and kept it and made it grow. Wait a minute . . . here's the sheriff."

He rose and slipped softly from the room, with only a faint, faint jingling of his spurs like the chiming of very distant bells, and the sheriff came in and sat down by the bed. He looked at the girl, then he stared into the open eyes of his son and saw the recognition in them.

"I've been downtown," said the, sheriff, "talking to a lot of men who want to put up a statue or something to you. I told them that they were a pack of fools. I told them that you only had done your duty. Because no Weller," he added, "can do more than that."

The son, still staring fixedly into the eyes of his father, suddenly smiled. "Thanks," he said.

"You understand?" whispered the sheriff, leaning closer.

"Aye," said Dick Weller. "I understand, at last."

There was a moment of pause. After that Dick put out his hand. It was not a good hand to look at, for sickness had blanched it, and the lack of blood showed in the blueness about the tips of the fingers, but the sheriff took that hand with a gentle reverence and held it for a long time. They did not need to talk. In their silence the souls of the two were being welded together at last.

About The Author

Max Brand® is the best-known pen name of Frederick Faust, creator of Dr. Kildare, Destry, and many other fictional characters popular with readers and viewers worldwide. Faust wrote for a variety of audiences in many genres. His enormous output, totaling approximately 30,000,000 words or the equivalent of 530 ordinary books, covered nearly every field: crime, fantasy, historical romance, espionage, Westerns, science fiction, adventure, animal stories, love, war, and fashionable society, big business, and big medicine. Eighty motion pictures have been based on his work along wit h many radio and television programs. For good measure he also published four volumes of poetry. Perhaps no other author has reached more people in more different ways.

Born in Seattle in 1892, orphaned early, Faust grew up in the rural San Joaquin Valley of California. At Berkeley he became a student rebel and one-man literary movement, contributing prodigiously to all campus publications. Denied a degree because of unconventional conduct, he embarked on a series of adventures culminating in New York City where, after a period of near starvation, he received simultaneous recognition as a serious poet and successful author of fiction. Later, he traveled widely, making his home in New York, then in Florence, and finally in Los Angeles.

Once the United States entered the Second World War, Faust abandoned his lucrative writing career and his work as a screenwriter to serve as a war correspondent with the infantry in Italy, despite his fifty-one years and a bad heart. He was killed during a night attack on a hilltop village held by the German army. New books based on magazine serials or unpublished manuscripts or restored versions continue to appear so that, alive or dead, he has averaged a new book every four months for seventy-five years. Beyond this, some work by him is newly reprinted every week of every year in one or another format somewhere in the world. A great deal more about this author and his work can be found in *The Max Brand Companion* edited by Jon Tuska and Vicki Piekarski.

Five-time Winner of the Spur Award

Will Henry

There is perhaps no outlaw of the Old West more notorious or legendary than Billy the Kid. And no author is better suited than Will Henry to tell the tale of the young gunman . . . and the mysterious stranger who changed his life.

Also included in this volume are two exciting novellas: "Santa Fe Passage" is the basis for the classic 1955 film of the same name. And "The Fourth Horseman" sets a rancher on the trail of a kidnapped young woman . . . while trying to survive a bloody range war.

A BULLET FOR BILLY THE KID

ISBN 13: 978-0-8439-6340-3

"Each of Randisi's novels is better than
its entertaining predecessor." —*Booklist*

Robert J. Randisi

Author of *Beauty and the Bounty*

When Lancaster rode up to the ranch house all he wanted was a little water. What he found instead was trouble.
Three men were beating and kicking a woman, and Lancaster couldn't let that be. As the gunsmoke cleared, the
three men were dead. Inside the house was another dead
man, the woman's husband. But who killed *him*? The
sheriff says Lancaster shot them all in cold blood. It's just
too bad for Lancaster that the dead husband was a town
deputy, that the three other men were his brothers, and
that all four were the sons of the local judge—the judge at
Lancaster's upcoming trial!

GALLOWS

"Randisi always turns out a traditional Western
with plenty of gunplay and interesting characters."
—*Roundup*

ISBN 13: 978-0-8439-6178-2

INTERACT WITH DORCHESTER ONLINE!

Want to learn more about your favorite books and authors?
Want to talk with other readers that like to read the same books as you?
Want to see up-to-the-minute Dorchester news?

VISIT DORCHESTER AT:
DorchesterPub.com
Twitter.com/DorchesterPub
Facebook.com (Search Pages)

DISCUSS DORCHESTER'S NOVELS AT:
Dorchester Forums at DorchesterPub.com
GoodReads.com
LibraryThing.com
Myspace.com/books
Shelfari.com
WeRead.com

☐ **YES!**

Sign me up for the Leisure Western Book Club and send my FREE BOOKS! If I choose to stay in the club, I will pay only $14.00* each month, a savings of $9.96!

NAME: _____

ADDRESS: _____

TELEPHONE: _____

EMAIL: _____

☐ I want to pay by credit card.

☐ VISA   ☐ MasterCard   ☐ DISCOVER

ACCOUNT #: _____

EXPIRATION DATE: _____

SIGNATURE: _____

Mail this page along with $2.00 shipping and handling to:
Leisure Western Book Club
PO Box 6640
Wayne, PA 19087
Or fax (must include credit card information) to:
610-995-9274
You can also sign up online at **www.dorchesterpub.com**.
*Plus $2.00 for shipping. Offer open to residents of the U.S. and Canada only.
Canadian residents please call 1-800-481-9191 for pricing information.
If under 18, a parent or guardian must sign. Terms, prices and conditions subject to change. Subscription subject to acceptance. Dorchester Publishing reserves the right to reject any order or cancel any subscription.